S0-BFD-062

L.G

**This Large Print Book carries the
Seal of Approval of N.A.V.H.**

THE BOSS OF
SANTA YSABEL

Center P
Large P

THE BOSS OF
SANTA YSABEL

Arthur Henry Gooden

CENTER POINT LARGE PRINT
THORNDIKE, MAINE

This Center Point Large Print edition is published
in the year 2012 by arrangement with
Golden West Literary Agency.

Copyright © 1949 by Arthur Henry Gooden
in the British Commonwealth.
Copyright © 2012 by Golden West Literary Agency.

All rights reserved.

First US edition: Center Point Large Print

First UK edition: Harrap

The text of this Large Print edition is unabridged.
In other aspects, this book may
vary from the original edition.
Printed in the United States of America
on permanent paper.
Set in 16-point Times New Roman type.

ISBN: 978-1-61173-391-4

Library of Congress Cataloging-in-Publication Data

Gooden, Arthur Henry, 1879–1971.
The boss of Santa Ysabel / Arthur Henry Gooden. — 1st U.S. ed.
p. cm. — (Center Point large print edition)
ISBN 978-1-61173-391-4 (library binding : alk. paper)
1. Western stories. gsafd 2. Large type books. I. Title.
PS3513.O4767B67 2012
813'.54—dc23
                                                    2011050271

THE BOSS OF
SANTA YSABEL

Chapter 1

The stage from Deming was more than two hours overdue, a fact that was one of two reasons for the grim look on V. Crumm's face. She stood in the wide entrance of the livery barn, frowning gaze intent on the distant haze of dust—a square-built, granite-featured woman in the middle fifties. A battered, wide-brimmed Stetson covered short grizzled hair, and she wore a man's blue flannel shirt tucked carelessly into an ankle-length denim skirt. Standing there in her cowboy boots, she looked as rugged and immovable as the great red butte round which the stage suddenly appeared.

The second and more disturbing cause of the worry in her shrewd, sun-wrinkled eyes was the scrap of paper in the pocket of her voluminous skirt. To think of it made her see red.

V. Crumm wrenched her thoughts back to the approaching stage, and even at that distance her experienced eyes told her that something was wrong there.

She spoke over her shoulder, her voice a harsh rasp.

"Pilar—bring me the spyglass."

"*Sí, señora.*" An elderly Mexican hurriedly appeared from the cavernous dark of the barn. She snatched the long brass telescope from his hand and levelled it at the approaching stage.

"Looks like Cap Hansy's run into trouble," she said in a deeply worried voice. "Pullin' the stage with only three horses. One of his leaders must have died on him."

"*Sí,*" muttered Pilar. His keen eyes needed no telescope to tell him that a horse was missing from the team. "Thees *bandido* try for rob stage some more, no?" He slanted a squint-eyed glance at his glowering boss.

V. Crumm's fingers clenched hard over the scrap of paper in her pocket. She felt with grim certainty that Pilar's guess was too uncomfortably close to the truth. The attempts to hold up her stages were all part of the scheme to frighten her, weaken her resistance, force her to sell her stage lines, sell her store—her profitable livery and feed stables. She was not wanted in Santa Ysabel. She had been warned to leave or face ruin—*death*.

Her square, sunburned face set in granite lines. She had lived too many years in this border town to be scared away by a gang of envious crooks. She had started with almost nothing—a lone team of horses and one wagon, salvaged from the Indian raid that had left her husband's freighting outfit in flames and herself a young widow in this new and remote corner of the Territory of New

Mexico. She had brought prosperity to the sleepy little hamlet of Santa Ysabel. Her freighting business had grown, fed needed supplies to the mines and to the spreading network of great cattle ranches. Her aggressiveness, her shrewd business ability and dogged perseverance, had brought importance to the little border town. She loved the place, it was part of her very being.

Feet wide apart, hands on hips, she glanced up at the big sign above the wide entrance.

SANTA YSABEL FEED & STAGE STABLES
V. Crumm, Prop.

She was proud of that sign. Those big black letters told a heroic story of a woman's triumph over ruin and tragedy. She had made this savage and remote land pay well for its harsh treatment of her. She was Santa Ysabel's most prominent and powerful citizen. Ranchers and miners within a radius of a hundred miles knew and respected the name of V. Crumm. Only a few, less than she could count on the fingers of one hand, knew what the "V" stood for. It was a secret they respected because of their affection for her. They called her Vee or V. Crumm, but never by the name she felt went ill with her aggressive, pugnacious personality.

From where she stood she could see up Santa Ysabel's short, dusty street. At the far end was a small plaza lined with low-roofed adobe buildings that had been there some two centuries and more. The crumbling ruins of an ancient church showed through the green cottonwoods, and the bell, still suspended from the great beam, caught and held V. Crumm's harassed eyes. Not in her time had that bell ever sounded its call to saint or sinner. She felt a vague wonder in her, a disturbing sense of dissatisfaction. It was not right for that bell to rust its life away in silence. Courage and fortitude and sacrifice had placed it there to call all men to better things. It came to her dimly that those crumbling adobe walls enshrined an unseen power she had failed to use against the evil and violence now engulfing the town. She must do something about it.

The stage was rattling up the street, trailed by a slow drift of dust touched to golden mist by the slanting sunlight. V. Crumm thrust the telescope into the ostler's hands and went briskly to the store that stood on the corner opposite the plaza. The big sign across the front drew a brief glance from her, put a glint of pride in her eyes.

SANTA YSABEL EMPORIUM
GENERAL MERCHANDISE
V. Crumm, Prop.

She climbed up the steps to the low, wide porch and shouldered through the crowd already gathered to meet the long-overdue stage. There was no hint in her now of the ugly fears that squeezed her heart.

"Well, folks . . ." She spoke jovially. "We'll have the mail out in two shakes." Her voice, powerful, raspy, dominated them. Good-natured grins spread over their faces.

She came to a standstill in front of a window where a small sign said, U.S. Post Office, and now her beaming gaze met the hostile look of a heavy-set, sandy-haired man who was tying his horse to the hitching-rail in front of the store.

"Seems like the mail is always late these times," he said sourly. "We're needing a new postmaster in this town."

V. Crumm flared at him, hands on hips. "Meanin' you want the job, huh, Al Derner?"

He came slowly up the porch steps, his cold eyes on her, his smile ugly. "No, *Violet.* I'm a cowman, *Violet.*" There was derision in his voice. "I mean we want a new postmaster. That's all I mean, Violet."

V. Crumm's face crimsoned, then took on the grey look of cold rage. "You damn' four-flushing cow-thief!" she exploded. "You get away from my store before I throw you into the street!" Her freckled hands balled into capable fists. "Get out, you low-down skunk!" she shouted.

Derner grinned at her. "You can't throw me out of a United States post office. Quit your job as

11

postmaster if you don't like me around your store, *Violet.*"

"Shut your lying mouth," she stormed. "My name's V. Crumm. Next time you call me Violet I'll smack you cold."

Derner shrugged, said ominously, "Same goes for you, next time you call me a cow-thief." He shifted his gaze to the stage, now slowing to a standstill in front of the store.

V. Crumm flung him an outraged look, stamped hurriedly down the steps, and glared at the lean, stoop-shouldered man on the driver's seat, and of a sudden the anger was gone from her, and the harsh rasp from her voice. Cap Hansy had the look of a sick man.

"Run into plenty trouble, huh, Cap?" Her voice was gentle, concerned. "Road agents ag'in, huh?" She flashed a penetrating look at the girl sitting by Hansy's side.

Hansy nodded gloomily, shifted booted foot from the brake, and expertly shot a dark brown stream of tobacco juice from whiskered lips. "Two of 'em," he said. "Fust shot took my nigh leader plumb in the head." He jerked a leathery thumb behind him. "Young feller inside dropped the varmint, and the other hombre hightailed it pronto."

He climbed down stiffly and reached a helping hand to the girl, but V. Crumm's attention was on the four men emerging from the interior of the dusty Concord. Two of them were cowboys, who gave her friendly grins as they started across the street towards the saloon. The third man was a stranger, a smooth-looking individual, whose manner and clothes indicated that he was probably a professional gambler. The last to climb out was a slim youth of medium height. At least that was V. Crumm's first impression. A second look told her he was older than he seemed. There was an unmistakable quality of quiet resoluteness in the poise of his lean, hard body, and something in the quick, almost casual glance he gave her had the impact of a bolt of lightning. His were the tawny eyes of a mountain lion, watchful, fearless; and that brief, forthright look told her that he knew who she was. Wondering, conscious of a quickening heartbeat, she returned her attention to the girl, now safely on the ground. She was suspicious of young girls who arrived without escort in Santa Ysabel. Too many of them had been coming of late.

Her now appraising look immediately banished her fears. This was no painted hussy, and there was weariness and a hint of panic in the blue eyes that met her interested look. She had dark, almost black hair, and the blue eyes were set wide apart in a delicately boned face. A dainty, fragile flower to be coming to an evil-ridden border town like Santa Ysabel, V. Crumm thought compassionately. Her heart went out to the girl

13

and she came to a quick decision even before Cap Hansy's voice broke into her reflections.

"Says her name's Ellen Frazer," drawled the stage-driver. "Her brother should be here to meet her." Cap Hansy paused to drag the mail-sack from under the seat. He heaved it on to the porch. "Here y'are, Pete . . ."

A lanky, elderly man with receding grey hair and a pair of steel-rimmed spectacles perched on a bony nose snatched up the pouch and vanished into the store. Most of the bystanders followed him, impatient for their mail. Hansy's keen eyes took on a troubled look.

"Young Frazer should be here," he fretted. "Ain't seen him 'round, have you, Vee?"

V. Crumm shook her head. "Not for weeks, and he always comes to the post office when he's in town."

"Duncan knew I'd arrive to-day," the girl said. "I—I don't understand . . ."

V. Crumm's heart was warming more and more to the helpless appeal in those blue eyes. She was more than surprised at herself, succumbing so quickly and completely to this young stranger. Her discerning eyes noted with approval the modest travelling dress of dove-grey, with its tight bodice and long, full skirt. There was breeding in this little Frazer chick whose brother was not here to meet and care for her. And for all her natural confusion, her weariness after the long ride, with an attempted hold-up thrown in, there was the poise, the fine, brave dignity that went with good breeding.

V. Crumm voiced her decision. "You'll not stay at the hotel," she said. "There's a room for you at my own house, Miss Frazer. You're more than welcome to stay until your brother comes for you."

"You are very kind . . ." The girl hesitated, eyes doubtful. "Perhaps I can hire somebody to drive me out to the ranch—"

"No!" In spite of herself, V. Crumm's voice was almost rough, the big, harsh voice she used in conducting her business. The girl's blue eyes widened, and Cap Hansy, who knew the reason for that almost explosive no, said gently: "You listen to Vee, Miss Frazer. Awful long, hard drive out to your brother's ranch. Come to-morrow he may be in for you, and if he ain't, it's time enough then to hire a rig for the drive. Vee runs the livery barn, and she can fix you up with a safe driver."

"Well . . ." Ellen Frazer gave the big woman a faint, grateful smile. "I suppose that is good sense."

"Pete!" bawled V. Crumm, "Send somebody out here." She smiled happily at the girl. "My place is back of the store," she told her. "We'll take your bags right over, and you can get out of your clothes and get right into bed. You're all tuckered out, you poor little lamb."

15

"I am tired," Ellen confessed. "Those dreadful bandits—the shooting—" She repressed a shudder.

A fair-headed youth ran out of the store and down the steps.

"Bring the young lady's trunk over to the house, Johnny," V. Crumm told him crisply.

"Yes, ma'am." Johnny's fascinated eyes were on the girl, who smiled at him.

"It's that small trunk, but I'm afraid it's too heavy for you."

"Oh, no, ma'am—" Johnny threw out his chest. "I'm awful strong. That trunk ain't nothin' for me to shoulder."

V. Crumm gave him a look. "I'll remember that, next load of sugar-sacks we get in," she commented acidly. "You've got strong all of a sudden, Johnny."

She marched towards the corner, hand under Ellen's arm, and then, suddenly reminded by something the girl had said, she looked back at the stage. The young stranger with the disturbing tawny eyes was walking up the street towards the livery barn. He had a saddle slung over his shoulder and a blanket-roll tight-wrapped in an oilskin slicker. A cowman from all the signs. She noticed with a tingle of satisfaction the gun in its low-slung holster, and recalled Cap Hansy's laconic statement: "Young feller inside dropped the varmint. . . ." She had no need to question the girl about the attempted hold-up. The young

16

cowman now walking so briskly to the Santa Ysabel Feed and Stage Stables was undoubtedly the quick-shooting passenger who had killed the road agent. He was no tenderfoot, this stranger, for all the boyish look of him. He knew his way around, knew what a gun was for. And he knew who she was. The quick glint of recognition in his steady eyes had been unmistakable.

Tingling with curiosity, V. Crumm turned the corner with the girl. She was eager to make her guest comfortable and hasten over to the livery barn. Instinct told her that the young stranger would be waiting there for her to come. Whatever his business in Santa Ysabel, it was something very private and for her ear alone. He had been told about her. Her description was one he would readily recognize.

Satisfied that she was half-way to the truth, she now gave her attention to Ellen Frazer, who was looking interestedly at the old church across the plaza.

"The padres built it a couple of hundred years before you were born," V. Crumm informed her. "Indians raided the town years ago. Ain't much left save the walls and that old bell." She recalled her earlier thoughts about the bell. "Seems a pity that bell don't ring like it used to. Never heard it myself, but I aim to do somethin' about it one of these days."

She halted in front of a narrow door set in the

high wall under which they had been walking and fished a large key from her pocket.

"Always keep this door locked," she explained. "Usually go in and out through the store."

The bolt clicked, and V. Crumm gestured for the girl to precede her. She followed, paused to relock the heavy timber door, and turned a beaming, expectant look on Ellen.

"Like it?" she asked with a chuckle.

Ellen nodded. "I never dreamed it would be so lovely on this side of the wall." Her gaze travelled across the patio. "So many beautiful flowers— and shrubs—and that lovely fountain." She looked wonderingly at the low-roofed adobe building standing back in the trees. "It must be very old."

"Older than the church," smiled V. Crumm. "A wreck and ruin when I took hold of it. Bought the place from one of the descendants of the old don who built it." She indicated a grove of cottonwoods. "You wouldn't guess the store fronts on the other street back of those trees."

She led the way to the house and down a long *galería* to an open doorway. A brown-faced woman met them in the cool, dim hall. She gave the girl a wondering look, listened impassively to V. Crumm's directions.

"*Sí* . . ." The woman's dark eyes suddenly warmed, and she gave the girl a smile. "Like your own daughter, *señora*." She spoke in Spanish.

18

"If I had one," chuckled V. Crumm. She looked at Ellen. "Ynez will see after you, fix up a nice hot bath, and then you must rest a bit before supper." She frowned, gave the Mexican woman a thoughtful look. "She'll like your *arroz con pollo*, Ynez. And don't wait if I'm not back. Hell's bustin' loose in this damn' town and I don't know where I'm at one minute to another." Her face reddened. "Sorry, child." She gave Ellen a shamefaced smile. "Don't mind my talk. I get kind of crazy that way and don't mean nothin'."

Her distress brought a reassuring smile from the girl. "You have so much on your mind," she said. "I quite understand, Mrs Crumm."

"Call me Vee, spelled *v* double *e,*" the big woman said. "Folks don't use that *Mrs* handle on me. I'm just V. Crumm in this town." She threw up her head, listened intently. "Sounds like Johnny comin' with your trunk, so I'll be off. Got a lot of things to 'tend to."

Ellen's low voice halted her. "Mrs Crumm—I mean—Vee—I—I can't help wondering about my brother. I wrote Duncan to meet me—to-day."

Something like a shadow flitted over V. Crumm's weather-beaten face. Ellen decided it was only the deepening twilight. There was no doubting that reassuring smile.

"Don't you worry, child. Like as not he never got your letter. Cowmen are awful busy these times."

"You'd know if he got my letter," persisted Ellen. "You're the postmaster—"

"Hell's bells—" V. Crumm broke off, softened the rasp from her voice. "Pete looks after the mail, Miss Frazer. I wouldn't be knowin' if your brother got your letter."

The explanation seemed to satisfy the girl, and V. Crumm made a hasty departure by way of the short-cut to the store. She was uncomfortably aware that she had not told the truth about the letter.

Pete was finishing sorting the mail when she hurried into the long store by way of the back entrance. It was almost closing-time, and the two younger assistants were tidying up, replacing bolts of cloth on the shelves and rearranging numerous assorted articles in their proper places. The store carried an astonishing miscellany and was redolent with spicy smells.

She paused at the little cubby-hole where Pete was pushing his mail into various pigeon-holes.

"Pete—" Her voice was troubled. "Is that letter that come for young Frazer still here?"

Her assistant nodded, his attention on the letters he was distributing.

"Listen—" She spoke sharply. "If he shows up, grab him, and don't you give up that letter to anybody else who comes askin' for his mail."

She had Pete's attention now, and he gave her a

startled look over the steel-rimmed spectacles. "What's wrong, Vee?" He shook his head worriedly. "I got to hand out mail when folks ask for it."

"I ain't arguin'," she barked. "Nobody gets that letter but him, and if he shows up you grab him. I want to talk to him."

She stamped out to the wide porch, came to a standstill, and stared interestedly at the backs of two men at that moment disappearing into the lobby of the dingy hotel across the street. The man in the black coat was the smooth-looking stranger who had come in on the stage. His companion was Al Derner.

V. Crumm frowned, went on her way to the livery barn, conscious of a growing uneasiness in her, trying to find some reasonable explanation for what she had just seen. The two men had likely struck up an acquaintance in the saloon, the way men did.

The explanation left her dissatisfied. She was suspicious of anybody associated with Al Derner, and it was her shrewd guess that the smooth-looking stranger was in Santa Ysabel for no good purpose where she was concerned.

Her fingers tightened hard over the scrap of paper in her pocket. Trouble was headed her way, and coming fast. She felt it in her bones.

Chapter II

Pilar Rojo was washing the dusty Concord stage now drawn up in the yard. He looked up from the sponge he was sloshing in a bucket of water, grinned nervously at the big woman bearing down on him. V. Crumm was in one of her belligerent moods. She had the look of a battleship going into action.

"Where is he, Pilar?" she rasped.

The Mexican straightened up, dripping sponge in his hand. "Cap say he mooch seek, go for *siesta*. Say for tell you w'en you come."

"Not him," V. Crumm said impatiently. "I mean the young feller with the saddle."

Pilar lapsed into his native tongue. He could explain things faster in Spanish, and the boss was in a hurry.

"He is in the back corral looking at the horses. He wants to buy a good horse, and waits to bargain with you."

V. Crumm nodded, disappeared into the dark tunnel of the long barn. Wants to bargain with me, huh? Now I wonder what his real game is! Her thoughts raced, could find no answer. One thing was certain. He had more in his mind than wanting to buy a horse.

She found him draped on the corral fence, a vague shape in that deepening twilight. Flung over the same top rail was the saddle. The bed-roll leaned against a post. V. Crumm's sharp eyes saw the stock of a short-barrelled rifle peeping from its saddle.

The young man slid from the fence at her approach, stood watching her, an odd glint of mirth in his eyes.

She came to a standstill, hands on her hips, and deliberately looked him up and down. His mouth twitched.

She said resentfully, "What are you grinning at?"

"The way you look at me, all bothered and puzzled—and suspicious."

Her short temper was fraying to the danger-point. "Get down to brass tacks," she snapped. "Who the hell are you, and what do you want?" She went on, not waiting for an answer. "I saw you look at me back there at the store. Wasn't needin' anybody to tell you I'm V. Crumm, either."

He stood there, fingers busy making a cigarette, laughter in the depths of his tawny eyes. "Sure I knew you, and if you'd think a bit you'd know me." He put a match to the cigarette, gave her a smile. "A lot of years since you saw me, and I reckon I've changed in looks."

She stared at him, brows corrugated, then,

crisply: "I'm a busy woman. Ain't got time to waste on guessin' games."

"Was here some twenty years ago, stayed with my uncle. His name was Miles, and he owned the Bar M outfit—"

V. Crumm's whoop interrupted him. She flapped a limp hand, said weakly, "You're that Miles Clarke kid."

"The same," he said with a low laugh.

"The same, but growed up to man-size, and sure plenty changed." She inspected him appraisingly. "You ain't growed up soft, Miles." Her expression sobered. "The old Bar M has gone plumb to hell, boy."

Miles Clarke nodded, waited for her to continue, his eyes hard as agate.

"Jim Miles ain't running the ranch no more. Gone for good it looks like. There's talk that a lot of ropes were danglin' for his neck." She gestured, shook her head sorrowfully. "Goes ag'in the grain to think Jim was a sneakin' rustler, but that's the talk, boy. Ain't laid eyes on Jim Miles for 'most half a year."

He looked at her steadily, his face a cold mask in that gathering darkness. He said quietly, without rancour: "Uncle Jim is not a cow-thief, and you know it, Violet Crumm. He was my mother's brother, and she gave me his name, a name he would never shame with dishonour."

She chose to let the "Violet" pass. She could

24

take it from young Miles Clarke. His mother had been her best friend in the long ago. She said unhappily, "It was Jim's runnin' away that got me bothered. An innocent man don't run from trouble."

Miles shook his head. "That's the point. Uncle Jim didn't run away. It wasn't in him to run from trouble."

"Meanin' what?" She wrinkled her brows at him.

"Meaning that he's dead." The young cowman's voice was grim. "It's the only answer. He was murdered, and that is why I'm here. I'm going to get to the bottom of this affair, find the murderer—clear my uncle's good name."

V. Crumm heaved a sigh of relief. "I'm believin' you," she said simply. "You've put your finger smack on the truth." She paused, added thoughtfully: "If you're right about it, it's goin' to be some dangerous. Like as not they'll get you too."

Miles Clarke shrugged. "I've an idea they made a try for me to-day."

"To-day?" V. Crumm was puzzled, and then, in a suddenly hard voice, "You mean them road agents?"

Miles nodded. "I had a good look at the man I killed. Been hanging around in Silver City for the last few weeks." He smiled thinly. "They don't want me nosing around down here."

She thought it over for a moment, nodded her head, then abruptly: "How's your pa?"

25

"Dead the past five years."

"You're runnin' the ranch up there?"

"Half-shares with my brother Ed." He paused, added with another thin smile: "I'm Uncle Jim Miles' heir. If he's dead, the Bar M ranch belongs to me. That's another reason why I've come to Santa Ysabel. I'm not going to let Uncle Jim's murderers take his ranch and his good name too."

"Al Derner claims he owns the Bar M now, or most of it," V. Crumm told him in a curiously tight voice. She was watching him intently, saw the name meant nothing to him. "He's a skunk," she added fiercely.

"What do you mean—he owns most of it?" Miles asked.

"Another bunch has got hold of that range down on the border, your uncle's old Juniper Flats camp. Call themselves the Box DF outfit." She paused again, and after a long moment: "That girl up on the seat with Cap Hansy is sister to one of 'em, Duncan Frazer. He was to meet the stage for her. Ain't showed up. I took her over to my place, not carin' for her to stay at that mangy hotel."

She sensed a stir in him, and even in that semi-darkness saw the quickening glow in his eyes.

"She's right pretty. Was wondering what brought her to Santa Ysabel."

V. Crumm eyed him suspiciously. "So you *did* notice her, huh? Well, it's her brother that claims to own that Juniper Flats range." Her voice

26

softened. "She's a poor lamb and I'm worried sick about her. She's headed for plenty trouble."

Concern looked from his eyes. "You mean this brother of hers is no good?"

"He's mixed up with a bunch of cow-thieves," asserted V. Crumm. "I ain't sayin' he knows it, but he's awful simple if he don't. Got a pardner that's hang-tree fruit and that's the truth. Name of Jess Wellen."

"I'd like to have a talk with her." The young cowman's eyes narrowed thoughtfully. "You say her brother failed to show up to meet the stage?"

"That's right. What's more, he ain't been in town for weeks. The letter she wrote him is layin' in his box right now."

"Smells bad," muttered the young man.

"Sure it smells bad," agreed the big woman. "It stinks."

"I'd like to have a talk with her," he repeated.

She eyed him worriedly. "Won't be safe for you in this town, I'm thinkin'."

"I'm heading for Uncle Jim's ranch to-night," Miles said. His look went to the dark shapes in the corral. "I need a good horse—the best you've got."

V. Crumm nodded. "Got a red bay in that bunch you'd like. Tough as mesquite and can run all day. Got him in a trade from your Uncle Jim."

"How much?" asked Miles.

She hesitated, reluctant to lose an opportunity

for a shrewd bargain, then gruffly: "Nothin' to you, young feller."

He shook his head. "I'll pay your price. No telling what'll happen. Don't want somebody claiming I'm a horse-thief."

"Hand me a dollar and I'll make you out a bill of sale," V. Crumm said.

He began to demur and she put out a hand at him. "Don't fret yourself. You'll earn him plenty times over before you get done here."

Something in her voice sharpened his look. "Meaning what?" He spoke softly.

"There's things goin' on that's got me worried," she told him simply. "Like as not I'll wake up some mornin' and find myself murdered in my bed."

The seriousness in her voice told him she was not trying to be funny. She was giving him the grim truth. He said laconically, "I'm listening . . ."

V. Crumm shook her head. "This ain't a good place for us to talk too long. I've a notion I'm bein' watched."

Miles narrowed his eyes at her. "You mean—the Mexican?"

She grinned. "Not *him*. Pilar Rojo would slit your throat if you as much as looked cross-eyed at me. He's a good hombre." She paused, asked, abruptly: "Did you notice the feller that come in on the stage with you? The one that looked like a tin-horn gambler."

Miles nodded again. "What about him?"

28

"Seen him over to the hotel with Al Derner."

"Who's Al Derner?" asked Miles. "You mentioned him before, said he was a skunk."

"Wolf!" the big woman said bitterly. "That's the word for the skunk!" She wagged her head gloomily. "Ain't got a lick of proof ag'in the man. Calls himself a cowman, but he hangs 'round in town most of the time. Loans money out, and has picked up some ranches from the poor devils as don't pay up. Ain't got a lick of proof he's back of the scheme to run me out of town or that he's mixed up with your uncle's disappearance. Seems like your uncle was owin' him a lot of money. At least that's Derner's reason for takin' over Jim's Bar M, lock, stock, and barrel." V. Crumm sniffed. "Jim ain't showed up to say different."

"I'm getting the picture," Miles Clarke muttered.

"That gambler feller seen you headin' over to the barn with your saddle," V. Crumm said. "Seemed kind of interested in you."

"Never saw him before," asserted Miles.

"You said you was bein' watched in Silver City," she reminded. "You said you figgered that try to hold up the stage was on *your* account. How do you know but what this feller ain't one of 'em?"

"I don't," he admitted dryly.

"Listen—" She spoke briskly. "You was seen headed for the barn, and now you've got to be seen headed *away* from the barn."

"I savvy," chuckled the young man.

She gave him an approving look. "You get your rope on that red bay. That's him drinkin' at the trough now."

Miles was already unfastening the rope from his saddle. "You're smart, Violet," he drawled.

"Don't you 'Violet' me when folks can hear you," she told him good-naturedly. "I've had to play a man's game in this town and I'm plain V. Crumm. The Violet handle just don't sit well on a woman like me."

His eyes twinkled. "I'll remember," he promised.

"Quick as you get saddled head west out of town. If folks come askin' Pilar questions about you he'll tell 'em only what he knows—that you headed west some place. He won't know that as soon as you're hid in the dark you turned left into the canyon and followed the wash round to my side gate. I'll be waitin' there to let you in."

"I savvy," Miles said again. His tone was admiring.

She waited until he got his rope on the bay horse and led him from the corral. "I'll tell Pilar we made a deal," she said. "For all he knows you're just a stranger that has bought him a horse from me and is headed west to parts unknown. Don't want him to know a thing more about you right now. If he's asked questions it's best he don't know who you are or where you've gone."

"Sound tactics." He bridled the horse, reached for the saddle.

She watched him, approvingly noted his deftness, his unhurried, quiet efficiency.

"Sure you got it straight—about the gate?" Her voice betrayed the tension in her.

He looked round at her, his eyes steady, reassuring. "Head west until I'm out of sight in the dark, then swing left and circle back up the wash."

"There's a lone cottonwood just below the gate," she put in. And then, anxiously, "Watch yourself, boy."

He nodded, eased the saddle into place. "Don't you worry, V. Crumm. I've been around."

She became a vague shape in the deepening night, and presently he heard her voice in conversation with the Mexican.

"Got a good price out of him for that bay gelding, Pilar. Reckon that hombre's in a big hurry to get a long ways from here. Was all set to cut the price fifty bucks, but he wasn't wastin' time arguin'."

"The law on thees hombre's trail, no?" Pilar said.

"Looks that way." V. Crumm's voice showed indifference. "Ain't none of *our* business, I reckon." A pause, then: "Tell Cap Hansy he needn't come over to the house to-night, Pilar. I'll see him in the morning."

Miles Clarke smiled grimly as he drew the cinch tight, made the latigo fast. V. Crumm was taking no chances. Not even the old stage-driver was to know of his presence at the house that night. Nothing to do with Cap Hansy's loyalty or Pilar Rojo's loyalty, he guessed. Merely her habit to keep her affairs to herself, or else it was something else—a haunting fear that drew on her caution even to the exclusion of trusted friends. V. Crumm was afraid, believed she walked in the shadow of death.

Miles frowned, thoughtfully tied on the bed-roll, slid the carbine into its leather boot, and fumbled tobacco and cigarette-papers from his shirt pocket. His intended brief stay in Santa Ysabel was meeting complications. He had a shrewd suspicion the mystery of his uncle's disappearance was tangled up with V. Crumm and the slim young girl who had come in on the stage with him.

The thought of the girl sent a glow of excitement through him. He had noticed her up there on the seat with Cap Hansy. The other men passengers had noticed her too, their grinning speculations had aroused a blaze of anger in him. The hard contempt in his eyes had been a deadly warning that their ribald surmises were distasteful. They had discreetly kept their eyes and their thoughts to themselves.

He stood there for long moments, smoking the cigarette and thinking about the girl. Her name was Frazer and she had a brother who had failed to meet her. He felt a vast interest in this brother who seemed to think he owned the Juniper Flats range. This was one of the reasons why he wanted to have a talk with the girl. The other reason was less tangible—a vague desire in him to see her again.

He suddenly slammed the cigarette down, snubbed it under his boot-heel. No use fooling himself. The last reason was the *real* reason. Nothing intangible about it. The girl had attracted him beyond words, and thanks to V. Crumm he would soon meet her face to face. He had a feeling that her smile would be worth while.

His own smile came, and with an easy swing he was suddenly in the saddle. The horse stiffened, laid its ears back ominously.

Miles spoke softly, and the sound of his voice, the ease of him in the saddle, seemed to reassure the horse. The tenseness went from him and he arched his neck, struck an impatient shod hoof on the ground.

V. Crumm was not mistaken about the horse. Miles grinned contentedly. He must remember to ask her for that bill of sale.

Chapter III

The Mexican had lighted the big swinging lamp in front of the barn, and now as Miles emerged from the covering darkness of the back corral, he saw two men suddenly appear from the darkness in the street. One of them called harshly, "Hold it, feller!"

Miles pulled the bay to a standstill, aware of a sickening dismay. The guns in the hands of these two men showed they meant unpleasant business.

They forged up, stood one on either side of him, and now a cold rage grew in him as he recognized the smaller of the pair. His late fellow-passenger: the tin-horn gambler, V. Crumm had contemptuously called him. He impressed Miles as something considerably tougher. His eyes were watchful, and the lust to kill was plain in them under the light of the big lantern.

His companion spoke again, the menace in his voice unmistakable. "Climb down, mister."

"Any good reason why I should?" Miles forced a thin smile. "Looks like you've got the wrong man."

"This is reason enough." The man waggled the gun at him. "And we haven't got the wrong man."

"I say that you have," argued Miles patiently.

The man peered up at him, and the glow of the swing-lamp showed a beefy red face and prominent light eyes under reddish brows. He was big, heavy-shouldered, and had the look of a bull about to charge.

He said angrily, "I ain't arguing."

"Are you the sheriff, or something?"

The man's hand went into a pocket, flashed a shiny badge. "I'm a deputy," he said gruffly. "I'm taking you to gaol."

"You're crazy—" Miles felt his temper slipping.

The man on the other side of him said softly, "We're wasting time."

Miles turned his head in a brief look at him. The pulled-back lips, the hot glint in those unwinking eyes, warned him not to temporize further.

He said mildly, "Have it your own way," and slid from the saddle, felt the smaller man's hand grasp his gun, deftly lift it from its holster.

"What's the charge?" He managed to hang on to his smile.

"Murder," growled the big man who had flashed the badge.

"That's a lie!"

"You're the man who came in on the stage, ain't you?"

"I'm one of them," admitted Miles. His quick glance took in Pilar Rojo, watching from the barn door, a look of deep misgiving on his swarthy face.

"You shot a man in cold blood." The big man's gun indicated his companion. "He was on the stage, saw the killin'."

Miles' thoughts raced. This man who claimed he was a deputy sheriff was Al Derner. He was sure of it. V. Crumm had seen him in conversation with the tin-horn gambler. She had also frankly declared that Derner was no friend of hers, hinted that he was mixed up in the mysterious disappearance of Jim Miles. This business also indicated that Derner was involved in the attempted hold-up of the stage. He did not want the nephew of Jim Miles in Santa Ysabel.

He heard the smaller man's voice, an impatient snarl now. "We're wasting time," he repeated.

"I'm runnin' this show," Derner said gruffly. He was eyeing the bay horse.

"How come you got this bronc?" he asked Miles.

Miles guessed the reason for the question. The man was anxious to find out his connexion with V. Crumm. The worry in his prominent pale eyes was plain enough. He was hoping that V. Crumm had nothing to do with his prisoner's presence in the town.

It was a question that called for a careful answer. It was important to keep V. Crumm out of this business.

He said curtly, "The horse is mine. Bought him from the woman who owns this livery barn."

Derner glanced across to the Mexican watching from the barn door. "That right, Pilar?"

"*Sí.*" The Mexican nodded vigorously. "Boss—she sell thees 'orse."

"Somethin' smells here," Derner muttered. He stared hard at Miles. "Let's see your bill of sale."

Miles covered his quick dismay behind a nonchalant grin. V. Crumm had forgotten about the promised bill of sale. And then, before he could think of an answer, he heard Pilar Rojo's voice.

"Boss—she make paper for señor . . . leave paper in office."

"The bill of sale?" Derner looked disappointed.

"*Sí, señor.* Boss—she beeg 'urry, say for me to tell señor paper in office."

"I'm having a look," growled Derner.

Miles came out of his daze. He knew that Pilar was lying.

He knew for a fact that V. Crumm could not possibly have stopped at the office and written out a bill of sale. She had left the barn immediately after her brief exchange of words with the Mexican.

"That's right," he drawled. "She was in a rush to get back to the store. Told me she'd leave the bill of sale in the stable office."

"I'm having a look," repeated Derner.

"It's *my* bill of sale," reminded Miles affably. "I'm going to feel easier with that piece of paper in my pocket."

Derner made no demur, gestured with the gun for him to walk in front. "No tricks," he warned.

From the corner of his eye Miles saw that Pilar Rojo was trailing them from the barn door, tried desperately to divine the purpose in the Mexican's lie about the bill of sale. There was no bill of sale. One thing was certain. The crucial moment was approaching. He must be ready for lightning action, keep his mind cool for the opportunity he sensed the Mexican was planning to create for him.

Conscious of Derner's gun prodding his spine, he pushed open the office door and stepped inside. A small kerosene lamp on the table diffused a dim light. He halted, heard Derner's voice behind him.

"Don't see no bill of sale layin' on the desk." His voice was heavy with fast-growing suspicion. "See any paper that looks like a bill of sale?" he asked his companion.

The man shoved past Miles, stood close to the desk, gun lowered in hand. His soft, precise voice said, "No paper here."

"Those drawer," Pilar said, pointing a brown hand at a rough, unpainted wooden chest that stood against the end wall.

Derner stepped forward, reached a hand to the top drawer. His companion's gaze followed the motion, and Pilar added softly, "Maybe thees drawer, no?" He was looking significantly at

Miles, and his hand made a swift, almost imperceptible gesture.

Miles saw the saddle in that same fleeting instant. It hung from a peg on the wall, within reach of his hand, and in almost the same instant his fingers closed over the butt of the .45 Colt that peeped from the holster slung over the horn of the saddle. Pilar's play had won him the opportunity he needed.

Derner's friend, standing close to the desk, had carelessly shifted his attention to Derner. With the same motion that plucked the gun from its holster Miles swung the heavy steel barrel against the man's head. The sound of the blow spun Derner around from the wooden chest. He went rigid, stared at Miles with aghast eyes.

Miles gave him a frosty smile over the prone body of the senseless man. With an effort he refrained from addressing him as Derner. He must say nothing that could involve V. Crumm. He was supposed to be a stranger in this town.

He said, quietly, "Drop your gun, mister."

The stupefied man let the gun slip from his lowered hand. He was too shocked for words.

"Stretch out on the floor," Miles told him. "Face down."

Derner obediently lowered himself to the floor. Miles moved close to him, kicked the fallen gun from possible reach.

"You, too, feller," he said to the Mexican, who

had stood motionless. "I'm tying you up along with the others." He gave Pilar a sly wink. It was not his intention to give Derner any idea of this honest Mexican's part in the affair.

With a hint of a grin on his dark face, the Mexican bellied on the floor. It was plain he appreciated the thought Miles had for him. He pretended loud-voiced indignation, made the most of V. Crumm's also pretended suspicions of the gringo who had bought the red bay horse.

"Boss—she say you bad hombre . . . she say you beeg 'urry go to border. *Por Dios!* Boss—she no wr-rong about you."

"Shut up," rasped Miles. He suppressed a grin, snatched a rope from a peg on the wall, and in a few moments had both men tied hand and foot. He drew the knots tight for Derner, left the Mexican's comfortably loose, but not too loose.

He next turned his attention to Derner's unconscious friend, decided to take no chances, and swiftly repeated his binding operations. For good measure he gagged the trio, using strips he tore from a soiled towel V. Crumm had neglected to remove.

Perhaps five minutes had passed since he had walked into that dingy little office, Derner's gun nudging his spine. Thanks to Pilar Rojo the situation had changed with startling suddenness. He wondered about Pilar. The Mexican's part in the affair puzzled him. For all Pilar knew he actually *was* an outlaw on the dodge. V. Crumm had seemed to encourage the idea for Pilar's special benefit. It was odd that the Mexican should have sided with him against a prominent townsman like Al Derner. He would have to question V. Crumm about the man.

He looked grimly down at his bound and gagged victims, and another thought took shape in his mind. Pilar had told Derner that V. Crumm had left a bill of sale for the horse on her desk. The lie must be substantiated or else the Mexican would be suspected of treachery. Derner would kill the man if he had a glimmer of the truth.

Miles went to the wooden chest and looked in the drawer that Derner had started to search. He saw a stack of old bills tucked in a corner. He snatched one, said loudly for Derner's benefit: "Queer place to put my bill of sale. Looks like the old lady figgered I'd ride off without it."

He made a show of crackling the paper noisily into folds before pocketing it, hastily gathered up the two guns from the floor, then stood for a moment, his hard smile on Derner, whose head had twisted round in an infuriated look at him.

"Well, gentlemen"—he spoke in a mirthful drawl—"thanks for helping me find my bill of sale. I'd have gone off without it." He laughed softly. "Was needing that bronc to finish my little trip to the border. *Adiós, señores.* My next address is any place in Old Mexico."

41

He turned down the lamp-wick, blew out the feeble light, took the key from inside the door, closed it behind him, locked it, and pocketed the key. He would hand it over to V. Crumm when he reached the house. In the meantime he had done his best to keep her and Pilar Rojo above suspicion. His comment about V. Crumm's apparent attempt to conceal the mythical bill of sale would go a long way to convince Derner that she was ignorant of his identity. Derner would be puzzled, but satisfied that his intended victim was in full flight for the border. He would be completely mystified about the .45 Miles had suddenly produced. Apparently neither of the men had noticed the filled holster. They had no reason to suspect Pilar Rojo.

Hugely contented, he swung up to his saddle and turned the bay into the street. He had an appointment to keep with V. Crumm and a slim young girl whose name was Frazer. He found himself speculating about her first name.

Lamplight glowed from windows, and horses were gathering at the long hitch-rails in front of saloons. A pair of cowboys passed him, dust-grimed, but cheerful with expectancy. He gave them an anxious backward look, was relieved to see them pass the livery barn. He guessed that a saloon was their first objective, a drink or two to cut the dust from parched throats.

He pushed on until a bend in the road hid the

town from view. A swing left brought him to the sandy wash, and he had to keep the horse at a slow walk now, mindful of deep holes and great boulders that leaped out from the black curtain of the night.

A mile up the wash brought the cottonwood into view, a vast, vague shape. He swung the horse up the slope, and suddenly he saw dimly the high mud wall—the gate.

He halted, slid from the saddle, and now the gate opened, so silently that he guessed the hinges were kept well oiled.

A big shape loomed in the blackness. He saw a beckoning hand. He led the horse through the gate, which closed as silently as it had opened.

V. Crumm's voice said in a gruff whisper, "You've been a hell of a time gettin' here. Began to think you'd hightailed it away from this town."

Miles Clarke peered at her. "I wouldn't be leaving without that bill of sale," he said laconically.

She stared back at him, and something she sensed in him drew a dismayed gasp from her. "You—you run into trouble—back at the barn?"

"Well . . ." He was suddenly smiling. "You might say that your friend Al Derner did."

V. Crumm flapped a limp hand at him. For once she had no words.

Chapter IV

Ellen Frazer awoke suddenly. The room was in pitch darkness, and somebody was knocking on the door. Momentary fright held her rigid.

A voice spoke softly: "*Señorita.*"

Ellen sat up. "Who is it?"

The door opened and light flowed in from the lamp in the hand of a Mexican woman. "I am Ynez, *señorita.*" She placed the lamp on a table, struck a match, and lit another lamp that stood on the bureau. "You 'ave nize sleep."

Ellen slid from the bed. "What time is it?" she asked.

"Past eight o'clock," Ynez told her. "Señora say you come now and 'ave supper weeth her." She picked up her lamp and moved to the door. "I tell señora you come soon."

Ellen waited until the door closed, then went to the bureau and stared at her reflection in the mirror, ran fingers through her thick, dark hair. She looked surprisingly refreshed, the worry lines smoothed from her face, her eyes clear. She had felt like an old hag when she climbed from the stage.

The thought of the stage sent a shiver through

her. The attempted hold-up—the dead bandit sprawled in the dust—the hard, bright eyes of the young man who had used his gun with such deadly efficiency.

The affair had drawn heavily on her already spent strength. And then the arrival in Santa Ysabel—and no Duncan. His failure to meet her had seemed more than she could bear.

She glanced at the trunk Johnny had carried over from the stage office. She would not even unstrap it. Her one desire now was to continue her journey, get out to the ranch Duncan had bought in partnership with a man named Jess Wellen. Wellen had put no cash into the venture, only his experience as a cowman and knowledge of the country. His wife was keeping house for them.

Duncan's first letters had been so enthusiastic, urging her to join him. Ellen and he would live in the new wing he was planning to build on to the present ranch-house, which he described as not more than a log cabin. She would have a garden, with flowers and vegetables and trees for shade. It seemed that there were few trees, only patches of scrubby junipers and vast stretches of brush. Twenty thousand acres, with free range reaching to the Mexican border.

Ellen reached abruptly for her handbag and extracted a letter. Worry deepened in her as she read the familiar scrawl, tried to make sense of it:

. . . and the way things look I'm not sure you should come. Several puzzling incidents have happened and I don't know what to make of them. Maybe I'm wrong, but I don't know, Sis. Jess Wellen puts on a grin when I ask him to explain, says I'm only a tenderfoot and need to grow my horns and that there's no sense getting scared about what I don't *savvy*, to use his word for it. Just the same I *am* uneasy and I can't help feeling that something is awfully wrong. I'll write again, soon. In the meantime don't think of coming—yet. Not until you hear from me. . . .

Ellen stuffed the letter back into her bag, stood there, conscious again of those old sickening fears that had been with her from the moment she had first read it. She had waited a month for further word from Duncan, and then written to him, saying she would leave New York the following week, and asking him to meet the stage at Santa Ysabel. Either he had never received her letter, or something dreadful had happened to him. She could find no other explanation. Duncan would not have disappointed her wilfully.

She recalled V. Crumm's curious expression when asked about the letter. V. Crumm was the postmaster and was likely to know if the letter had reached Santa Ysabel. The big woman had hesitated the merest instant explaining that her

46

assistant looked after the mail and that she wouldn't be knowing about it.

Ellen went slowly to the door, opened it, and stepped outside. She stood for a moment, accustoming her eyes to the darkness and wondering miserably about V. Crumm. Perhaps she had been a little too hasty in accepting the woman's hospitality.

Ugly suspicions were stirring in her. V. Crumm had lied about the letter. She knew all about it, knew that Duncan Frazer's sister was expected to arrive on the stage. It explained why she was waiting there when the stage halted in front of the store. She had refused to let Ellen go to the hotel, insisted upon hurrying her away to her own house.

The door was open now, and fear crept in. Ellen suddenly knew that she was frightened, knew that she desperately wanted to get away from this place.

She looked about frantically, realized she was completely lost in the black night that mantled the patio. She had no idea where to look for the gate in the old wall opposite the church. If she could find the gate she would have no difficulty in making her way to the hotel. Once safe in the hotel, she could send for her trunk.

She turned into the room, hastily put on her little bonnet. Her hands trembled and she could hardly tie the ribbons under her chin. Bag in hand, she hurriedly left the room, came to an abrupt stand-still. Somebody was approaching up the long gallery. Ynez, carrying a lantern.

The Mexican woman was smiling apologetically. "I forget breeng—" She was suddenly silent, and, lifting the lantern, she peered curiously at the bonnet.

Ellen said, quietly, "Thank you for bringing me a light, Ynez. I was wondering where the gate is, and it's so dark."

"The gate, *señorita*?" Ynez took a backward step, her smile gone now, her eyes suspicious.

"I want to take a walk, see the town," Ellen said. "Show me the gate, please, Ynez."

"You 'ave no eat," expostulated the Mexican woman. "Señora—she wait for you—"

Ellen repressed the impulse to snatch the lantern and run. She was suddenly impatient with herself. It was no time to give way to panic. She must keep her wits, and use them.

The thought steadied her, and she felt a warming flow of courage, a new and stiffening self-confidence.

V. Crumm looked at her shrewdly as she followed Ynez into the dining-room. Something had happened to the girl. Her eyes were bright, and a bit hard, and there was a resolute lift to her chin—a fighting look to her—that won V. Crumm's instant approval.

Ynez disappeared into the kitchen, and V. Crumm

48

said in her big, genial voice, "Sit down, child—"
She broke off, surprised look on the bonnet.
"What's the idea, puttin' on your bonnet just to
come and eat?"

Ellen said unsmilingly, "I'm leaving, Mrs
Crumm. If I can't get somebody to drive me to my
brother's ranch to-night I'll stay at the hotel."

V. Crumm stared at her curiously. "What's got
you so scared all of a sudden, child?"

"I'm not scared. I—I'm worried." Ellen was
watching her intently. "It's very strange that you
don't know anything about that letter."

V. Crumm interrupted her. "Your brother never
come for it. I was askin' Pete, and he says the
letter's still layin' in his box."

Ellen's hand went blindly to the chair. She
leaned against it for a moment, then slowly sat
down. Her legs felt trembly and weak.

"You was thinkin' I lied about the letter."
V. Crumm spoke gently. "I wasn't sure, honey.
That's why I put you off. Wanted to ask Pete if
your brother had been in for it. Pete says he ain't
seen him in weeks."

Ynez made her soundless appearance from the
kitchen with loaded plates. She placed them on the
table, gave Ellen an anxious look, and hurried out.
Ellen thought she heard a man's voice in the
kitchen as the door closed behind her.

V. Crumm took up knife and fork, sniffed
appreciatively. "You'll feel a heap better when

49

you've et some of this *arroz con pollo*," she said
loudly. "Ynez has 'em all beat when it comes to
arroz con pollo."

Ellen eyed her plate listlessly. *Arroz con pollo*
was chicken and rice with other things mixed in,
she saw. It looked appetizing enough, but the
thought of food revolted her at that moment.

"I'm not hungry," she said.

"Don't get foolish!" V. Crumm glared at her.
"You'll not fight trouble any easier for not eatin',
and by all the signs—there's plenty trouble
hornin' your way." She smiled grimly over her
fork. "I've got more kinds of trouble you can
shake a stick at, and *I'm* eatin'."

Ellen felt a sudden shame. She was behaving
like a little coward. Where was her pride, her
courage? She would get nowhere if she kept on
giving way to weakening fears. She picked up
knife and fork.

"I'm afraid I'm being silly," she said.

"No call for you to blame yourself." V. Crumm
spoke sympathetically. "Awful shock for you,
landin' in a strange place like Santa Ysabel and
your brother not showing up to meet you."

Ellen nodded. The chicken was delicious, and
she was surprised to find that she was suddenly
ravenous.

"It's my guess you was some worried before
you got here," V. Crumm continued. She gave the
girl a shrewd look. "You was uneasy in your

mind about your brother . . . some news he sent you in a letter."

Ellen nodded again. "He wrote me that queer things were happening . . . told me not to come."

"And you wrote back and said you was comin' west right off and for him to meet you at Santa Ysabel." V. Crumm's look went momentarily to the kitchen door behind Ellen. "You got scared when he didn't show up, and got to thinkin' I was lyin' when I told you I didn't know about the letter. And then you got to thinkin' I was mixed up in the business that was worryin' your brother, and that was why I hauled you over here from the stage like I done. The more thinkin' you did, the worse scared you got, and you figgered to get away as quick as you could."

Ellen was silent for a moment, then her eyes lifted in a steady look. "I'm sorry—for doubting you. I don't any more. Please forgive me." She gestured despairingly. "I—I feel so—*helpless*."

"You just don't know which way to turn," V. Crumm said gently. "The trails look all alike, twistin' off into the scrub to goodness knows where."

"I can't sit around doing nothing. I've got to get to the ranch to-night, find out about Duncan." Her voice faltered. "I'm afraid something has happened to him . . . something dreadful."

"Nonsense!" V. Crumm pretended an optimism she was far from feeling. "Lots of things can happen on a cow ranch to keep a man from gettin' to town."

"I must go to-night," insisted the girl. "Please arrange it for me, Mrs Crumm."

V. Crumm pursed her lips obstinately. "Mighty long ways to the Juniper Flats country. Keep you travellin' most all night, way the roads are."

"I won't mind."

"Ain't carin' to risk one of my rigs on a dark night like this. You wait until mornin', child."

"I can try the hotel, find somebody else who'll rent me a buckboard and driver." Ellen's face hardened with determination.

V. Crumm glared indignantly, then of a sudden a smile softened her rugged face. "You're tough-minded, for all your flower face," she chuckled. "I like your spirit, child. Good, clean metal in you, and that's what it takes in this country." Her voice lifted. "Miles—you come and talk to Miss Frazer. She's got me licked with her stubbornness."

Ellen turned her head in a quick look at the kitchen door. Her ears had not deceived her. She had heard a man talking to Ynez.

V. Crumm's voice was saying: "Miles Clarke come in on the stage with you, Ellen. He's an old friend—known him since he was a yearlin'."

Ellen was living again those tense moments on the mountain grade—the dead bandit sprawled in the dust, the smoking gun in the hands of the young man now gravely returning her startled look from the kitchen doorway. Something he saw in her amazed eyes disturbed Miles. He read fear there, a hint of horror. She was afraid of him.

He closed the door behind him, looked doubtfully at V. Crumm. She beckoned him to the table.

"Sit down," she said. "I'll tell Ynez to bring you a fresh cup of coffee."

Miles shook his head. "No more, thanks." He pulled out a chair opposite Ellen and sat down, careful to keep his face averted. "I've finished supper," he said.

"Well?" V. Crumm was frowning. "Ain't you got a word for Ellen Frazer? What's wrong with you all of a sudden? You act like you swallowed a poker along with the chicken Ynez fixed for you."

"I remember seeing Miss Frazer on the stage." Miles felt in his shirt pocket, drew out tobacco and cigarette-papers. "What is it you want, Vee?"

V. Crumm's puzzled frown deepened. "What's got into you young folks, actin' so hostile?"

"I don't know . . ." Miles paused, looked curiously at Ellen. "Unless Miss Frazer is thinking about that hold-up," he finished gloomily.

"Nonsense!" exploded V. Crumm. "She ain't holdin' *that* against you. If you hadn't acted so quick she would likely have been killed herself."

Ellen found her voice. "I'm not used to such things. It seemed dreadful—that man lying there —dead."

53

"You'll get used to it if you stay in *this* country," V. Crumm told her grimly. "Don't get fool notions about Miles Clarke. He ain't no killer. He only done what was right. You thank your lucky star he was along when them low-down wolves jumped the stage."

"I—I suppose you're right." Ellen's face went suddenly pink, and her eyes lifted in a fleeting look at Miles.

"You bet I'm right," barked V. Crumm. "Miles Clarke is good poison to have handy when killin' wolves is doggin' your trail."

Ellen's head lifted in another look at Miles, and her eyes were contrite now. "I'm sorry," she said. "I'm afraid I've been a prig."

His smile came, warm, reassuring. "I don't blame you, Miss Frazer. It was ugly business." His face sobered. "We have no benefit of law in this Santa Ysabel country. Some day the Law will come, and when it does I'll be among the first to welcome it with a handclasp."

"Huh!" V. Crumm nodded vigorously. "I'm thinkin' it'll be yourself that'll bring law and order to the Santa Ysabel country. Won't be easy, but you've got the guts for the job." She flushed, added apologetically, "There I go ag'in with my rough talk, and this young lass fresh from the East."

Ellen smiled. "Don't mind me. I'm learning fast."

Miles, watching her intently, felt an odd thrill of satisfaction. Ellen Frazer's smile quite fulfilled his dreams. It emphasized a little dimple in her left cheek and was worth any man's time and efforts to win for himself.

He became aware of V. Crumm's shrewd, discerning look, realized that he was wearing what must have seemed like a silly grin, and hastily put a match to his cigarette.

She smothered a grin of her own, and then, crisply: "Ellen's got the fool notion she wants to get out to her brother's ranch to-night. She's worried sick 'cause he ain't showed up to meet her."

"I really must," Ellen said. Her chin lifted resolutely. "Mrs Crumm doesn't want me to go—for some reason."

"It's a fool notion," insisted V. Crumm. "I ain't sendin' one of my rigs over them roads this black night. All of twenty-five miles to the Box DF." She was looking at Miles. "That's her brother's outfit," she added significantly; "over Juniper Flats way."

Miles nodded, guessed she had purposely refrained from telling the girl of her suspicions about the Box DF outfit. He was recalling her words: "He's mixed up with a bunch of cow-thieves. . . . Got a pardner that's hang-tree fruit. . . . Name of Jess Wellen."

He felt reasonably certain that V. Crumm had

good cause for her suspicions. She would not lightly call a man a cow-thief. He knew, too, that she would shrink from giving even a hint of her fears to Ellen Frazer. She could only do her best to keep the girl in town, at least overnight. It was unthinkable to let her reach the ranch in the dead of night, alone, unsuspecting.

He said slowly, uncomfortably aware of Ellen's appealing eyes on him, "I think Vee is right, Miss Frazer. Can't do any harm to wait until morning. There's a chance your brother will show up."

"I must go—to-night," reiterated the girl. "I—I feel that something is wrong—that Duncan is in danger." Her face was suddenly pale. "You see— we're twins—and very close." She got out of her chair, a slim, straight little figure in close-fitting bodice and full skirt, and her hand lifted in an impatient gesture gave a settling pat to the little poke bonnet on her dark hair. "If Mrs Crumm won't hire me a rig and driver, I must try the hotel. Surely there's another livery barn."

"There ain't," V. Crumm said gruffly.

Miles Clarke broke his silence. "I'm riding out that way to-night. Can easily drop in at the Box DF, tell your brother you're in town."

She considered the suggestion, blue eyes holding his, and suddenly her smile came, turned his heart over: "I've a better idea than that," she said. "You can take me with you."

V. Crumm caught Miles' quick glance. She

exclaimed harshly, "*No!* I ain't hirin' out no buck-board and team for that drive to-night. And who's to bring the rig back to the stables?" She glared at Ellen. "And it ain't fair to make all that trouble for Miles. He's got business of his own to 'tend to."

Ellen stood there, rigid, her face white under its cloud of shining dark hair. Miles felt he could not bear to see her so miserable. He was on his feet now, heard his own voice, a bit unsteady:

"Now, Vee—"

The kitchen door pushed open violently and Johnny rushed in. He was breathless, the freckles big on his white face.

"V-vee," he stuttered. "Somethin' awful wrong at the barn!"

V. Crumm was out of her chair and bearing down on him. "Now, Johnny—you get your breath back."

"Looks like Pilar's dyin' or somethin'," Johnny continued excitedly. "Couple of fellers went to stable their broncs. Wasn't nobody 'round and the office locked up, no lights burnin'."

V. Crumm gave Miles a sly glance. "Nothin' to get all excited about," she said. "Pilar's likely gone off to get him a drink."

"No, ma'am," Johnny shook his head impatiently. "It's plenty worse than that. These fellers stabled their broncs their own selves in the dark. And when they come past the office they heard somebody groanin' awful queer. They was afraid

57

to bust the door down, and went off to get the town marshal. I reckon Dan Heeler's there by now, and he won't stop at bustin' a door."

V. Crumm was already moving towards the kitchen. For a big woman she was amazingly quick on her feet. "I reckon I'd better see what's goin' on," she said over her shoulder. "No—" as Miles started to follow, "the barn ain't no place for *you* right now, young feller. You stay here with Ellen until I get back." She disappeared, Johnny stamping at her heels.

Chapter V

Ellen went slowly to her chair and sat down. She was puzzled by V. Crumm's parting words: "The barn ain't no place for you right now." A strange thing to say to Miles Clarke, and bore only one interpretation. It was dangerous for Miles Clarke to be seen at the barn—or in Santa Ysabel.

She stole a look at him. He seemed suddenly older, his face lean and hard, and he was staring with narrowed eyes at the door that Johnny had slammed shut when he ran after V. Crumm.

He muttered an exclamation, drew a key from his pocket, gave it a startled glance, and moved quickly to the kitchen door.

Ellen came out of her chair. "Where are you going?" Alarm put a shrill note in her voice. "Mrs Crumm said you must stay here—with me!"

Miles came to a standstill, looked back at her. "I forgot to give her the key," he said. He held the key up. "She won't like it if the town marshal smashes the door."

"I won't stay here alone," Ellen said.

He was not waiting to argue with her, and after a moment's indecision she ran into the kitchen, followed him into the darkness of the patio, conscious of a startled exclamation from Ynez, busy with her dish-washing.

Miles heard the quick beat of her feet on the worn flagstones. He halted, waited for her to overtake him.

Her fingers fastened on his arm. "I'm afraid to stay alone—"

They stood there, vague shapes in that darkness, and after a moment she heard his voice, low, not quite steady: "All right."

Her hand dropped from his arm, and she was aware of an odd, exciting glow in her from the momentary touch; and then they were moving through the darkness, following a light that twinkled and danced ahead of them through the cottonwood trees.

They reached the rear of the big store building. Miles suddenly halted. He was acting like a fool, letting this girl's nearness, the touch of her

59

hand, put his mind in a whirl, confuse his thoughts.

He spoke again, his voice harsh: "Not safe for you to be seen on the street."

She made no answer, just stood waiting, her uplifted face a pale blur in the night.

"All right," he said again, but this time he could not force harshness into his voice. "We've got to hurry—but don't make more noise than you must."

A big kerosene lamp suspended from a chain sent a dim light through the store, and they made their way quietly to the street door. Miles tried it gently, found that V. Crumm had left it unlocked. In another moment they were outside and moving cautiously down the plank sidewalk.

Lamplight glowed from saloon windows, and Ellen could see the vague shapes of horses at hitch-rails. From one of the saloons came the squeak of a fiddle, the pound of dancing feet, a woman's shrill laugh.

Miles hurried her along, his hand on her arm now, to keep her from stumbling on the rough planking. Ahead of them lantern lights danced like fireflies in front of the big livery barn, and they heard V. Crumm's voice, loud, belligerent.

"You ain't bustin' my door down, Dan Heeler. You wait a moment. I got a key some place—"

"Ain't waitin' for no key," answered a man's voice. "Somebody go get an axe."

V. Crumm's voice became a bellow. "No damn

sense wreckin' my door. I got a extry key back at the house. Johnny—you run back to the house and get that key from my desk. You know where it is."

"Somebody's layin' dead or dyin' in there," argued the man's voice. "If the axe gets here ahead of your key I'm bustin' the door."

"I'll sue you for damages," raged V. Crumm. "Johnny—you get runnin' for that key."

Johnny was already running. He came pounding up the board-walk, and Miles, crouching back in the deep shadows with Ellen, reached out a hand.

"Johnny," he whispered. His hand fastened hard on the boy's arm, drew him close.

"Here's the key," he thrust it into Johnny's hand. "Pretend you found it lying in the street."

Johnny recovered his breath. He had no idea who Miles was, but the sight of Ellen reassured him. "I *savvy*," he gasped, and went pounding back to the barn.

"Found it layin' in the street!" he yelled to the little group waiting in the lantern flare.

"Sure got owl eyes, spottin' that key in the dark," commented the town marshal, his voice heavy with disbelief.

Johnny was discreetly silent, and Heeler drew his gun, standing watchful while V. Crumm unlocked the door.

Miles was in a fever of impatience to get Ellen away from the street. Excited shouts, the clatter of approaching feet, warned that the rumour of trouble at the livery barn was drawing a crowd from the saloons. Escape back to the house by way of the store was cut off.

"Come on," he said to Ellen. "We've got to get away from here."

Her hand slipped into his, and they ran into the big yard and hid behind a high-sided freight-wagon drawn up close to a straw stack. If they had been noticed, they were only two more people running to the scene of the excitement; vague, unrecognizable shapes in that darkness.

They crouched there, between the pile of straw and the big canvas-hooded Conestoga. The door was open now, and the office aglow with lantern light, and they heard the town marshal's voice uttering loud and profane comments.

"Who the hell done this, Al?"

Al Derner was on his feet, rubbing chafed lips. "Ain't knowin' for sure," he answered in a rage-thickened voice. "Young feller that come in on the stage."

"How come you tangled with him?" asked the town marshal. He stared curiously at Miles' late fellow-passenger, now getting to his feet and also rubbing a sore mouth. "Who's this hombre, Al?" He indicated the man.

"Friend of mine," Derner told him curtly. "Come in on the stage with the feller I was tellin' you about."

"Seems like you'd better do some talkin', Al

Derner," loudly declared V. Crumm. "Looks like you've been up to some funny business." She jerked Pilar Rojo to his feet. The Mexican's grin could have meant anything.

"Señor Derner teenk thees hombre steal 'orse, ask for see beel of sale."

"Left it here in the office for him," V. Crumm said, remembering Miles' account of the affair. "He wasn't no horse-thief, Al Derner. Maybe he was on the dodge, but I wasn't askin' him questions. Paid me a good price for that geldin'."

Derner glowered at her. It was plain that he was reluctant to talk. Pilar Rojo, catching her covert glance, took up the tale.

"Señor Derner try for arrest thees hombre for murder—"

"Shut your mouth!" growled Derner. He grinned uneasily at the attentive town marshal. "Ace Stengal"—indicating the black-coated stranger—"come in on the same stage and got suspicious about that killin' up the road. He figgered the feller got scared when he saw them riders pop out of the brush and pulled off his gunplay thinkin' they was the law."

Dan Heeler transferred his attention to Stengal. "That right?" he asked.

Stengal nodded, his smooth, dark face an unreadable mask. "I'm sure I've seen him before . . . don't remember just where." Stengal paused, a frown gathering, as if trying to force his memory. "Was on the dodge all right," he finished in his thin, precise voice. "Admitted he was heading for the border and that his address would be any place in Old Mexico."

V. Crumm broke in gruffly, belligerent look on Derner: "How come *you* got the right to go arrestin' folks?" she wanted to know. "You ain't the sheriff of this county, Al Derner."

Derner glared at her. "Any citizen has the right to question a suspicious stranger!"

"You could have had Dan Heeler ask the questions," fumed the woman. "You might have got Pilar killed with your bull-headed ways."

"I carry a deputy sheriff's badge," Derner angrily retorted.

"Huh!" V. Crumm's rage was making her reckless. "I reckon there ain't much poor Jake Renn won't give *you* for the askin'."

"I'll tell Sheriff Renn what you think about him." Derner's smile was back. He rolled amused eyes at the town marshal.

"He's just another poor devil you've got squeezed under your thumb!" shouted V. Crumm.

Dan Heeler was eyeing her uneasily. "Now, Vee—" he shook his head at her. "Ain't right for you to talk loose thataways." He darted the grinning Derner a furtive look and seemed to take courage from something he read in the man's eyes. "You can get into plenty trouble with *that* kind of talk."

V. Crumm pushed out her chin at him. "Ain't trustin' you neither, Dan Heeler. You're just another of 'em that minds when Al Derner cracks his whip." She lifted her hands in a sweeping gesture of disgust. "This town's gone to hell!"

A guffaw came from the crowd that jammed the doorway. The town marshal's face reddened and he swung round, glaring angrily at the grinning men. "Get away from that door!" he roared. "When I'm needin' help I'll ask for it."

V. Crumm gave Derner a nasty smile. "You should swear in a posse and go chase the young feller that tied you up. You'll maybe catch him before he hits the border."

Derner's eyes went suddenly cold, thoughtful, and he stood there looking at her, fingers gently touching the sore corners of his mouth.

"Who's the young lady you yanked off the stage so quick?" he asked.

His soft-spoken words were inaudible to Miles and Ellen, crouched behind the big freight-wagon, but they sensed he had said something to alarm V. Crumm. She stood there, rigid, tense, eyes fastened on Derner's dark face.

Evidently catching a wordless message from Derner's quick look, the town marshal stamped heavily to the door, hand on the gun in his holster, eyes menacing the lingering crowd.

"All right, fellers. Let's get away from here. Vee ain't wantin' her yard all cluttered up." His tone

65

lightened. "I'm headin' for a drink." He pushed through the door, and in a moment the board sidewalk resounded to the tramp of booted feet as the crowd followed him up the street.

Only Derner and Stengal remained now, and Pilar and Johnny, their faces uneasy as they watched V. Crumm. It was plain they too had sensed her panic.

Derner was watching her intently. He darted Stengal an oddly triumphant look, spoke again, loudly now; and there was malicious amusement in his voice.

"I was asking about the girl, *Violet*."

"You damn skunk!" exploded V. Crumm. "I warned you I'd smack you next time you called me Violet." Her hand swept up.

Derner tried to duck the blow. He was too late, and the flat of her big hand caught him on the cheek. He staggered, managed to hold on to his taunting grin.

"You ain't answerin' my question," he said. His voice roughened. "You damn old wildcat!"

"You bet I'm a wildcat!" she told him grimly. "I sure ain't one of your tame cats tied to your string." She put out a hand, seized Johnny by the arm as the boy thrust himself between her and Derner. "You keep out of this, sonny. I'm wildcat enough to chew this skunk and spit out his stinkin' bones."

"Ain't lettin' him harm you," Johnny gasped.

66

"Take more'n his kind to harm *me,* sonny." Her voice softened, but her eyes were hard and bright as she stared at the two men. "You pair of skunks get out of my office," she added roughly, her fists doubled. "Ain't needin' help to throw the two of you out on your necks."

Derner shrugged, rubbed his reddened cheek, and moved towards the door. Stengal followed him, wary eyes on the big woman whose nostrils quivered as she looked at him.

She said bellicosely: "And I'm tellin' you now I ain't wantin' your tin-horn gambler friend on my property no more."

For the first time something like emotion showed on Stengal's face, a fleeting venomous amusement in the quick lift of his eyes at her, and then he was outside in the dark, waiting for Derner, who halted in the doorway, head turned in a backward look.

"You ain't foolin' me one cent's worth." His bruised lips took on an ugly twist. "I know all about the girl. She's Duncan Frazer's sister, and he asked me to meet the stage for her. You were too quick for me—while I was in the post office." He paused, added softly, "Frazer will want me to look her up, and I'm doing the same even if it means getting out a warrant to search your house."

He followed Stengal into the dark night, left her again rigid, speechless; and it was Johnny who broke the silence.

He said, gruffly, to hide his own alarm, "Got to talk to you, Vee." He looked uneasily at Pilar.

She read his thoughts, said gently, "No need to mind speakin' in front of Pilar"—she gave the Mexican an affectionate smile—"Pilar's awful smart, sonny. You ain't half guessin' how smart."

The elderly Mexican's face was one broad grin. "*Sí, señora*, you bet I fool those Derner hombre." He gestured contemptuously. "Those Derner hombre beeg r-rascal, no?"

"Rascal!" she snorted. "He's hell's own pet rattlesnake." Her inquiring gaze was on Johnny: "All right, sonny."

Johnny went quickly to the door, stood for a moment listening, then, reassured, he said over his shoulder, his voice hardly more than a whisper: "She's here, Vee, hidin' back of the wagon."

V. Crumm stared at him, her expression bewildered. "What's this crazy talk. . . ."

"There's a feller with her," Johnny went on. "Was him as grabbed me, give me the key. They ducked behind the wagon when them fellers come on the jump to see what was goin' on."

V. Crumm was suddenly brisk. She relighted the office lamp, picked up her lantern, and strode to the door.

"You stick here in the office, Pilar," she told the Mexican in a loud voice. "Bisco's due to relieve you at nine o'clock, and then you can go home."

"*Sí, señora*."

"You come along with me to the barn, Johnny. I'm takin' a look at the roan I took in trade from Jim Winters. I've a notion he'll be in shape for Cap Hansy to use in place of the horse that skulkin' road agent killed."

Miles grinned to himself in the dark, tightened a reassuring hand over Ellen's. V. Crumm's purposely loud voice was intended for his ears.

The lantern-light danced like a firefly across the yard; and hand in hand Miles and Ellen followed it through the blanketing night.

The girl's thoughts were in a sickening whirl. She had no idea who Al Derner was, but it seemed that Duncan had asked him to meet the stage, and that would mean he was a friend of Duncan's.

It was also apparent that Miles Clarke was the man "on the dodge" who had overpowered Derner and the others, left them bound and gagged, and supposedly fled for the border. Only he hadn't ridden for the border. He was close by her side, his hand holding hers, leading her through the darkness, following that dancing light to perhaps more unknown terrors. After all, what did she really know about these people? Al Derner had plainly accused V. Crumm of kidnapping her in an attempt to keep her from reaching Duncan.

Ellen was suddenly hanging back against the pull of Miles' hand. She said in a low, frightened voice, "I don't like this. . . ."

They came to a standstill, and Miles spoke in a concerned voice: "I don't blame you."

"That man said Duncan asked him to meet me."

"He's probably lying."

"I want to talk to him." Ellen tried to pull her hand from his clasp. "Please let me go."

Miles said sharply, "Don't be crazy—"

"But he knows Duncan," her voice was low, furious. "He knew I was expected to arrive on the stage—"

"He couldn't have known you were arriving to-day," Miles pointed out. "You wrote your brother to expect you, but the letter is still in the post office —unclaimed." His voice hardened. "Derner evidently knows about you, but it's my guess he's lying when he claims your brother asked him to meet you."

Ellen was silent for a moment, obviously impressed by the argument, and then, almost tearfully: "I must get out to the ranch to-night. I can't bear it, waiting here and Duncan perhaps sick and needing me. If Mrs Crumm won't help me I'll have to ask Mr Derner."

"I'm taking you out to your brother's ranch myself," Miles said.

He heard the quick intake of her breath, and then: "You mean it? You really will—take me—to-night?"

"To-night," Miles said. "I was going to tell you

70

I would when Johnny interrupted us back at the house."

He felt her eyes on him, appraising, considering. "Of course I know it was you who tied up those men in the office," she said. "They say you're on the dodge from the law—think you plan to escape across the border. It's very mysterious," she added. "You—you don't seem like a desperado. . . ."

"*Gracias.*" The dark hid his grin, and then, his voice suddenly grim: "It's mysterious all right. I think Derner planned to kill me."

Ellen shuddered. "It's terrible—and he claims he's a deputy sheriff—that he's the law."

"There is no law in the Santa Ysabel country," Miles said. "I told you back at the house that we are without benefit of law." His voice softened. "Yes, it must seem very terrible to you, but you must trust V. Crumm, Miss Frazer—and, if you can, try and trust me, and believe me when I say that I'm not on the dodge from anything." His hand was again gently urging her towards the big barn. "Vee is waiting for us. Her talk about the black horse was only to let us know she wants us to join her. We've got to make plans in a hurry."

She made no further protest, and they moved on, keeping close to the high corral fence and following it round to the glimmer of light that showed from a small side door.

They slipped inside, and Johnny, waiting, quickly closed the door and dropped the bar. He

71

gave Ellen an excited grin, pointed down the long line of stalls to another door.

"She's waitin' back in the granary," he whispered.

V. Crumm gave them a grim look as they followed Johnny into the granary. She said to Johnny, "Cover the lantern with a grain-sack. Don't want light to show, now you've got here." She frowned at Miles. "Took you an awful long time to get over here. Began to think you hadn't caught on when I spoke out loud I was comin' to have a look at the black horse. Johnny said you was hidin' behind the wagon."

"Miss Frazer was worried," Miles explained. "You can't blame her, Vee—"

"Huh!" V. Crumm stared at Ellen with shrewd eyes. "Heard Derner's lyin' talk about your brother askin' him to meet you, and that letter you wrote your brother still layin' in the post-box."

"He seemed to know about me," reminded Ellen.

"Seems like he does, worse luck." V. Crumm shook her head unhappily. "I'll tell you this, Ellen, he don't mean no good by you, and that's why we've got to do some smart thinkin'. Derner's got Sheriff Renn in one pocket and that dumb Heeler in the other. They dance to any tune he sets, or else he can strip 'em clean as a skinned maverick. Renn's got a ranch he'd hate like poison to lose. He ain't sayin' no to nothin' Derner wants of him." She gestured gloomily: "He'll rig up some kind of paper and force his way into my house . . . do his best to get his hands on you."

"I'm leaving for the ranch," Ellen told her. "I won't be there if he comes looking for me."

V. Crumm ruffled like an angry hen: "You'll not be goin' with *my* help. I was figgerin' on kind of smugglin' you clean away from here—to Silver City. Know folks there that can take good care of you." She broke off, looked keenly at Miles, who was smiling reassuringly at Ellen. "Huh! You two have been cookin' up some crazy scheme, I'll bet," she charged.

"That's right," grinned Miles. "She's determined to go to her brother's ranch, and I'm taking her."

"Of all the fool notions," grumbled V. Crumm. "Well—if she's set on goin' she can't do better than have you along." She studied Ellen curiously. "You heard what was said about Miles, didn't you? How do you know they wasn't tellin' the truth? Ain't you afraid to trust with him?"

"No," Ellen said. She looked at Miles. "He told me he was not on the dodge from anything. I believe him, and I—I trust him." Her smile came, confident.

"He's on the dodge, all right," grumbled V. Crumm. "On the dodge from wicked men who figger to kill him. He ain't so safe to be seen with."

"I don't care," Ellen said soberly. Something like admiration was in her eyes. "I saw what he did to those men."

73

"I reckon Miles can take care of himself if any man can," admitted V. Crumm. She chuckled: "One ag'inst three, he was, only Pilar Rojo don't really count."

"I'm wondering about Pilar," Miles said quietly. "He thinks I *really* am on the run from a sheriff's posse. I haven't figgered out why he helped me get hold of that gun."

"He hates Derner's guts," V. Crumm said frankly. "Pilar's ready to side with anybody that Derner's out to get. That Mexican loves Derner the same way he loves a pizen rattlesnake." Worry deepened the harsh lines on her face. "How do you figger to get Ellen out to the ranch? Derner will have the roads watched. Don't you under-estimate that hombre. He's crafty as a wolf and a heap more dangerous."

"We won't use any road," Miles told her.

"Figger to ride, huh?" V. Crumm looked at Ellen doubtfully. "How do you know she can set a saddle without fallin' off?"

"I've ridden horses all my life," Ellen said indignantly.

"Huh!" V. Crumm wrinkled a scornful nose. "I reckon all the ridin' you done was in a park. Some different, out here." She eyed Ellen thoughtfully. "I've got a couple of side-saddles in the barn, but you cain't be seen in that outfit you're wearin', and goodness only knows where I can lay my hands on a ridin' skirt. Ain't got one. Ride straddle, myself, like a man."

"Well," Ellen's chin went up resolutely, "I've never ridden straddle, but I will if I must."

"Not in them clothes," snorted the older woman. "You'll need pants. . . ." Her face brightened. "You're slim-built, and I'm bettin' Johnny's pants will fit you fine. Johnny, ain't you got another pair of pants over to the house? If you ain't I'm skinnin' them pants you're wearin' right off of you."

Johnny, embarrassed and stuttering, admitted he had an extra pair of jeans at the house.

"Run over and fetch 'em. Go the back way, and don't let nobody see you. And Johnny, bring that new blue flannel shirt I give you, and she'll need them boots you're wearing and the loan of your pinto bronc and saddle."

Johnny, an appalled look on his freckled face, nodded and turned to go. Ellen called to him, "I'll need my little bag. Ask Ynez to get it for you."

"And bring Miles' horse back with you," added V. Crumm.

Johnny nodded again, vanished through the granary door.

V. Crumm looked at Miles. "Ain't safe for you to go back to the house for the horse," she said with a grave shake of her head. "No tellin' but what Derner's already watchin' the place."

"You think of everything," admired Ellen. "You—you're wonderful!"

75

V. Crumm's answering smile was something to see in that dim lantern light. It made her rugged, weather-beaten face seem extraordinary kind and gentle.

"You're a brave lass," she said softly. "If it wasn't for Miles Clarke here ridin' with you I'd tie you up before I'd let you go to Juniper Flats this dark night or any other time. That's what I think of you, lass; and may God ride close to the pair of you." Her voice was brisk again. "I'll be throwin' Johnny's saddle on his pinto. You'll want to get away quick as you can when he gets back with his pants and things for Ellen. You stay here with Ellen, Miles. You've got to keep out of sight."

She picked up the lantern and disappeared into the stable, leaving them alone in the darkness of the granary.

Chapter VI

Ellen marvelled that Miles Clarke could find his way through the darkness of the gorge. She could see nothing of their surroundings in that blackness, only the vague outline of the man in front of her, the slow-moving horse under him.

She sensed from the back-pull of her weight in the saddle that the trail was making a steady climb. Miles had put the mare on a lead-rope, warned her to ride with a loose rein. Ellen was thankful enough to leave it to the lead-rope to keep her on the trail. She would have been quickly lost if the mare had taken it into her head to wander.

She recalled with some amusement the relief on Johnny's freckled face when V. Crumm had at the last moment decided not to use his pinto horse, and selected instead the sleek chestnut mare.

"That paint horse of yours has got some ornery tricks, Johnny," she had said. "I reckon Ellen will be a lot safer on Ginger. Goin' to be dark as sin down in the gorge, and Ginger's awful steady. She'll follow good on a lead-rope, and that's what Old Paint ain't likely to do. He'll get to jumpin' and throw the girl."

The trail steepened, and Ellen heard the rattle of stones under scrambling shod hoofs. She leaned forward in the saddle, held her breath, reins loose in her hand, and suddenly they were on level ground and at a standstill.

She heard Miles' voice: "We'll rest a bit," he said. "Let the horses get their wind back."

Ellen suspected that the rest was for her benefit. The mare was breathing quite normally, despite the steep climb. She was glad enough, though, to relax in the saddle.

Miles spoke again, a hint of concern in his voice: "How are you making out?"

"All right," she answered, and then her face lifted in a wondering look at him. "I don't see how you can stick to the trail in this darkness, or know where you are going."

"Only one way to go, up this canyon." She felt rather than saw his smile on her. "Another mile or two will bring us out on the flats, and then we'll make better time." He slid from his saddle. "Get down and stretch," he advised. "A long way to Juniper Flats."

Ellen climbed from her saddle, and he came close to her side, went on talking: "Moon coming," he said. "We'll have good moonlight on the mesa, once we get out of this canyon."

She looked up at the patch of sky above the dark mass of the cliffs. The stars were less bright, and there was a luminous glow widening down from the rimrock.

Miles watched her, marvelled at the change in her made by Johnny's trousers and blue shirt, the battered Stetson that concealed tight-braided dark hair. She looked like a slim boy in that darkness.

Ellen felt his scrutiny, and her face came round to him, her smile faintly challenging.

"Will I pass inspection?"

He was silent for a moment, stirred by her nearness, and dismayingly aware that not even Johnny's clothes and the hat could deceive anyone. She was too completely feminine. He said, almost gruffly, "If nobody gets too close for a good look at you."

"Well"—her tone was matter-of-fact—"I'm not wanting to make anybody think I'm a man. I'm wearing these clothes because long skirts aren't practical for this ride."

Miles said thoughtfully, fingers busy making a cigarette, "We don't want to risk anybody knowing you are a girl, not with Al Derner on the watch for Duncan Frazer's sister."

"I don't quite understand"—Ellen paused, hand caressing the mare's velvety nose. "Why must I be afraid of Duncan's friends?"

"We don't know—yet." Miles lit the cigarette, and even in that darkness she saw the bleakness in his eyes. "We don't know the answer," he continued. "We only know that your brother has not been seen for weeks, and after what happened to me at the livery barn to-night we know that Al Derner is up to mischief."

"You're trying to frighten me," she said resentfully.

"I'm trying to warn you." His tone was gentle. "I want you to be prepared for—*anything*."

"I don't understand," she repeated. "In what way am I connected with Mr Derner's attempt to arrest you? You are not mixed up in Duncan's affairs. He never mentioned your name in his letters."

Miles hesitated, miserably aware that it was

impossible at that moment to divulge his suspicions. She was already too overburdened with anxiety about her brother. It was no time to tell her that Duncan Frazer was either hand-in-glove with a rustler outfit, or else a helpless victim of a ruthless conspiracy. He preferred for the moment to believe that Ellen's brother was an innocent party to the mysterious and sinister pillaging of Jim Miles' Bar M ranch.

He answered her with a question. "Didn't your brother ever mention Al Derner's name?"

Ellen shook her head. "No . . ."

"He never told you from whom he bought the Box DF?"

"No," she repeated. "I haven't seen the—the papers." She was peering at him, trying to read his expression. "Why do you ask?"

"V. Crumm told me you had a worried letter from him. He told you there were things he didn't understand."

Ellen said in a low voice, "You—you make me frightened."

"I'm sorry." Miles snubbed the cigarette under his boot-heel, forced a cheerful grin. "No use for us to speculate until we know more. Let's be on our way." He turned to his horse.

Her voice held him back. "Wait a minute. I want to know why you are so interested in Duncan's affairs—why you want to know who sold us the ranch."

His head turned in a long look at her. "You were determined to go out to the ranch to-night," he reminded. "I agreed to take you. I'm sorry—if I seem too curious."

Ellen sensed that he was evading, and she moved close to him, peered into his face. "It's so dark," she complained. "I can't really see your face, read your expression." Her hand lifted in a despairing gesture. "Please, Mr Clarke! I'm half crazy with worry. What brought you to Santa Ysabel? And why am I in danger from Mr Derner? And why do you want to know who sold the ranch to Duncan and me? I *do* want to trust you."

Her hand was on his arm, and the feel of it turned him rigid. He said, huskily, "You've *got* to trust me—"

"I want to trust you." Her hand tightened imploringly. "Only don't keep things back . . . don't try to save my feelings. Tell me the truth."

He thought desperately for some answer that would satisfy her, felt his way cautiously: "I came to Santa Ysabel to look into the disappearance of my uncle. V. Crumm suspects that Derner knows something about it. After what happened to-night, I've reason to believe he does. Derner doesn't want me in Santa Ysabel, asking questions about Jim Miles. I'm quite sure that he planned to kill me. I'd never have seen the inside of that gaol. It was a trick to get me away, kill me."

"Kill you!" she said in an appalled whisper. "Oh, Mr Clarke—I shouldn't have let you come with me."

"That's right." Miles smiled at her. "I'm dangerous company."

"I didn't mean that!" flared Ellen. "I meant it's dangerous for you, out here. You might be followed, and if it wasn't for me you could be safe at Mrs Crumm's house, or some place."

"I didn't come to Santa Ysabel to hide out," Miles said grimly.

She stood there, looking at him intently, and he saw that her lips were parted, her eyes wide with growing apprehension. Far above them, the lifting moon dripped silver on the rimrock, but down in the canyon where they faced each other the night was a black cloak about them, a still and silent world, touched only by the beating of their own hearts.

Ellen broke the silence. She said in an odd little voice, "It was Jim Miles who sold the ranch to us."

"That is why I asked who sold you the place." Miles kept his voice level. "You see—my uncle has been missing almost half a year."

He heard her quick gasp, then her frightened voice: "You—you can't be right. Duncan wrote me about buying the ranch only four months ago. Your uncle *must* have been alive then or he couldn't have signed the papers."

The panic in her voice hurt him. He said gently, "Don't worry too much about my uncle. I'll find out the truth, and I'll not let the truth harm you —or your brother. You must believe me, and trust me."

She was too bewildered for more words, and without further demur she got back into her saddle; and their horses moved on at the same slow walk, up the dark trail, and suddenly they were on the moonlit flats.

Miles untied the lead-rope. "We can make faster time now," he said, and then, a hint of a smile touching his grim-set mouth: "Your hair shows. Can you fix it?"

Ellen frowned, took off the battered Stetson, and tightened the coils of dark hair. "Johnny's hat is too small," she complained.

"He doesn't have a lot of hair to cover," grinned Miles.

"I should have cut it off," mumbled Ellen, a hairpin between her lips. "Like V. Crumm."

"Not if I can stop you."

His indignation seemed to please her. She smiled at him. "Well—I might have to, if you don't want me to look like a girl."

They rode stirrup-to-stirrup now, through the moonlit chaparral, and twice Miles drew to a standstill, and as he listened Ellen sensed growing uneasiness in him. The second time he stopped, she asked apprehensively: "What is it?"

"I don't know—" His head was turned away from her, but she saw his hand go down to the gun in his holster. "Thought I heard horses. . . ."

They continued to wait, Ellen straining her ears now. At first she could hear nothing, only the sigh of the night wind in the sagebrush, and then, distinctly, she picked up the sound, the muted thud of shod hoofs. Her pulse quickened and she gave Miles a startled look.

"Could be anybody," he said, "or somebody we don't want to run into. If my guess is right, they've come up Duck Creek Canyon from Santa Ysabel."

"You mean they're looking for us?" Ellen whispered the question.

"No telling." Miles swung his horse. "Let's get away from here."

They took cover behind a heavy growth of sagebrush, got down from their saddles, and found an opening that gave them a clear view of the moonlit landscape.

"Might be anybody," Miles said again, "or it might mean that Al Derner is losing no time. If he suspected we headed up Apache Canyon he'd likely figure we'd have to cross these flats."

Ellen pressed closer to him. There was comfort in the nearness of this quiet-spoken man. She was afraid, felt she must draw on the deep wells of his courage.

The hoof-beats were more distinct now. Something drifted across a patch of moonlight, a slinking, ghostly shape, and Ellen heard Miles' low whisper, "Coyote . . ."

She glimpsed the horsemen now, three of them, trailing one by one over the low ridge. Voices touched her ears, and she was suddenly tense, straining to catch the import of the low-rumbled words.

"Ain't easy to read sign in this moonlight." The rider in the lead halted his horse, waited for his companions. "Let's set quiet for a bit, fellers. If they're down in the canyon we'll mebbe pick up sound."

"Looks like the broncs smell somethin'," observed one of the riders, watching the nervous twitch of his horse's ears.

"That coyote we jumped," the first speaker surmised.

There was a long silence, the men motionless in their saddles, faces turned towards the deep gorge of Apache Canyon. Ellen pressed closer to Miles. He gave her a brief, warning look.

"Don't hear nothin'," one of the men finally said. "I reckon they're ahead of us, Nevada. We're wastin' time."

Nevada made no answer. He seemed to be turning something over in his mind. Apparently he was the leader of these men. It was up to him to make decisions.

"Ain't so sure we're wastin' time, Boone." His

voice was low, hardly audible to the listeners crouched behind the clump of sagebrush, and they saw that he was absorbedly watching the quick play of his horse's ears. His look went to the other horses. Their heads were lifted, and like his own mount they were showing interest in the thick clump of sagebrush that concealed Miles and Ellen.

Nevada spoke again, his tone thoughtful: "Sure act like they smell somethin', like you said, Boone."

"That damn coyote," Boone commented. "Reckon he didn't run so fur after we jumped him back of the ridge."

"Circled round and is waitin' for us to git away from here," guessed the third man. "Likely got some pups back there and ain't wantin' to git too fur from 'em."

Nevada said something, too low for Miles to catch. A brief silence followed, and the faces of the riders turned in a long look at the tall sagebrush.

"Waal—let's git goin'." Nevada's voice was loud, far-reaching again. "Reckon you're right, Boone. That old coyote's hangin' round close. It's him the broncs have winded."

He rode on, followed by his companions, their horses moving at a slow walk, and in a few moments they were lost to view.

"Thank goodness," Ellen whispered. "They've

gone. I was frightened stiff. I thought they'd surely ride over here for a look."

"I'm not so sure they've gone," Miles said soberly. "I've an idea that Nevada guessed the truth. He knows it wasn't a coyote that interested their horses. It was our own horses they smelled."

"You mean they'll be back?" Dismay stiffened her face.

He nodded, his expression grim. "I've got to leave you alone for a few minutes." He took her hand, led her deeper into the thicket that enclosed a tumbled mass of boulders. "Stay here until I get back, and don't move or make any sound."

"Yes . . ." Her voice was a faint whisper.

"Don't move from here, no matter what happens, or if you hear shooting. They'll be stalking us on foot, crawling through the chaparral. I've got to head them off."

She said again, in the same stifled whisper, "Yes—I understand."

He left her, silent as an Indian, seemed to melt into the moonlit chaparral, and she crouched there between two huge boulders, listening tensely. She could hear no sound, only the thumping of her own heart.

Chapter VII

Miles knew that the moment of crisis was on them. He had not been deceived by Nevada's loud-voiced decision to ride on, continue the chase. His words were intended to trick his quarry, leave them unprepared for the ambush he planned. They would return, on foot this time, stalking their unsuspecting victims. Or so Nevada thought—only he was going to be disappointed. If Miles could manage it, Nevada and his friends were due for an unpleasant surprise. An ambush was in the making, but not the kind of ambush they would relish.

Cautiously, soundlessly as any coyote, he drifted through the great clumps of sagebrush, ears and eyes alert, his forty-five readied for instant action. These men were hard-bitten killers, ruthless, without pity. They had been sent to kill. For Ellen Frazer's sake he would have to be equally ruthless. A bitter and hard solution. He could not afford to be squeamish.

It was difficult to see distinctly in that tricky moonlight. Miles knew these men were wily, would take advantage of every bush and boulder and bristling cactus. Anything motionless melted into that landscape, became a part of it. His only chance was to watch for movement, keep his ears sharp for some betraying sound.

Hugging the shadows of a big mesquite, he came to a split boulder and flattened behind it for a careful survey of his surroundings. Nevada and his friends would ride only far enough to make their quarry believe the coast was clear. They would be in a hurry to work their way back before it was too late to pull off the ambush.

Miles crouched there, gaze searching, analysing the moonlit terrain. Some fifty yards on his left was a thick growth of scrubby juniper-trees; and now, of a sudden, he became aware of movement in the shadows there. A shape appeared, slid into the concealing darkness of the sagebrush that circled back towards Miles.

He continued to watch, saw two more shapes, vague, fast-moving, soundless as leaves in the wind. And now his straining eyes could see nothing, only the tall clumps of sagebrush, their shadows drawing away to the east.

A coyote suddenly slunk across a patch of moonlight, vanished swiftly into another clump of brush. Miles' lips drew back in a thin smile, hand lifted, finger on the trigger of his gun.

He heard a low, muttered oath: "That damn coyote, ag'in—"

It was apparent the speaker was confident in the success of this ambush, had no suspicion that the stalkers were in turn being stalked.

Another voice spoke, Nevada's harsh rasp: "Tie up your lip, Boone—"

"They cain't hear us, yet," muttered the man sulkily. "What the hell's got you so scary?"

"You keep your mouth shut, or stay back with the broncs," rasped Nevada angrily.

"Ain't likin' the way you sling talk." Boone's voice was thin-edged. "Sure I'll stay back, and to hell with you."

A dry twig snapped under an impatient foot, a shadow moved, melted back into the juniper thicket.

"The damn' no-count fool," grumbled Nevada, indignation loudening his voice. "Gettin' too fresh. I'll sure fix him proper after we get this job done."

They were close now, within fifty feet, but still invisible in the shadowing sagebrush. Miles pressed close to his boulder, gun-hand lifted.

Nevada's remaining companion broke his silence. "Only two of us." He spoke doubtfully. "You had orter call Boone back, Nevada. He's awful fast with a gun. I'd like him with us."

"To hell with him," Nevada retorted. "You and me can handle this business. We hold all the aces. We've got that Clarke hombre fooled. He won't be lookin' for us to head back on his hide-out."

Miles kept his eyes hard on the clump of brush that still concealed the stalkers.

"The gal's a good-looker," the other man said. The leer in his voice sent a shiver of cold fury through Miles. "Sure is stuck-up. Wouldn't give me and Boone a look when we rode in from Deming with her. I'd sure like to get my rope on her, break her good."

Miles narrowed his eyes thoughtfully. This man and Boone were the two cowboys who had arrived in Santa Ysabel on the Deming stage. It was plain that he had been watched better than he knew.

He waited, tingling with impatience, resolve hardening, and there was no shred of scruple in him now. It was up to him to stop these desperadoes, keep their filthy hands off Ellen Frazer. He must choose to regard them as dangerous wolves, fit targets for the long-barrelled Colt in his clenched fingers.

He heard Nevada's obscene chuckle. "We'll cut cards for her, Chino."

"Was allus lucky, thataways," Chino said, with a satisfied laugh.

A stone rattled under careless boot-heel, a snarl from Nevada: "Watch your step, feller. . . ." Miles held his breath, realized with dismay a sudden growing darkness over the scene.

A muttered exclamation came from the bushes. "Damn that cloud. Cain't see a thing. We'll have to wait."

Miles relaxed, finger light on the trigger of the forty-five, and slowly the cloud drifted on its way. He saw a shadow move, a tall, vague shape.

He waited, kept impatience in check. He wanted both men under his gun. He knew his own ability, his deadly swiftness.

A second shape emerged from the dark cover of the sagebrush. Miles tightened trigger-finger and the night's stillness was shattered with two quick reverberating gunshots that flared red fire from the long barrel of the forty-five.

He heard an agonized shout, and again a cloud darkened the moon.

Miles waited, ears keyed to catch any whisper of sound in that blanketing silence. Another man was somewhere back in the juniper scrub. A man named Boone, who was deadly fast with a gun. The play was not finished, not with Boone still alive.

A sound broke the stillness, a low groan, and after a moment moonlight again touched the landscape. He saw the two men who had taken his bullets prone on the ground. One of them was moving, crawling for a covering bush.

Miles spoke in a rasping whisper: "Stop!"

The crawling man flattened, let out another groan. Miles circled round, keeping to the shadows, came close to him.

The man's head lifted in a look. He said in a hoarse, strangled whisper, "Damn you . . ."

Miles recognized the voice. The wounded man was Nevada. He would not have known one man from the other in that deceptive light, but Nevada's harsh rasp was enough to identify him.

A quick glance at the other man was enough. Chino was dead, stretched face down on the ground, gun lying near his hand.

Cloud shadows drifted, moonlight and darkness. Miles continued to wait in the shrouding blackness of the mesquite, ears alert for some sound of movement in the juniper scrub. One man lay dead, another seriously wounded, helpless, but Boone still lurked in the cover of those concealing junipers.

His attention was suddenly drawn back to Nevada, and just in time he stooped, wrenched the gun from the man's hand.

Nevada went limp again. "Heard tell you was a smart hombre, Clarke," he gasped. "Wasn't figgerin' you savvied our play."

Miles considered him with some compassion. The man was a scoundrel, but he was well supplied with nerve.

"You were wrong about holding all the aces," he said. "I'm no dumb maverick, easy to rope."

"That kid's face you wear had me fooled," groaned the desperado.

"Hurt bad?" Miles asked.

"My laig's broke . . . feels like your lead landed some place in my belly. I'm bleedin' to death."

"Your own fault," muttered Miles. He was

feeling sick. "Al Derner hired you to kill me, didn't he, Nevada?"

"Ain't tellin' you nothin'," muttered the man.

"I'm leaving you here," Miles said in a harder voice. "One of your friends is back in the junipers. I'm not letting him get away."

He left the wounded man mouthing curses at him, moved stealthily through the scrub. Boone would be a tough customer, and now, warned by the shooting, he would be on his guard. The fact that no sound had come from the junipers indicated the man still lurked in the vicinity. The two gunshots would have him puzzled, wondering what had happened. He would not know that the quarry his companions were stalking was so close, would probably decide the coyote had startled nervous trigger-fingers. He was not likely to investigate too quickly, for fear of drawing their fire on himself. Any movement in the brush was suspicious. Boone would be too wary to risk a hastily flung bullet. He would be on the watch, though, his gun ready.

Miles waited for every shifting shadow, took no chances, and at last he was crouching close to the twisted, gnarled trunk of a juniper.

He stood for several moments, accustomed his eyes to the play of moonlight that came and went from behind the gathering cloud-drift. Thunder rattled from distant hills and he realized with some dismay that a storm was in the making. The thought worried him. He must get back to Ellen. She would be suffering torments of anxiety.

His probing gaze found what he was looking for, the three horses, vague shapes in that elusive maze of the shifting shadows. Boone would be somewhere close. He would not get too far from his horse.

No sound touched his ears, only the low rumble of thunder. He must do something, and quickly; and yet he feared to move. For all he knew, Boone was watching him, waiting for the chance to fling his shot.

Desperate now, he ventured an old trick, picked up a small stone, tossed it into the brush. Gunfire flared in answer, and in that fleeting instant he saw the man, squeezed the trigger.

Stillness settled down, and then he heard Boone's voice, uncertain, tinged with fear: "Was that you shootin', Nevada?"

Miles spoke softly. "I've got you covered, Boone. Drop your gun, step into the open—and keep your hands up."

Another long silence while Boone thought it over. He had no reason to believe that Miles lied, but feared to take a chance that he lied. As a matter of fact, he was invisible in that tricky light.

He spoke again, and the crack in his voice showed that his nerve was breaking under the strain.

"Don't shoot, feller. . . ."

Miles saw him now, a dark shape against the boulder that had covered him, his hands up above his head.

"Move this way," Miles said. "No tricks."

"Ain't tryin' any," muttered the man.

He came slowly across the narrow clearing. Miles stepped from behind his tree, moved swiftly behind him, pressed gun-muzzle against his spine, reached with his free hand and plucked a second gun from the man's low-slung holster.

"Reckon you're the Clarke hombre," Boone said huskily. "You're some wolf, feller."

Miles studied him, dawning recognition in his cold eyes. The twelve-year-old boy he had once played with had changed a lot, was a tall, sandy-haired man of twenty-seven—his own age. It was fifteen years since that spring on his uncle's Bar M ranch. Boone Haxson used to meet him down on the creek and they would hunt rabbits, quail, sometimes trail along with the round-up crew. Jim Miles did not quite approve of Boone. The Haxson family were a bad lot, he would tell his nephew. The older Haxson, Boone's father, ran a small spread west of the creek, and Jim Miles suspected him of cow-stealing when opportunity offered.

His prisoner saw the recognition in his eyes. "Yeah," he drawled, "I'm him, I'm the same Boone Haxson, only some growed." A mirthless grin creased his hard face.

"I should kill you," Miles muttered. He knew

he could not. The thought of more bloodshed sickened him. He had already killed one man, and Nevada would soon be dead.

He abhorred the thing he had done. There had been no alternative. Ellen Frazer's life, and more, had demanded the deadly ambush. His own death would have left her at their mercy, and there would have been no mercy. The man Chino had said enough to convince him of *that*. For Ellen's sake he had been forced against his code to shoot first, and shoot to kill.

Boone Haxson spoke again: "Heard the shootin'," he said. "Wasn't figgerin' it was you jumped 'em."

"Chino's dead," Miles informed him. "Nevada won't last an hour. I had to do it," he added grimly. "Didn't like doing it, Boone. I'm not your kind of low-down killer."

Boone's reckless young face took on a troubled look. "We wasn't fixin' to kill you," he said earnestly. "Was only fixin' to get the drop on you, take you down to gaol." He hesitated, lowered his eyes under Miles' cynical silence. "Leastways that was Nevada's talk," he mumbled.

"You know better," Miles said. "I'd have been dead by now if I hadn't beat Nevada to it."

"Nevada had me fooled." Perspiration beaded Boone's face. "I'm tellin' you the truth, Miles. I ain't no low-down bush-whacker." His twisted smile came again. "At that, I wasn't knowin' it was *you* we was after."

"You knew my name," Miles reminded. "You called me 'the Clarke hombre.' "

"Wasn't couplin' you with the Miles Clarke I used to know down on the Bar M," insisted the young cowboy.

"You and Chino came in on the Deming stage with me. You were trailing me."

"Wasn't knowin' you from Adam," reiterated Boone desperately. "Wasn't trailin' you. Nevada sent word he had a job for me ridin' for Al Derner over to the Bar M. Ain't knowin' how deep Chino was mixed up in the business. Chino wasn't one to talk much. Never did like the skunk, no more'n I liked Nevada. Nevada got to ridin' me from the start, and I was all set to say *adiós* to his damn' job."

"He was all set to fix *you*," Miles told him grimly. "You wouldn't have lived long enough to say *adiós* to him." He paused, added wearily, "You can put your hands down, Boone. Maybe I'm a fool, but I've a notion you're telling the truth."

The cowboy dropped his hands with a relieved grunt, and he stood rigid for a moment, a look of shame and gratitude softening his hard face. "You're a white man," he muttered. "I sure feel like a skunk, Miles. Wouldn't have blamed you none if you'd gunned me, same as the others."

"I've got to think this thing out," Miles said, half to himself. "I'm in a hurry, Boone, and damned if I know what to do with you."

Boone glanced off at the horses, now hardly visible under the increasing darkness of the clouds. Lightning ripped the blackening sky overhead, was followed by a reverberating roll of thunder.

"Let me fork my bronc, and I'll head off a long ways from here," he said. "You won't need to worry none about *me* no more."

Despite his haste to get back to Ellen, a thought came to Miles, held him: This man had known Jim Miles. He could use him—perhaps. He said, bluntly: "I'm looking for my uncle. What do you know about him? Your dad was his neighbour."

Boone Haxson hesitated, his eyes refusing to meet Miles' direct look. "I—I wouldn't be knowin' about Jim Miles." His tone was embarrassed.

"I've heard talk," Miles went on. "Doesn't listen good to me." His voice hardened. "You know well enough that Jim Miles wouldn't turn cow-thief."

"He skipped out," muttered Boone.

"He's dead," Miles said. "That's the only answer, Boone." He paused, added quietly: "Tell me what you know, or must I choke it out of you?"

"Don't know nothin'," Boone said again. His eyes lifted in a steady look. "I'd talk quick enough if I knowed what happened to the old man. Him and my pappy wasn't good friends . . . reckon old Miles figgered Pappy was hang-tree fruit . . . went round tellin' folks he was a cow-thief. I sure hated his guts for the way he run down the Haxson family."

Miles nodded. Jim Miles had never hesitated to express his contempt for the Haxson tribe, or of anybody else who smelled like a cow-thief.

"Maybe your dad knows something," he suggested curtly.

Boone shook his head. "He wouldn't. Pappy's been daid more'n five years." He gave Miles his crooked grin. "Lead poisonin'," he added laconically.

Miles wondered briefly if the lead poisoning had belched from a Bar M gun. He was disposed to believe that his uncle had good reason for his suspicions of the elder Boone Haxson's activities.

Boone spoke again, his tone thoughtful: "Yeah, I hated your uncle's guts, but me and you was good friends when we was kids. If you think there's murder been done I'd like mighty well to throw in with you." He paused, added shyly, "If you can trust me."

Miles studied him, thoughts racing. He *must* come to a decision . . . he could not keep Ellen waiting in her agony of fear. She was likely thinking him dead.

He said brusquely, "You've been running with the wild bunch, huh?"

Lightning flared and he glimpsed Boone's eyes, pale blue agates in the brown of his face.

"What for you want to know?" The cowboy's tone was guarded, almost sullen.

"Can't use an outlaw."

"Ain't no warrant out for me, if that's what you want to know."

"Nevada figured he could use your fast guns, wasn't that it?"

"Mebbe he did. I like excitement—"

Another flash of lightning forked venomously overhead. Miles lifted his voice against the crackling thunder. "I can use those fast guns of yours, Boone, and I've a notion you've the tough guts you'll need if you throw in with me."

"It's a deal," Boone said laconically.

They gripped hands, and Miles said harshly, "I'm trusting you a lot, Boone."

"I've shook hands on it." Boone's voice showed emotion. "You're white clean through. I'm set to ride to hell and gone with you."

"I'm believing you."

"*Gracias.*" The cowboy's grin was no longer crooked. Even in that cloud-veiled moonlight Miles saw the change in his face: a new self-respect, an eager radiance, and something like awe. "I'm stickin' with you till hell freezes," Boone declared. "I'll mebbe amount to somethin', ridin' 'long with you. Ain't never had much use for the Law, but if you're ridin' *that* range, ain't carin' how many tin stars you figger to pin on me."

Miles grinned. "No stars yet, Boone. Right now all the law we've got is home-made." His voice sobered: "Some day we'll have the real thing. I'm counting on you to help."

"You bet!" chuckled Boone. "I'm for wranglin' old Johnny Law till he rides right pretty in this pasture."

Miles handed him the confiscated six-gun. "Look around for the one you dropped," he said.

He waited impatiently while Boone searched in the scrub for the other gun. There were hundreds like Boone, hesitating on the border-line. A push one way or the other and they would be riding either with the wild bunch, or with the Law. He hoped he was making no mistake with Boone, believed he was not. He was familiar with his breed, loyal to the death once a pledge had been given. And he sensed, too, a gratitude in the man. He knew that Miles could have killed him. Instead he had extended the hand of friendship, given him his trust.

Boone's tall shape emerged from the chaparral, and both low-slung holsters were filled now. He said, a jubilant note in his voice, "I'm all set to go, boss."

"You won't like your first job," Miles told him.

"Don't matter a damn what I like or don't like."

"You're tying two dead men on their horses and taking them back to Santa Ysabel."

Boone's jaw sagged. "You—mean it, boss?"

"You've got to do some lying," Miles continued. "You're telling Al Derner that Nevada and Chino got to quarrelling, went for their guns, and shot it out. Derner musn't know you ran into me up here on the flats."

Boone let out a long breath. "Some lyin'," he said, dubiously.

"Nevada and Chino can't tell him you're lying," reminded Miles.

"That's right," muttered the cowboy. "Never did know a dead hombre as could talk."

"It's up to you to make Derner think you're still on his pay-roll. You can help a lot, Boone, scouting around, keeping your eyes and ears open."

"I'll be needin' to get in touch with you," Boone said. "Won't be easy."

"You know V. Crumm?"

"Sure do, only I reckon she ain't got much use for me. Figgers I'm a plumb wild hombre."

"Watch your chance, slip her a note for me. Easy enough for you to run into her at the store or the livery barn. You won't need to talk to her. Just slip her a note when you want to see me. She'll see that I get it."

"I savvy . . ." Boone hesitated. "Won't say nothing about runnin' into you up here." He paused, cleared his throat nervously: "Nevada was talkin' about a girl—the one that come in on the stage with us."

"She's all right," Miles told him curtly.

"Ain't wantin' to be nosey," mumbled the cowboy. "Was wonderin' how come she's mixed up in this business."

"I haven't the answer for that one—yet," Miles said. "She's a nice girl, Boone, and we've got to look out for her."

Boone nodded: "I'm believin' you. Wasn't carin' for the way Nevada and Chino talked. Was all set to horn in on their play if they got to actin' rough with her."

"Thanks, Boone." Miles spoke warmly. "We'll shake on that."

They gripped hands again. "I've dealt you the cards," Miles said. "It's up to you to play the hand."

"I'm sure backin' our play to the limit—and then some," Boone assured him grimly.

"Take your time getting back to town," suggested Miles. "I'm *needing* time."

"I'm campin' here till mornin'," Boone decided. "Come mornin' I'll rope them dead hombres across their saddles and head for town. Be to-morrow night before I'm tellin' Derner how come Nevada and Chino got to smokin' guns at each other." He chuckled. "Lucky I got my tarp along," he added, glancing up into the dark sky. "Sure is goin' to storm."

Miles left him, in haste now to get back to Ellen. Moon and stars were blotted out and it was slow work finding his way through the darkness fast deepening across the chaparral.

He called her name softly as he neared the place, and after a moment heard her answering voice.

He was afraid she would attempt to meet him, lose herself in that blackness. "Don't move," he called again. "I'm coming."

He pushed through the thick growth of sagebrush, finally made out her dark shape against the great split boulder. She saw him at the same moment, was suddenly moving towards him. He heard her voice, shaken, touched with hysteria.

"Oh, Miles . . . I've been terrified!"

It was the first time she had used his name. Hardly knowing he did so, Miles drew her inside the circle of his arm, held her close. It was an instinctive gesture of protection, comfort, and she accepted it as such, seemed not to notice.

"That shooting," she whimpered. "I—I thought they'd killed you. Oh, Miles—I was so dreadfully afraid—for you." She pressed against him, head limp on his shoulder.

"It's all right," he said. "They won't trouble us again."

"You were gone so long . . ."

"Less than twenty minutes."

"It seemed an eternity"—Ellen broke off, seemed suddenly aware now of his arm, tight round her slim waist, and the fact that her head was on his shoulder. She pulled away, said confusedly, "I hardly know what I'm doing, clinging to you like a frightened child."

"It's all right." He managed to keep his voice matter-of-fact, resisted the impulse to draw her back into his arms. "Looks like a storm coming," he went on. "We must get away from here, find shelter."

He sensed growing curiosity in her, an urge to ask questions, went on quietly: "We won't be running into that outfit again. I've a notion they'll be heading back to town."

Her silence told him she was not quite convinced. The darkness hid his bleak smile.

Lightning forked from the black clouds, thunder shattered the stillness, violent blasts of sound that drew a startled exclamation from the girl; and suddenly swirling gusts of rain moaned through the brush.

Miles got her into her saddle, untied his slicker, and threw it over her shoulders. She sat rigid, felt the beating rain cold on her face.

"But where can we go?" she asked apprehensively.

A flare of lightning lit the scene, and its white glare showed her that Miles was again holding the mare's lead-rope as he swung into his saddle.

"Used to be an old cabin somewhere on these flats," he answered. "Years ago, when I was a kid, my uncle and I were up here, deer-hunting. We camped there one night. Make good shelter—

if it's still got a roof on, and I can find it."

They moved slowly through the black night, and over them the clouds spat vicious snaky tongues of lightning. A gust of rain drove into Ellen's face, drew a gasp from her. She was not afraid, though, not any more. She sat lightly erect in her saddle, face lifted defiantly to the storm. She did not care much whether or not they found the old cabin. She was learning things about Miles Clarke. He was protection enough for her from any danger. His explanation about the three riders had not deceived her. They were dead. Those shots had come from his gun. But it was not murder. He had calmly risked death for her sake, destroyed a blood-lusting wolf-pack. Ugly business, yes, but what else could a man do? She recalled his blunt words: "We have no benefit of law in this Santa Ysabel country. . . . When it comes I'll be among the first to welcome it with a handclasp."

Ellen's eyes were bright in her wet face. V. Crumm was right about it. It would be Miles Clarke who would bring law and order to the Santa Ysabel.

She heard his voice above the crackling thunder, quiet, reassuring.

"All right—Ellen?"

"All right—Miles," Ellen said. She smiled contentedly into the slanting rain.

Chapter VIII

The old prospector's cabin was still there on the bluffs overlooking the deep gorge of Apache Canyon, a low log building, hardly visible in the crowd-ing juniper-trees. Miles noted with some surprise that the small pole corral and horse-shed showed signs of quite recent repair.

Mystified, he got down from his horse and tried the door. It opened to his push and he stepped inside. The smell of undisturbed dust and long disuse was unmistakable. The place had not been occupied in many months.

Ellen slid down from her saddle, came up, a hand holding the long oilskin slicker against the blowing rain. She followed him into the room.

Miles lighted a match, saw a lantern on the crude home-made table. He picked it up, shook it, heard the splash of kerosene in the tank. He struck another match and lighted the wick, swung the lantern close to the floor. Dust lay deep, unmarked except for their own footprints, the rain-drip from their clothes that made little wet balls of mud. He replaced the lantern on the dusty table, gave the girl a contented grin.

"We're in luck," he said. And then, "I'll be back

in a few moments. Want to get those horses under the shed." He vanished into the wet night.

Ellen stood motionless, eyes taking in the details of the cabin as well as she could in that dim light. She saw a small, rusty cooking-stove, its chimney pushed through a hole in the log wall. There were some pots and pans, two home-made cots with lumpy straw-filled mattresses, a wooden bench on one side of the table, and a couple of wooden stools. Other objects littered the floor: a pile of empty sacks, pieces of old canvas, a much-worn broom, a short-handled shovel, and what she guessed was a miner's pick. A box near the stove was filled with short pieces of juniper wood, into which was tucked a dust-covered newspaper. A cupboard stood in a corner, the seams in its rough boards sealed with strips of tin. Cobwebs were everywhere.

Miles came in, stamping mud from his boots. "Might as well sit down." He snatched up one of the sacks, wiped off the dusty bench.

Ellen removed the dripping slicker, saw a nail in the wall, and hung it up.

"You're soaking," she worried. "I'm hardly damp. Your slicker covered me like a tent."

"I'm used to it," grinned Miles. His gaze fell on the wood-box. "I'll have that stove going in no time." He reached for the newspaper. It was folded tight, apparently had never been opened. He hesitated, carried the newspaper close to the lantern, and stared fixedly at the name scrawled on the wrapper. "J. Miles"—his uncle's name.

Ellen, watching, saw his suddenly grim expression. She exclaimed quickly, "What is it?"

"I don't know—yet." Miles dropped the newspaper on the table, rummaged again in the box, found more paper, stuffed it into the stove, and piled on some of the bone-dry twigs.

The stove began to send smoke into the room. He fiddled with the damper and in a few moments had a roaring fire.

"Better get your feet dry," he said to Ellen. "I'll pull the bench over."

She got up and he dragged the bench from the table, set it close to the stove. She sat down again, held out her damp boots to the warmth.

Miles stood silent, eyes on the folded newspaper lying on the table, fingers making a cigarette. He lighted the cigarette, then, careful not to tear the wrapper, he removed it and opened the newspaper.

"The *Santa Fe Republican*," he said to Ellen. "The date is last August—nearly six months ago, and it's never been opened—read."

"Yes?" Her eyes were on him, puzzled, questioning.

"My uncle disappeared just about six months ago," Miles said. "He was accused of rustling cattle. The talk is he fled to save himself from a lynching party."

"Your uncle—a cattle rustler?" Incredulity widened her eyes.

"A lie! Jim Miles was no cow-thief. He hated a cow-thief."

Ellen indicated the newspaper in his clenched fingers: "What has that to do with his—his disappearance?"

"It confirms my belief that he was murdered; and the thing began here—in this cabin."

He came close to the stove, now glowing red from the fierce-burning juniper. Steam rose from his soaked flannel shirt.

Ellen said again, worriedly, "You're awfully wet. Won't you take that shirt off—get it dried out?"

He shook his head. "We get used to these things—out on the range." He dropped the cigarette on the hot stove, watched it curl into ash, his eyes moody. "Uncle Jim used to come up here deer-hunting. I told you I came with him once, years ago when I was a kid. I've a notion he came up a lot since then. That's why he kept the cabin in repair—the corral—the horse-shed. You see, the Bar M takes in this mesa, runs several miles the other side of Apache Canyon."

"It's a big ranch," Ellen commented. "Why—it's enormous!"

"Used to take in Juniper Flats," Miles said.

She wondered uneasily at the odd look he gave her.

"That's where Duncan's ranch is," she said quickly.

"Yes." His tone was curt, and he shifted his look, went suddenly to the closed door, stared at it intently.

"What is it? Do you hear something?" Ellen stood up, her eyes apprehensive.

Miles made no answer. He picked up a sack, rubbed the iron-strapped planks of the door vigorously. Ellen, curious, moved to his side. His face turned in a glance at her.

"The old Bar M brand." He smiled. "Uncle Jim's brand. He let me burn it on, the time I came up here with him. A lot of cattle wear that iron-mark on their hides—or did."

Ellen nodded. "Duncan has a brand," she said. "Mr Wellen worked it out for him. A Box DF. Duncan sent me a sketch of it. I have it in my bag."

Miles looked at her thoughtfully, and then, abruptly: "Let's get back to that hot stove."

They returned to the bench. Ellen sat down, but he continued to stand, his back to the stove, and she saw that he was looking at her with an intentness almost rude.

She stirred, uncomfortable under the prolonged stare, lowered her eyes; and there was a deep silence, disturbed only by the steady drumming of the rain. She felt suddenly afraid.

Miles broke the silence. "This mystery seems to

involve both of us, Ellen. V. Crumm too. She's been warned to get out of Santa Ysabel."

Ellen raised her eyes. The hardness had gone from the look he still kept on her. She read an odd pity there, a disturbing pity.

"You—you mean Duncan is—too?" Her voice was not quite steady.

He seemed to be searching for an answer, finally said cautiously: "It's strange his not getting your letter, but perhaps there's an explanation."

She looked down at her boots, sending out steam from the heat. "Don't evade. . . ." Her voice was low, but steady now. "You think something has happened to him."

"We don't know the answer—yet."

"I'm beginning to think you—you doubt him." Her eyes lifted in an angry look.

"I don't know your brother—"

"Duncan is fine. . . . He—he's wonderful. He's my—my twin!"

Miles was silent, and she saw a fleeting tenderness in his eyes, and her anger passed, left her trembling, confused.

At length he said gently, "Don't worry, Ellen. I'm your friend before anything else, and I'll want to be Duncan's friend. Keep on trusting me, no matter what happens, or seems to threaten."

She nodded, unable to speak, sat there watching while he took his gun from its wet holster, started wiping the long steel barrel with his handkerchief. A chill crept over her, a frightening chill. The boyishness was gone from the face bent over the gun. It was hard-set with implacable purpose, and there was a deadly deliberateness in the pain-staking way he sought out every drop of moisture, polished the weapon dry. He was making sure the gun would not fail him. The trails ahead of them were dark, ambushed with dangers—with death. She wondered miserably how many more times must he use this terrible, home-made law. She had seen a man die that afternoon under its blazing thunder, and within the last hour more men had died from its deadly hail of lead. She did not believe those three riders were heading back to Santa Ysabel as he had implied. They were lying somewhere in the rain-soaked chaparral—*dead*.

Miles replaced the gun in its holster, went to the door, opened it a few inches and peered into the night. Wind drove a flurry of rain into his face. He slammed the door shut. "No sign of letting up," he said. His hand lifted. "Listen. . . ."

Ellen heard a low whispering of sound, recognized the snarl of unleashed waters. She gave him a startled, questioning look.

"Wolf Creek," he said. "Running bank-full, empties over the bluffs into the Rio Apache. We'll likely have some trouble getting across—if the storm continues overnight."

She considered him, growing dismay in her

eyes. "We have to cross, to get to Juniper Flats?"

Miles nodded. "We must hope the rain will let up soon. Once the rain stops it won't take long for the flood waters to go down."

"I simply must get out to the ranch." Ellen gestured despairingly. "I can't bear it—waiting, and Duncan perhaps lying out there—ill—helpless." She stood up from the bench, faced him, hands clenched, eyes bright with impatience. "Can't we do something?"

His expression softened as he gazed at her, so slim and straight in Johnny's flannel shirt and faded blue jeans. The appeal in her drew hard on his resistance. He yearned to take her in his arms, but instead sought safety in apparent harshness.

He said gruffly, "Don't be a baby."

She recoiled as if he had slapped her, sank back on the bench, turned her head away from his look, and so missed the quick remorse in his eyes.

Miles was completely horrified at himself. He said huskily, "I'm sorry."

Ellen kept her face averted. "I deserved it." Her voice was low, bitter with self-reproach. "I shouldn't make things harder for you."

Miles fumbled in his pocket, found cigarette-papers and tobacco. His fingers were shaky, spilled tobacco down his shirt, and, suddenly impatient with himself, he thrust tobacco-sack and papers back into his pocket.

"Look here," he spoke cheerfully. "What we

could do with right now is a pot of hot coffee."

Ellen said in a muffled voice, "Where's the coffee?"

"It's time we have a look round." Miles picked up the lantern. "No telling but what Uncle Jim kept a few things for an emergency, or left them behind after a trip here."

Ellen turned, looked at him, smiled through wet lashes. "I'm a good cook—if there's anything to cook."

"Me too," chuckled Miles. "You should see me toss a flapjack."

Ellen followed him to the closed cupboard she had noticed earlier. Miles slid the wooden catch and opened the door. There were three deep shelves, and they were not empty.

"Beans!" ejaculated Miles. His hand closed on a tin can. "And good old Arbuckle."

Ellen snatched at the coffee. "I'll make it," she said. "You can warm up the beans—" She broke off, added in a dismayed voice, "We'll need water."

Miles laughed, slammed the cupboard door. "Gallons of water, dripping from the roof," he reminded. "Won't need to use it, though. I'll throw on my slicker and fill a bucket from the spring, back of the cabin."

"I'll stoke up the fire," Ellen called after him as he stepped outside.

For some reason she was suddenly light-hearted,

almost gay. At least she was doing something, and action was what she needed to take her mind off her worries. She wondered if that had been Miles' deliberate intention, to build for the moment a defensive wall against crushing, weakening fears. She began to hum to herself as she piled chunks of juniper into the stove.

Miles was soon back with a brimming bucket of spring water. He rinsed out and filled a small tin kettle, placed it on the stove.

Ellen mixed the coffee, found two tin cups in the cupboard, and washed them clean of dust, while Miles did the same with the frying-pan. He opened the can of beans, emptied them in the pan, and set it on the stove.

Ellen found knives and forks and spoons in the cupboard, packed in a wooden box. Somebody, perhaps Jim Miles himself, had burned the mark of the ranch brand on the cover, a Bar M, like the one on the door. She carried the box to the table to show Miles. He grabbed a knife, began to stir the beans to keep them from burning.

The table next demanded attention. Ellen washed off the dust with a wet cloth, wiped it dry with another rag. Miles emptied the sizzling beans into tin plates, Ellen poured into the cups, and they were ready to sit down.

They lifted the steaming cups, looked at each other solemnly, and drank.

"That was good!" Ellen set her cup down and

began on the beans. "Didn't know I was so hungry." Her dimple came. "You know how to make plain, ordinary beans taste good."

"Cowboys get a lot of beans," Miles said dryly. "We get so hungry—anything tastes good."

They scraped their plates clean, emptied the coffee-pot to the last drop. Miles relaxed on his stool, reached again for cigarette-papers and tobacco. Ellen watched him, aware of odd emotions in herself. She was alone with a man she had seen for the first time only that same day, cooped up with him in a remote cabin that had once been the abode of some whiskered old prospector. Life had plunged her suddenly into a strange and bewildering world. She could hardly believe her senses. So much had happened since the moment she had climbed down from the dusty stage in front of V. Crumm's store. To think of the sequence of swift-moving events made her mind whirl. It was incredible—but it was real. She was not dreaming. These things were actually happening to her.

She stole a glance at Miles, sensed his own thoughts were racing. There were tiny furrows in his brow, and he was staring gloomily at the cigarette between his fingers. He seemed to have forgotten her, so absorbed were his thoughts.

Ellen held herself very still. She knew he was struggling with a mystery that dangerously touched them. She would not give way to another emotional outburst. She must learn from this quiet-voiced man who could be so calm in the face of deadly peril—and so amazingly quick to act. He was different from any man she had ever known, and she had known many men. None quite like him. There was a quality in him that bred confidence, a certain efficiency in his every movement, a warming reassurance in his nearness.

She felt his gaze on her, met his faint smile. "Not raining so hard," he said, and dropped the dead cigarette into the tin cup. "These storms come this time of the year. Cowmen, and Indians, pray for them, but right now I'm one cowman praying different."

Ellen listened, growing excitement in her. Miles was right. The rain had slackened its fury.

She asked quickly, "When can we start?"

Miles shook his head: "Not yet—not for hours. Too risky trying to ford Wolf Creek in the dark. We must wait for daylight."

She hid her disappointment: "You know best." And then, determined to keep cheerful, she drew his attention to the wooden box she had found in the cupboard. "It's got the Bar M brand on the cover."

Miles looked at it, and there was memory in his slow smile. "I did that. . . ." He drew the box close, ran a finger over the burned scars. "Uncle Jim wanted me to know the feel of the Bar M iron—said I would be the big boss of the ranch some day . . ."

He was suddenly silent, forefinger poking at something inside the box. He turned the box over, emptied its contents, and extracted a piece of brown wrapping-paper.

"That was only used to line the inside of the box," Ellen said.

"Got writing on it," Miles told her. "Uncle Jim's writing." There was repressed excitement in his quiet voice. He smoothed the creases, held the paper close to the lamplight. "Listen . . ."

He read the pencil-scrawled words aloud, slowly:

"DEAR MILES,

"There's a chance I won't get away from here alive. I've got something they want and they're after me hard. You'll remember that little gully, where Wolf Creek empties into the river—where we got the mountain lion that time. Those cliffs are loaded with rich copper ore. I've known about it for a long time, but I'm a cowman, not a miner, so I've kept quiet, not wanting a lot of crazy folk stampeding all over my Bar M range. Reckon I've been a fool. There's a crooked bunch riding my trail, trying to locate where the ore is. Looks like the showdown. They've got me holed up here, trapped. No water, and no chance to get to the spring. Nothing I can do but make a break for it when it's dark—shoot my way out. I don't know who the king wolf is, but I'm counting on you to track him down some day and get his hide. If anything happens to me, the ranch is yours, all clear—no debts. Wrote my will years ago. V. Crumm has it in her safe at the store. She knows nothing about the ore business. I'm hiding this note in the old knife-box, the one you burned the Bar M iron on. You'll be up here, sooner or later, looking for me, reading sign. You won't overlook the old knife-box. *Adiós*, nephew. Good luck."

Miles was suddenly silent, and he began slowly folding the piece of brown paper into its original creases. Ellen guessed from the stony look in his eyes that he dared not trust himself to speak. He was fighting for self-control. She kept very still.

The story was taking shape, beginning to make sense to Miles. He recalled something V. Crumm had said: "Al Derner claims he owns the Bar M now, or most of it. . . . Seems like your uncle was owing him a lot of money . . . that's Derner's reason for takin' over the Bar M lock, stock, and barrel."

Miles Clarke narrowed thoughtful eyes at the piece of brown paper his fingers were folding into its creases. There was contradictory evidence here, in those words Jim Miles had scrawled so hastily: "The ranch . . . is all clear—no debts." The implication was sinister, pointed a sure finger at Al Derner. No doubt now about the identity of the "king wolf." It was Derner who had done Jim Miles to death in an attempt to possess the secret of the copper lode. He had cloaked the cold-blooded killing under a loathsome lie with the intention of deliberately destroying an honoured reputation. A double murder, taking not only Jim Miles' life, but his good name.

There was a stillness in the little cabin. Miles was suddenly aware that the rain had stopped its monotonous patter on the roof. He looked at Ellen, met her anxious eyes.

She smiled faintly, said: "I've been afraid to speak. You look so—so stern."

Miles gazed at her. She was in it too, an innocent pawn in this mysterious devil's game. Perhaps her brother was one of the wolf-pack, or perhaps he was just another unsuspecting victim.

He said quietly, "It's stern business—terrible business." He tapped the folded brown paper in his fingers. "This explains a lot that's puzzled me, gives me the name of my uncle's murderer. Uncle Jim gave no name, but these last words point to the man."

"Last words?" Ellen's eyes were full of pity. "You mean—"

Miles nodded: "I mean he's dead, murdered,

probably shot down on the doorstep of this cabin when he tried to escape."

Worry visibly deepened in her, and after a moment her head lifted in a steady look at him: "You—you suspect my brother is mixed up in it?"

He wanted to reassure her, found himself awkward, stumbling for words. "We don't know anything about it—yet. It's senseless to speculate."

"Please don't pretend . . ." Ellen spoke quietly. "You *have* been speculating, wondering about Duncan."

He tried to evade: "I'm speculating about the murderer of my uncle."

"I want a straight answer," Ellen said. "I can stand the truth."

Miles said nothing, went to the cot, and carried the mattress outside. Moonlight flooded in when he opened the door. He shook the mattress vigorously, took it back to the cot, and smoothed out the lumps.

Ellen watched him, her face pale, a growing fear in her eyes.

She said to his back, her voice unsteady, "I know why you won't answer me. You think that Duncan is—is dead."

He turned, looked at her, and what she read in his eyes was answer enough. She went slowly to the cot and flung herself face down on the straw mattress.

Miles hesitated. He wanted to say comforting

words, but could find no words. Instead he went back to the open door and gazed into the night. The sky was clearing. Moonlight—and shadows —stars. The storm was over. Dawn would see them continuing the journey to Juniper Flats.

Chapter IX

They rode steadily into the west, the mid-morning sun hot on their backs. The rain had been light here, and drying sun and wind had already absorbed the moisture. Dust riffled under the horses' hoofs, drifted lazily in their wake. The junipers, though, had a fresh-washed look, and there was a spicy tang in the air that added to Ellen's growing excitement. This was the Juniper Flats country, and soon she would have her first glimpse of the little ranch-house Duncan had described to her. Despite her anxiety, her fears, she was thrilled by the thought.

Miles stole glances at her as they rode. The few hours sleep had done marvels for her. The haunting fear was gone from her eyes, and there was a new, undismayed bearing in her, an unafraid readiness to meet anything the day could bring. She was going to need all she had in her, Miles reflected. Her brother was either dead or a prisoner. There could be no other answer. Also this vast reach of juniper-covered mesa was actually Bar M range. Ellen Frazer thought it was the ranch Duncan had bought with her money. He knew he would never have the heart to tell her that the sale was fraudulent, not even if Duncan Frazer was still alive. Some day he would clear the title for them with a quit-claim deed.

Ellen pointed: "Smoke—over there," she said.

He said, "Yes—that's the place."

She gave him a quick look. "You don't want me to expect—too much."

He was remembering the grim answers drawn from those long hours of self-communion while waiting for the dawn. He said, briefly, "Not too much."

"I'm not afraid," Ellen said. She gave him a faint smile that had a touch of hardness in it. "I'm not the same girl who climbed down from that stage."

A turn in the trail brought them in sight of the cabin, a weather-beaten ancient log structure. Miles heard a smothered exclamation from Ellen, understood her keen disappointment. The Box DF ranch-house was still an old-time cow-camp, a bleak, lonesome place of wide-spread corrals, the old cabin as he remembered it, crude log walls chinked with mud. No trees for shade, and even the scrubby junipers cleared away. He could not blame the girl for that shocked little cry.

A hound winded them, and his vociferous

clamour caused a commotion in the cabin. The door opened, framed a woman who watched their approach, hand lifted to shade her eyes against the sun. Her voice, sharp, nasal, commanded the dog to silence, and, tail down, he slunk back to the door, stood there, teeth bared in a snarl.

They drew to a standstill, and Miles, after a quick glance at Ellen's stiff face, asked laconically, "Duncan Frazer home?"

The woman remained silent, her eyes suspicious, hostile. Miles repeated his question.

"He ain't to home," the woman answered, reluctance in her voice. "What for you folks is askin' for him?" She moved back, held the door ready to slam shut.

Miles lifted a hand, indicated Ellen: "His sister," he explained. "Miss Frazer." The woman's hand tightened on the door, and her gaze fastened on Ellen an oddly disturbed look. She said in a tight voice, "I told you he ain't to home." She started to shut the door. Ellen's exclamation held her, and her look went again to the girl, uncertain, almost fearful.

"You must be Mrs Wellen," Ellen said, and smilingly added, "I've come all the way from New York to see Duncan. You see, Mrs Wellen, I'm one of the partners."

The woman hesitated, turned her head and spoke to somebody inside the cabin: "Says she's Dunc's sister, Jess."

A man's voice rumbled an indistinct reply, and now the woman's smile came. She said, with an attempt at genial hospitality, "I reckon you'll want to come in and set, Miss Frazer. We wasn't expectin' you. Dunc will sure be red-eyed he wasn't here when you come. He's talked a lot about you to Jess and me."

Ellen was sliding from her saddle: "Oh, Mrs Wellen—I've been so worried. Duncan didn't get my letter."

Miles dropped from his horse, stood close to her, watchful eyes on the woman. She stared at him suspiciously.

"He your friend? Ain't seen him before?"

Ellen correctly interpreted the quick warning in Miles' glance. He did not want his name known. She said, casually, "The livery stable people sent him along to show me the way and take the mare back."

"You fixin' to stay?" Mrs Wellen looked dubious.

"Of course." Ellen spoke impatiently. "I'm Duncan's sister—his partner. Of course I'm staying." She edged closer to the door.

"We're awful crowded," Mrs Wellen said. "My man is bad hurt." Her voice took on a sullen note. "We just ain't got the room. Like I said, we wasn't expectin' for you to git here so quick."

"Well—" Ellen glanced at Miles, caught his slight nod. "Now I'm here I'd like to come in, Mrs

Wellen. I want to talk with Mr Wellen—if he's not too ill."

The man's voice answered from inside the cabin: "Sure—let her come in, Minnie. I ain't too sick to talk to her." Mrs Wellen stood away from the door. "Come right in, folks." She made an apologetic gesture. "Things is in a mess, me not expectin' you, and Jess layin' 'round with his hurt leg."

They followed her inside. Ellen gave Miles a quick look of dismay. Mrs Wellen was not a tidy housekeeper. The girl repressed a shudder of disgust. Poor Duncan . . . forced to live in such a filthy pigsty. Her look went to the man lying on the bed, a torn and dirty blanket drawn up to his chin.

Ellen's heart sank as she gazed at the swarthy, unshaved face. She wondered wildly how Duncan could have formed a partnership with so repellent a creature. With an effort she forced a smile, said feebly, "How do you do, Mr Wellen? I'm so sorry to find you not well."

Wellen's eyes had been on Miles, wary, suspicious, and now he shifted his look to the girl.

"You sure dropped in awful sudden, Miss Frazer." His grin showed tobacco-stained teeth. "Dunc ain't here. Reckon he'll be some upset, him not bein' here when you come."

His guarded look went back to Miles, and there was a furtive movement under his blanket.

Perhaps he caught the flicker in Miles' eyes; he explained with another grin: "Bronc pitched me, like to have broke my laig. Been laid up most a week."

"Tough luck," Miles said. "How about letting me have a look. I could tell you if she's broke. Might be I could fix a splint for you."

"Ain't needin' no help, mister." Wellen's tone showed odd alarm. "All this laig of mine needs is some rest. I'm gittin' along fine."

Ellen sat down on a chair Mrs Wellen pushed at her. "When will Duncan be back?" she asked worriedly.

Wellen's cold eyes went back to her. He shook his head. "No tellin'," he answered. "Me bein' laid up like this, he keeps right busy doin' two men's work."

"Don't you know where he is?"

Wellen withdrew a hand from under the blanket, reflectively rubbed his black bristle of beard. "Talked some of roundin' up a bunch of strays down in the canyon." The man paused, looked at his wife. "Seems to me he said somethin' about headin' round to the Bar M, didn't he, Minnie?"

"I wouldn't be rememberin'," the woman answered. She turned to the stove, began slamming pots and pans. Miles sensed fear in her, a reluctance to talk.

"I'll tell Dunc you was here," Wellen continued. "If he headed over to Bar M he'll likely stay there for quite a spell. Figgers to pick up a bunch of yearlin's."

"I'm staying, now I'm here," Ellen said.

"Well, ma'am—" Wellen glanced at his slatternly wife. She shook her head. "Well, ma'am," he repeated in a harsher voice, "don't seem a good idee for you to stay, way we're fixed. We're some crowded for room."

"I can make up a bed outside," Ellen suggested. And then, firmly: "I don't mind roughing it, Mr Wellen. I'm terribly anxious to see Duncan."

Mrs Wellen dropped a frying-pan with a loud clatter. She turned, faced the girl angrily. "It just don't suit us for you to stay, and if you've got good sense you'd head back to Santa Ysabel and put up at the hotel. We'll tell your brother just as quick as he gets in."

"You forget something." Ellen's tone was icy. "I happen to be one of the partners. My money bought this ranch, and I'm not going to be told I can't stay here."

Mrs Wellen began a retort, was stopped by an exclamation from her husband. "I reckon she's hit the nail square, Minnie. Ain't for me and you to tell her she ain't stayin' if she wants to." His placating grin was on the girl. "I reckon we can make out some way, Miss Frazer, if you don't mind sort of campin' outside. Got some old wagon sheets Minnie can rig up a tent with." He chuckled. "I'm bettin' my chips Dunc'll hustle you back to Santa Ysabel as quick as he gits in."

"I'll send word to have my trunk sent out." Ellen looked at Miles: "You'll do that for me?"

Miles pretended an uneasiness he was not far from actually feeling. "You figger to stay, ma'am? Don't seem like a smart idee, you sleepin' under the stars. Rain comes snortin' along fast these times."

"You're sure shoutin' the truth," agreed Wellen from the bed, a hint of approval in the look he gave the stranger.

Mrs Wellen said sulkily, "I reckon she's set on stayin'. I'll go drag out those wagon sheets." She flung Ellen an indignant glance and stepped into the sunshine.

Wellen said in an amused tone, "Minnie's some peeved." His eyes were taking in the girl, appraising her from head to foot. "You sure look like a boy in them pants," he added with a chuckle. "Figgered you was a young feller when I seen you ridin' into the yard." He hastily amended his statement: "I mean Minnie figgered thataways when she got sight of you through the window."

Miles' quick look at Ellen told him she had not noticed the slip. He said diffidently, playing his role of livery-stable-hand, "You'll want to settle for the mare and my time now, ma'am?"

She guessed he wanted her out of the cabin, wanted to talk to her alone. She was not ready yet, and, frowning worriedly at Wellen, she asked,

"How is Duncan, Mr Wellen? I was upset—finding he hadn't been in town and got my letter."

"Dunc's fine as silk," the man assured her. "Sure will make a bang-up cowman time I git done with him. Can handle a rope 'most good as me."

Ellen got up from the chair. "All right," she said to Miles. "My bag is tied to the saddle. I might as well pay you off now."

Miles followed her outside to the horses. Mrs Wellen was working a long-handled pump and some half-dozen horses were crowding round the trough, nosing at the spurts of water that came with the down-sweep of her arms. She looked across the yard at them, called out shrilly, "Clean forgot to fill the trough, what with Jess takin' up so much of my time 'tendin' to him."

Miles felt Ellen's quick glance; he called back genially, "Reckon I can do some pumpin' for you, ma'am. Ain't in no rush to get to town."

Mrs Wellen stood back as he approached the pump. "Mighty nice of you, mister." She watched him for a moment, then moved off towards a small shed. "I'll go take a look at them wagon sheets. Like as not they're full of rat-holes. Jess ain't used them in a coon's age."

She disappeared inside the shed. Ellen came up, halted close to Miles. "What's a wagon sheet?" she asked.

"Canvas they use to cover loads on wagons," he told her. His voice lowered. "I'm not wanting you to stay, Ellen. I don't like this outfit."

The girl's mouth set stubbornly. "I'm staying— and Miles, I can't tell you how relieved I am about Duncan." Her voice broke. "He—he's all right, and I've been so frightened for him."

Miles kept his gaze on the water gushing into the trough. His silence disturbed her.

She said, uneasily, "You—you think something is wrong, but I don't care. I'm going to stay here until Duncan comes."

The long trough started to spill over. Miles dropped his hand from the pump-handle, and his head turned in a steady look at her.

He said gravely, "I can't force you to leave."

"No . . ." Ellen's chin lifted. "Nothing you can say will make me change my mind." She broke off, turned her gaze on Mrs Wellen, who was hurrying from the shed. Her feet sent up little riffles of dust that the wind caught up, flurried against dragging skirts.

"The wagon sheets ain't so good, but I reckon they'll do for fixin' up a tent," Mrs Wellen said. She threw Ellen a sulky look, hurried on to the cabin.

"She doesn't like me," Ellen guessed. She frowned. "I wouldn't stay here a minute if it were not for Duncan. These Wellen people are horrid. I don't understand how Duncan ever took such a man as Jess Wellen for a partner."

"Smooth talker," Miles said. "Your brother

wouldn't be knowing much about men—not Wellen's kind."

"His good sense should have warned him," fretted the girl.

"Wellen's cow lingo would seem the real stuff," Miles pointed out. "I've a notion Wellen can be pleasant enough when he wants something. He's crafty. I don't trust him."

"You're trying to frighten me," Ellen complained.

"He gave himself away," Miles continued in a relentless voice. "He saw us ride into the yard, was watching from the window."

"He said he meant that his wife saw us," reminded Ellen, weakly defensive.

"He was lying, and that means he's pulling off a trick, wanting us to believe he's too lame to move from his filthy bed." Miles was watching the cabin door, eyes narrowed, alert. "He's no more sick than I am."

"You're trying to frighten me," Ellen repeated. Her face was suddenly pale.

"He had a gun on us," Miles went on quietly. "I saw his hand move under the blanket. He was ready to shoot. One wrong move from either of us, and we shouldn't have left that cabin alive."

Ellen gazed at him with appalled eyes. She wanted to tell him he was wrong. He had to be wrong, because so much depended on his being wrong. *Duncan.* She could not bear to think it out, stood frozen with horror, listening while Miles' voice came to her as from a far distance.

"I can't let you stay here," Miles was saying. "I smell danger here—*death*."

Ellen found her voice, weak, sick with fear: "You—you think he's lying—about Duncan?"

"Yes." There was grim finality in Miles' low voice. "The man lies, Ellen." His pitying look embraced her. "It is no use for you to stay here. Duncan won't be coming back—" His hand went out, steadied her.

Ellen went rigid, and after a long moment, "Thank you, Miles. I—I promised not to make things harder."

"Right," he said. "You won't." The sunlight drew a flash from his tawny eyes. "You've got what it takes." Admiration deepened his voice.

"What must we do?" Ellen was aware of an odd amazement at herself, her sudden command of a trembling body, the steadiness in her voice. Miles Clarke was an immovable rock of strength. His indomitable courage flowed into her, sustained her at this dreadful moment. She watched him, saw that his vigorous mind was already shaping plans, making ready for immediate action.

Voices reached them from the cabin: Mrs Wellen's shrill, nasal tones, her husband's deep-throated growl, a sudden hard laugh from him.

Ellen shivered, for all the hot sun on her.

Anything could happen out here in this remote and hostile land. If Miles was right about Jess Wellen, the man was actually a desperado, a killer. He would not let them get away if he suspected that Miles had guessed the truth, that death crouched by his side under the covering dirty blanket. To merely climb into their saddles, ride away, would not solve the problem. Wellen's suspicions would break into full flame. He would reach for the rifle she had noticed leaning against the wall. They could not ride fast enough to get away from rifle bullets.

Miles said, slowly, "We've got to take this easy, keep him thinking he has us fooled. The woman is dangerous too."

Ellen nodded. She found herself wishing she knew how to use a gun—only she had no gun. She gazed, fascinated, at the Colt forty-five in Miles' holster. *Would he again be forced to use it in her defence?* Her heart began to pound.

"We mustn't stand here," Miles went on. "They'll get suspicious. We've got to keep them fooled, play their own game."

She nodded again, and at his gesture made her way back to the cabin. Miles followed, close on her heels, and she heard him in a low voice telling her what she must do.

"Say you've been thinking it over, and that after all it seems best to follow Mrs Wellen's advice and go back to the hotel in Santa Ysabel."

"Yes," she said in a whisper, not looking back at him. "I understand."

"Don't get between Wellen and me," Miles warned. "And watch the woman. I'll take care of Wellen—only don't get between us."

"Yes," she said again. "I understand."

She stepped inside the dark, smelly room, a bright smile on her face now, and no hint in her of the cold prickles of fear chasing up and down her spine. Wellen's look passed her, fastened on Miles, and again there was a furtive movement under the blanket.

"Thought you was headin' back to town," he drawled, surly suspicion in his voice.

Ellen spoke quickly. "I've been thinking it over. It doesn't seem right to put Mrs Wellen to so much trouble—and you sick in bed."

"Meaning what?" Wellen demanded.

"I mean I'm going back to Santa Ysabel," explained Ellen. "You can tell Duncan—when he comes." Despite her attempt to keep her voice steady, the mention of her brother's name made her falter. Wellen's cold eyes narrowed.

"Ain't no trouble, puttin' you up here," he said gruffly. "Minnie ain't mindin' none. Ain't that right, Minnie?" He flashed her a warning glance.

"All right with me for Miss Frazer to stay." Mrs Wellen forced a smile. "I done told her she's welcome."

"You are both very kind." Ellen found herself

137

stumbling. "I—I—well, I'll be saying good-bye, and thank you—"

Wellen interrupted her: "Seems like you changed your mind kind of sudden. Mebbe it was this hombre you got with you changed it for you, huh?" Again the furtive movement under the blanket. "Ain't so sure Dunc would like for you to go off with this hombre. Dunc'll likely give me hell if I let you."

Ellen hardly heard him. She was watching Mrs Wellen, saw her quick, sly glance at something in the corner behind her—a shotgun, almost within reach of the woman's hand. Ellen's mind was suddenly cool, racing. She must manage somehow to keep Mrs Wellen away from that shotgun. The crisis was roaring down on them. She dared not give Miles a look. Instead, her look, her smile, held the woman motionless.

"You've been so kind, but I can't think of putting you to so much trouble, Mrs Wellen." She moved towards the woman, hand outstretched. "I *must* say good-bye . . ."

Mrs Wellen hesitated, looked blankly at the girl's hand, and then her eyes shifted in another glance at her husband.

Wellen did not see the questioning look. He was watching Miles, and now, his voice a snarl, he said, "You git out, feller. You ain't takin' the girl away."

Miles was close to the empty chair Ellen had

used. His foot lifted, sent it hurtling at Wellen's head. Smoke and flame poured through the blanket, but Miles was crouching to one side now, his own gun making thunder.

Ellen kept her mind only on Mrs Wellen—the shotgun. She flung herself forward, seized the woman's reaching hand, felt steel-hard fingers clawing at her throat. She fought desperately, kept herself between the woman and the shotgun, glimpsed Jess Wellen, fully clothed, a long, gaunt-framed man, black-bristled face a mask of rage. He was backing towards the open door, bloody hand dangling and useless. Gun-smoke veiled the scene, choked her with its acrid bite, and suddenly the woman struggling with her went limp in her grasp.

Ellen released her hold, leaned against the wall, gasping for breath. She saw Miles, framed in the sunlit doorway, gun in lowered hand. His head turned in a look at her, and now he was running to her.

"Hurt?" Anxiety made his voice tight.

Ellen shook her head, hand feeling at her throat. "She tried to choke me."

Miles looked at Mrs Wellen, limp, sobbing in a chair. "Your man got away."

The woman's face lifted in a dazed look at him, and after a moment she said in a whispering voice, "Wish you'd killed him dead. He's pizen mean."

"You were doing your best to help him." Miles eyed her curiously.

"I've lived with Jess long enough to do what he tells me. Jess wasn't past killin' *me* if I didn't mind him." She made a despairing gesture. "Wish you'd killed him."

Miles was inclined to agree. He had wanted Wellen alive, for questioning, and had purposely placed his bullet to disable, not to kill. The man was tough, active as a cat. Ellen's desperate struggle with Mrs Wellen had distracted Miles, and Wellen had managed to escape into the chaparral with only a bullet-smashed hand to show for the encounter. Luckily there had been no chance for him to get to the horses.

Mrs Wellen pulled up her apron, wiped her hot face, looked apathetically at Ellen. "Wasn't fixin' to harm you. Had to mind Jess—do what he said."

Ellen found herself unable to cope with the strange situation. She gave Miles a helpless look. He seemed equally at a loss. Mrs Wellen's efforts to help the man she apparently hated made a baffling problem. He went back to the bed, picked up Wellen's fallen gun. A forty-five, like his own. He ejected two empty shells, replaced them with cartridges from his belt, and returned to Ellen, still guarding the shotgun.

"Here's a gun for you." He handed her the loaded weapon.

Ellen took it from him, her expression a bit horrified. "I hate the things," she said, and then, with a hard little smile, "but they're useful."

Miles picked up the shotgun, crossed the room and secured the rifle resting against the wall near the bed. Mrs Wellen watched him with listless faded blue eyes. "Jess can git plenty more," she said dully. "Too bad you didn't kill him, mister."

Ellen wondered if the woman's odd humility, her outspoken hate for her husband, was all pretence. There were questions she wanted to ask her, questions she almost dreaded to hear answered. She looked down at the gun in her hand. Wellen's gun. Perhaps this same gun had done murder—murdered her brother. The thought horrified her. Clenched fingers went limp, allowed the Colt to thud on the floor. She felt she could never bear to touch the thing again.

Miles heard the clatter, and, startled, he ran to her, saw her stricken look at the gun and guessed her thoughts. He gave her a remorseful look, picked up the gun, and spoke abruptly to Mrs Wellen.

"I want you to explain why your husband tried to trick us."

"Jess seen you comin', figgered to find out your business." Fleeting, malicious amusement glinted in her faded eyes. "Ain't the first time he's pulled off that trick. Gives him the chance to git in the first shot." Her mouth twitched in something like a smirk. "Jess don't usually miss. You sure beat him to it, mister."

"You mean he used that same blanket trick on some other man? You saw him kill somebody—the way he tried to kill me?"

Mrs Wellen darted a sly look at Ellen, hesitated, tightened her lips. "I ain't tellin' what I seen Jess do."

Miles' eyes were on her, hard, uncompromising. "You saw him use that trick on Duncan Frazer—kill Duncan Frazer."

"Ain't tellin' you nothin'," repeated the woman, sullenly. She hung her head, began to tremble.

She had no need to tell them more. The great fear in her was enough. Ellen knew now that her brother was dead, killed by the same gun Miles had just picked up from the floor.

She heard her voice, a faint, grief-stricken whisper, "Duncan—*poor Duncan*—" And then an arm was round her, a strong, comforting arm, and she hid her face against Miles' shoulder.

Chapter X

Pilar Rojo leaned on his pitchfork, apparently absorbed in the antics of two young mules on the other side of the corral fence. Actually his attention was slyly on the lanky, sandy-haired man who came sauntering into the yard.

The Mexican's eyes were narrow slits under heavy grizzled brows. *Por Dios*! He comes again, this gringo. Three times now, and always he looks into the office for *Señora*.

Pilar scowled. He did not trust this Boone Haxson hombre. He was a wild one, and there was talk that he was not above stealing a horse. It was well to watch him.

"Hi, hombre! *Cóm' está*?" Boone halted, dragged cigarette-papers and tobacco from his shirt pocket, lip lifted in a grin that found no reflection in singularly watchful eyes.

"*Cóm' está*?" Pilar's answering grin hid a growing uneasiness. He lifted a lean, dark hand, casually pushed up the brim of his steeple-crown hat. An innocent enough gesture, but really to assure him that his razor-edged machete was in its proper place inside the back of his shirt. One never knew, and it seemed that *Señora* had mysterious enemies who meant her no good.

"You wan' somet'ing, *señor*?"

Boone leaned over the fence, waved a hand. "That buckskin yonder. Was wonderin' what V. Crumm is askin' for him."

Pilar recognized this for subterfuge. His smile stiffened. "*Quién sabe*?" He thrust his fork deep into the straw pile. "You ask *Señora*."

"Been waitin' for her to show up," Boone told him. "Nice bronc, that buckskin. Mebbe me and V. Crumm can make a deal."

The firm tread of booted feet approaching up the planked sidewalk saved Pilar from continuing a conversation he found disturbing. His relieved look went to the big woman turning into the yard. V. Crumm could handle this hombre who pretended he wanted to buy a horse. She would spit in his eye, send him running. V. Crumm was afraid of nothing—man or devil. *Por Dios*! She was a mighty one, even if only a woman.

Despite his reassuring thoughts, Pilar Rojo wriggled his shoulder-blades, took added comfort in the feel of the big machete. *Caramba*! He would use it quick if this *pícaro* tried any funny business with *Señora*.

V. Crumm came to a sudden standstill, and there was no friendliness in her eyes—or her voice.

"What for you loafin' here, Boone Haxson? I'd just as soon you didn't hang round my barn."

"Now, ma'am"—Boone spoke in a good-natured drawl—"no need for you to get on the prod." He lounged towards her. "A friend of yours asked me to hand over this piece o' paper."

V. Crumm glanced suspiciously at the folded paper in his fingers. "Me and you don't have the same friends," she snorted, thinking of another piece of crumpled paper still in her pocket.

Boone grinned. "You'd be surprised, ma'am. *This* friend come in on the stage with me sundown yesterday."

V. Crumm snatched the note from his extended hand, muttered a surprised exclamation as she glanced at the pencilled scrawled name.

"This ain't for me!"

"That's right," drawled the cowboy. "It's from me to him." His eyes went hard, warned her. "We ain't lettin' nobody know about it. Savvy?"

"Comin' from *you,* I don't," she snapped. She thrust the note deep into a pocket, gave him a worried look. "How come you met up with him, Boone? Or ain't you talkin'?"

"Ain't talkin'," Boone said laconically.

"All right—get out!"

He shook his head: "I'm buying me a horse, ma'am. Cain't risk bein' seen over to your barn without I make a dicker for a bronc. Savvy?"

V. Crumm studied him with cold, shrewd eyes. She believed she had good reason to distrust this lanky, sandy-haired cowboy. The Haxsons had always been known as a bad lot. His father had been a petty cow-thief and died with a Bar M bullet in him.

Her hand closed over the note in her pocket. Boone was going to a lot of trouble getting it to Miles Clarke. And Boone didn't want it known that he was sending notes to Miles Clarke. It was all very confusing. She couldn't make head or tail of it.

"You should do some more talkin', Boone," she complained. "You're dealin' me cards and askin' me to play 'em blindfolded."

The cowboy shook his head, said softly, "I'm obeyin' orders, ma'am. *His* orders." He dropped his cigarette and snubbed it under his boot-heel. "Had to do some figgerin' how to get this note to you without makin' talk. Figgered it would be a right smart play to buy me a horse from you." His gaze slid over the corral fence. "What you askin' for that buckskin, ma'am?"

V. Crumm pursed her lips. She was used to making swift decisions. "I'm taking a gamble on you, Boone," she said slowly. "Mebbe I'll be sorry, but you'll be more sorry—if this note is a trick."

"Listen," Boone's drawl was gone, and there was an odd tightness in his voice. "I've done throwed in with him, ridin' with him to hell and gone. It ain't no trick."

She was impressed, despite her doubts. "All right," she agreed. "I'm playin' the hand." She gave him a wintry smile. "So the deal calls for a horse-trade, huh?"

"Sure does," grinned Boone. "I spread it round that I was buyin' me a horse from you." His appraising look was on the buckskin.

"You would *pick* that buckskin," V. Crumm grumbled.

"How much you askin'?"

She named a price, watched with shrewd eyes for his reaction.

Boone merely grinned. "You sure think a lot of that bronc, but anythin' you say goes with me. Ain't *dinero* out of *my* pocket."

"Huh?" V. Crumm was startled. She said irritably: "Look here, young feller, you was just tellin' me you aimed to *buy* a horse. I don't *give* 'em away."

"You can collect from the feller that's got his name on that note I handed to you." Boone's grin widened, but did not reach his eyes.

Her face reddened. "Why—you doggone young—" She broke off, studied him intently. Something in him warned her that he was in deadly earnest.

She gestured helplessly, "Oh, go get a rope on him and get out." Sarcasm crept into her voice. "Or do you want I should throw in a saddle and bridle?"

"All I'm needin' is a bill of sale," drawled the cowboy. He gave her a knowing wink. "Makes the trade look bona fide, like the law sharks say."

V. Crumm nodded, went briskly into the office, and by the time Boone came by with the buckskin on a rope she had the paper ready.

She stood in the doorway of the office, thoughtful gaze following man and horse as they left the yard. Pilar Rojo crossed over from the straw-pile with his pitchfork.

He said, cautiously, in Spanish, "I am much puzzled, *señora*. You sell a good horse to this man, but take no money."

V. Crumm met his worried look, and the hint of a grim smile played over her rugged features. "I have been dealt a blind hand of cards, Pilar. It is possible I'll hold an ace or two." She broke into English. "Hell's bells, ain't the first time I took a long chance and raked in the jackpot."

"Thees jackpot beeg, no?" muttered the Mexican.

"Life—or death, I'm thinkin'," V. Crumm said grimly. "*Quién sabe?*"

"*Quién sabe?*" Pilar spoke softly, a sudden glitter in his eyes. He touched his shoulder. "I carry sharp steel, *señora*. The ace of death for those who would harm you."

She looked at him affectionately. "You're a good hombre, Pilar. Now you get busy and shake down some hay. Stage is due soon, and Cap Hansy'll yell bloody murder if you ain't ready for him."

She went back to her big office-chair. It creaked ominously under her. She frowned. She'd have to get Pilar to wire the legs or some day she'd find herself flat on the floor.

Her hand fumbled in a pocket, brought out the note Boone Haxson had given her, and she gazed at it with puzzled eyes. A message for Miles Clarke. She yearned to open it, satisfy her curiosity. Ingrained honesty restrained her, and after a moment's hesitation she thrust the note back into her pocket. Her fingers encountered another piece of paper. Her face hardened. This note crumpling under her fingers was addressed to herself, warned her to leave Santa Ysabel, promised unpleasant things if she ignored the warning. She had been given ten days to make up her mind.

It was hard to down the sickening fears that persisted in lifting ugly heads. She was not afraid of danger, of enemies who came out in the open. She was a two-fisted fighter and demanded odds from nobody. This thing, though, was getting her down. She was walking in the dark, never knew just when she might step on a rattlesnake lurking unseen in the trail.

V. Crumm exploded a deep sigh, shook her head, angry at herself for allowing weakening fears to beset her. She had learned long ago that the only way to meet a difficulty was to wade right in to the middle of the stream and find out how deep it was. Action was the answer, not sitting there, mooning, wondering, getting herself scared to death.

Her mind went back to the puzzle of Boone Haxson's tie-up with Miles Clarke. Boone had arrived on the same stage with Miles, but Miles had not mentioned any interest in the sandy-haired cowboy. Something must have happened since Miles and Ellen had ridden away the night before.

A recollection came to V. Crumm as she frowned over the mystery. Miles' visit to Bar M long years ago when he was a boy. He had made friends with old Boone Haxson's kid. It was possible the friendship still persisted, despite the fact that young Boone was supposed to be mixed up with a shady bunch, swinging a too-wide loop.

V. Crumm nodded to herself. She felt she had the glimmer of an answer that might explain the mystery. At any rate she had chosen to accept Boone as an ally, let him walk off with a valuable horse, given him a bill of sale she would have to stand by. She wondered gloomily if she were getting soft in the head with advancing age. In less than twenty-four hours she had given away two of her most prized horses merely for the asking. First Miles Clarke and now young Boone Haxson. And she had involved herself with the affairs of a young girl whose brother was probably a bad lot, a cow-thief.

V. Crumm grunted explosively. No sense letting crazy notions worry her. She'd climbed to the saddle, had to make a good ride of it, stick it out to the finish.

Pilar Rojo poked his head inside the door. "Stage—she come," he said.

The usual crowd was gathered in front of the store when she strode up the steps to the porch. "Hello, folks." None there would have guessed her gnawing anxieties. "Cap Hansy sure is right on time like he always is 'cept when he runs into road agents or washouts."

"Cain't blame Cap for *them* things," sagely observed a lank, grey-bearded man. "Them things is acts o' God."

"Huh?" V. Crumm snorted sceptically. "Nobody with good sense can blame God for hold-ups, Tom West. Them things is acts of human wolves. As for floods and washouts, we got to expect 'em as natcheral. I don't hold with blamin' God for nothin'. Huh! Acts o' God! That's fool talk."

Al Derner climbed the porch steps, and V. Crumm's brief glance told her that he was in an ugly frame of mind. Red-eyed as a bull on the prod, she thought uneasily. Looks like he's been hit where it hurts.

She wanted to intercept him, thrust the crumpled piece of paper under his nose, challenge him then and there to deny that he was responsible for the cowardly threat. Something held her back, caution whispering, warning against rashness. She must not wade out too far, not yet. She felt vaguely that she would want Miles Clarke standing by on the bank, lest she go beyond her depth.

The stage rattled up, dust drifted past. Cap Hansy wrapped the reins around the brake, reached for the mail-pouch, and tossed it to Pete.

Cap climbed down, and, with a wink for V. Crumm, gave his immediate attention to the pair of young women who had shared his seat.

V. Crumm sniffed disdainfully. No doubts about *these* girls and what *their* business was in Santa Ysabel. Brazen, painted hussies for Mat Ryber's dance-hall. She darkly suspected that Al Derner was the *real* owner of that prosperous place of sin.

As always, she mentally tabulated the passengers climbing from the big Concord's interior. Six men, two of them cattlemen she knew. Three were strangers, hard-looking men with guns in their holsters who lost no time making for the saloon.

V. Crumm involuntarily glanced behind her, but Al Derner was in the store waiting for his mail. She heard his impatient, arrogant voice nagging at Pete.

The last of the passengers climbed from the stage, an old man who wore the brown robe of a Franciscan. He seemed very feeble, and stood there gazing about him, an odd, remembering smile on his thin, deeply lined face.

V. Crumm stared at him as if he were something dropped from the skies. The sight of him made her think of the bell in the crumbling tower of the old church, the bell too long silent. She had wanted to do something about it, felt now that her longing was an unvoiced prayer this venerable brown-robed priest would fulfil.

Her feet moved with the swift pace of her excited thoughts. She bore down on the newcomer, hand outstretched.

"Welcome to Santa Ysabel, padre." She beamed, spoke in her best voice, the harshness subdued. "Been kind of hopin' you'd be along."

The old Franciscan looked somewhat astonished, but took her hand, held it lightly for a moment. "Indeed, daughter—" a kindly smile warmed the thin face—"I had not sent word—"

V. Crumm smacked her bosom with a big hand. " 'Twas my heart told me you'd be along," she said earnestly. "I've lived here in this backyard of hell for close on thirty years and never heard the bell ring. 'Tis time the bell rings again, padre." She nodded vigorously. "And rings damn' loud." She reddened. "Excuse the langwidge. You can blame it on the bell for not ringin'."

He looked at her, interest deep in his eyes, and said slowly, almost sadly: "Ah, yes, the bell . . . so many years now—so many years." His eyes closed for a moment, his lips moved as if in soundless prayer.

V. Crumm watched him, struggled with her conscience. She was Protestant herself. But this old man was a priest, ready-made for the work she wanted done, and, after all, it was *his* kind of priest who had reared the ancient adobe walls now crumbling to ruins.

"You'll stay in my own house," she said firmly. "Got plenty room in that old place Don Mario Salgado built a couple of hundred years ago. Big as a monastery, and Ynez will look after you good." She chuckled. "Ynez is some back in makin' her confessions on account of the old church not doin' business."

The Franciscan was listening intently. "Ah, yes," he murmured, a far-away look in his eyes. "The old Salgado place. Yes, daughter, I have been there many times."

"Huh?" V. Crumm gaped. "You know this town?"

"I was priest in charge forty years ago, until the raid destroyed the church." He smiled gently at her astonishment. "I was a long time recovering from many wounds, and then later transferred to a charge in Mexico City. This town is American now, but I longed to come back, visit old scenes." He paused, added quietly, "I am Father Valdez."

"Pleased to know you . . ." V. Crumm hesitated. "Folks here call me V. Crumm." Her face cracked in a brief smile. "Pilar and Ynez call me *Señora.*"

She became aware of Al Derner's interested gaze from the post office doorway, added hurriedly, "You will stay at my house, padre?"

He inclined his head. "Until I can make arrangements, *señora.* You are most kind."

She seized the little bag he held in his hand. "Just around the plaza, padre. I'll take you there myself."

Al Derner's frowning gaze followed them until they disappeared round the corner. He drew a cigar from a pocket, bit off an end, struck a match, and applied the flame, then, his expression thought-ful, he went down the steps and crossed the street.

Boone Haxson and several men were discussing the buckskin horse tied to the hitch-rail in front of the saloon.

Derner halted on the steps of the hotel porch, called softly, "Boone—come here."

The cowboy hurried up, a wide grin on his sunburned face. "Sure bought me a good bronc. Sim Hogan's ridin' me hard for a trade. His bay colt and ten dollars to boot. Nothin' doin'."

"I bet the Crumm woman stuck you plenty," commented Derner.

"She's sure one smart horse-trader." Boone grinned complacently. "Ain't so slow my own self."

Derner nodded. "She's a damn' nuisance." He looked morosely at the end of his cigar, suddenly flung it into the street. "You see that monk hombre, the feller in the brown robe?"

"Sure." Boone nodded, waited for the other man to continue.

"The Crumm woman took him off with her.

I've a notion he'll be over at her house." Derner paused. "Find out about him, Boone. I want to know his business here and if she sent for him to come."

"I savvy," Boone said.

"We don't need *his* kind in this town," Derner grumbled. He paused again, then: "Right now I'm sendin' you out to Renn's JR. Tell the sheriff I want him in a hurry—and, Boone, see if Dan Heeler and Ace are in the saloon. I want 'em over at my office pronto."

He continued up the hotel porch steps and disappeared inside the lobby. Boone watched him until the screen-door slammed shut. The cowboy's eyes were narrowed slits, his mouth tight. He turned on his boot-heel, went clattering towards the swing-doors of Mat Ryber's Palace Bar.

V. Crumm found she must slacken her vigorous stride to keep pace with the frail old Franciscan. He walked slowly and with a noticeable limp.

"An old wound," he explained, observing her look at his dragging leg. "An Indian arrow—" He smiled, shook his head. "I was young, and strong, then. Now I am old—" He broke off, stood gazing across the plaza at the church, and V. Crumm saw pain in his eyes. "I should have returned," he said, half to himself. "Yes—I was needed here. I should not have stayed in Mexico because of the treaty of Guadalupe Hidalgo. What mattered the hoisting of a new flag? The Holy Cross is above worldly things, is for all the peoples of all nations." He bowed his head in silent prayer.

"The bell will ring again," V. Crumm said softly. "Santa Ysabel needs to hear the bell, padre."

He gave her a benign smile. "Yes, daughter. The bell will ring again for saint and sinner alike. While I live it shall be silent no longer."

V. Crumm unlocked the high gate, motioned for him to enter the garden. She followed him, a rapt expression on her face, a great contentment in her eyes.

Chapter XI

The horses moved at a slow walk through the blanketing darkness. Ellen knew that great cliffs rose on either side, but she could not see them. Stars twinkled overhead, trailed a glittering ribbon above the twisting course of the rimrock.

Miles rode in the lead, now and again glancing back at her. She had refused to let him put the mare on a lead-rope again. They were accustomed to each other now, her hand on bridle rein light and steady, the mare docile and instantly responsive. Miles had reluctantly consented, but his frequent glances told her that he was not liking it. His concern for her safety pleased her.

Miles halted his horse, waited for Ellen to draw alongside.

"Been a stiff down-hill trail," he said. "How are you making out?"

"All right." She relaxed in the saddle, sighed. "It was worse than last night going up." She was suddenly silent. Last night—only last night! Hardly twenty-four hours! Black hours of horror and despair and grief.

"We'll soon be out of the gorge," Miles said. He peered at the vague outline of her face, sensed her weariness, her despondent thoughts. "Another half-hour will take us up the slope to V. Crumm's gate." His hand reached out, closed over hers, where it rested on the horn of her saddle. "You've been mighty brave, Ellen."

She said nothing, sat there, limp, dejected, too weary for words.

Miles withdrew his hand, made and lit a cigarette, his mind busy. It would not be safe for Ellen to remain in Santa Ysabel. He must persuade her to return to New York. He would manage to smuggle her over to Silver City. If she objected to going back to New York, she would be safe at his brother's ranch. It was no time now to talk things over with her. She was too tired, her nerves frayed raw. She needed rest and sleep and good food. Mrs Wellen had grudgingly cooked a breakfast for them: tough steak, greasy fried potatoes, coffee. Ellen had hardly touched the food. She had been too shocked, too grieved about her brother. And the long hours, waiting there in the cabin of murder, had been an ordeal. The wait was unavoidable. They needed the cloak of darkness for the return down the canyon, and he had wanted her to rest, get some refreshing sleep. She had found sleep impossible, and instead had prowled round the ranch-yard with him. She knew, without asking questions, what he looked for, some clue that would lead them to Duncan Frazer's grave.

It was a useless search, and they soon desisted, dragged chairs out and sat in the shade of the lone juniper, from where Miles could watch the surrounding scrub and keep an eye on the cabin door. He suspected that Jess Wellen still lurked in the fringing chaparral, guessed from Mrs Wellen's sly looks that she was waiting for a chance to join her husband. He was quite certain now that her vicious outburst against Jess was a cunning attempt to keep her own skirts clean. She was a sly, dangerous woman and needed watching. Despite questioning, she continued to deny any knowledge of Duncan Frazer's whereabouts, refused to admit that Jess Wellen had murdered him.

Her frenzied protests failed to convince Miles. There were ominous stains on the floor between the bed and the door. Blood had been spilled there, and looking at them Miles could read the grim story they told. Duncan Frazer had learned something that must have enraged him, filled him with a bitter loathing for the man he had taken for a partner.

As Miles pictured the scene, Jess Wellen was still in bed when young Frazer rushed into the cabin, where Mrs Wellen was probably busy getting breakfast ready. Frazer must have warned Wellen that he was going to the Law with his story, and as he turned to leave the cabin Wellen had shot him in the back. The killing had been so easy that Wellen apparently thought it was a good trick to try on Miles. He failed because Miles already suspected the bed was an ambush.

One thing was certain. Mrs Wellen had witnessed the murder. Her own words convicted her: "Ain't the first time he pulled off that trick."

With the approach of sundown they had ridden away, leaving the woman alone in the cabin. There was nothing else they could do. No doubt Wellen was soon back in the cabin, having his wounded hand cared for, and cursing because Miles had confiscated his weapons and driven his horses from the corral. It would take him a long time to carry the news of the affair to Al Derner. It meant a tough walk to the Bar M ranch to get a horse for the ride to Santa Ysabel. The delay was invaluable, allowed time for Miles to get Ellen safely back to V. Crumm.

He pinched out his cigarette, gave Ellen an

encouraging smile, face bent close to hers. "Stiff climb up the slope," he said. "Sorry."

"I'm all right." Her slumped shape straightened in the saddle. She winced, added ruefully: "I'm stiff and sore with all this up-hill and down-hill."

Miles chuckled. "V. Crumm will soon have you in bed."

"I'll sleep—and sleep," Ellen said. "I won't need rocking. I've had rocking enough—in this big saddle."

They reached the massive timbered gate. Miles got down from his horse, found the great key V. Crumm had left concealed for him outside the adobe wall. Lock and hinges were well oiled and the gate swung open without a sound. Ellen rode through. Miles followed with his bay, closed the gate, and slid the heavy bolts.

He climbed into his saddle, was suddenly reaching for his gun.

"Somebody in the brush," he muttered.

They waited, tense, and Ellen now heard a faint whisper of sound. A shape appeared, vanished, and then they heard a low voice, startlingly close in that darkness—Johnny's voice.

"It's me, Mr Clarke."

The boy slid into view, stood in front of them, a dimly seen shape, carbine in lowered hand. "V. Crumm told me to watch the gate," he said. "She figgered you'd mebbe show up any time."

Miles managed a grin. "Good thing you called out, Johnny," he said, a bit grimly.

"Gosh!" Johnny was chagrined. "You seen me comin'?"

"Heard you," Miles told him laconically.

"I ain't so good yet," mourned Johnny.

"Things all right at the house?" Miles asked.

"Sure . . ."

They rode on through the trees and came to the patio gate. Johnny took the horses, led them away to the low adobe building V. Crumm used for her private stable.

Ynez, busy in the kitchen, heard their footsteps on the flagged walk. She held the door open, eyes wide with astonishment as she looked at Ellen in her man's attire. She muttered a startled exclamation in Spanish, smiled amusedly at the girl.

"You look mooch like boy, *señorita*."

They entered the big kitchen. Ynez closed the door, turned and gazed at them, her face sober now, eyes questioning.

"Where's Vee?" Miles asked, noticing her hesitation.

"Señora talk weeth padre," Ynez answered.

"Padre?" Miles was puzzled.

"*Sí*." Ynez nodded, a sudden light in her dark eyes. "Padre come on stage. Señora breeng heem to *casa*."

"Well, tell her we're back." Miles looked anxiously at Ellen, who had slumped wearily into

162

a chair. "Miss Frazer is dreadfully tired, Ynez."

The Mexican woman gave the girl a compassionate look. "I tell *Señora* queek." She hurried through a door and the whisper of quick-moving sandalled feet came to them from the corridor.

Miles waited impatiently, his gaze on Ellen. She looked so pale, so completely exhausted.

He said gently, "Vee will soon have you in bed."

Ellen nodded, smiled wanly. "I'm all right. Just tired—*tired.*"

Footsteps approached up the corridor, the firm, yet singularly light tread of V. Crumm. She burst into the kitchen, Ynez at her heels, and halted abruptly.

"My God! So it's the two of you—back!" She nodded. "Ain't surprised none." She was gazing at Ellen. "So you didn't find your brother, huh?"

"She's too tired to talk," interposed Miles. "Get her to bed, Vee."

"And no blame to her if she's wore to a frazzle," declared the big woman. "Ridin' sixty or more miles over trails a mule would balk at." She bent over Ellen:

"Come on, lass, it's back to your room you go this very moment. Ynez, you get her lamp lighted."

Ynez vanished, and helped by V. Crumm's big hand, Ellen got up from the chair.

"I'm so stiff"—her smile was rueful. "I'm one big ache all over."

"Ynez will get you a hot bath and tuck you in bed," V. Crumm told her. She was looking at the girl with keen eyes. "Hurts you to walk, huh? Miles, you carry her."

She led the way to the bedroom, lantern in hand, Miles following with Ellen in his arms. He was too concerned to wonder at his quickened pulse, but something in him drew a sharp look from V. Crumm. Her grim mouth softened in a fleeting, odd little smile.

She said to Ellen, gently, "Ynez will look after you, my lamb." She gave Miles a look.

Outside in the corridor she seized his arm. "Tell me quick! 'Twas bad things she found out, huh?"

"Yes," answered Miles. "Very bad."

"I could see it in her face, poor lamb," V. Crumm said sorrowfully. "It's her spirit that's weary, more than her body."

"Her brother is dead," Miles told her. "Murdered . . ."

"It's the answer that explains why he never showed up in town for his mail these last weeks." V. Crumm moved on down the corridor, the lantern in her hand making dancing shadows. "You and me has a lot of talkin' to do, Miles." She turned in at a door. "We'll set here in my office—" "She broke off, keen eyes on him. "You'll be starvin' for food."

"Food can wait," Miles said. He took a chair. "Derner been bothering you? He threatened to get out a warrant to search the place for Ellen."

V. Crumm made a scornful gesture. "Dan Heeler come nosin' round last night, pretended he had a paper. I booted him off, told him I'd use a shotgun on him next time he showed his ugly face inside my gate."

Miles grooved a cigarette-paper, dribbled tobacco from the sack. "Anything else—happen?" He shot her a quick look, shaped the cigarette, and scraped a match on his leg.

V. Crumm said tartly, "You know damn well there's somethin' else . . . wears the name of Boone Haxson."

Miles drew in a mouthful of smoke, let it trickle from his nostrils. "What about him?"

She fished inside a pocket, drew out a smudged piece of folded paper, threw it at him. "Got your name on it." She glowered.

"Boone give it to you?" Miles smoothed out the folds, read the brief scrawl, his face expressionless.

"Who else?" she snapped, adding with annoyance: "Ain't carin' for secrets."

He looked up at her, surprised. "Didn't you read it?"

"What do you think?" She pursed her lips indignantly: "I don't poke my nose into folks' letters!"

Miles grinned. "I didn't tell Boone for you not to read it. Says he has news soon as he can get in touch with me."

"He wasn't sayin' I could." Her indignation

mounted: "Wangled him a horse from me, said for me to charge it to you."

Miles struck a match, touched the flame to the note, carried the burning paper to the stove, and dropped it inside. "I suppose he had some reason," he said. He returned to his chair, squinted thoughtfully at her through cigarette smoke.

"That's right. He wasn't explainin' much, but I got the idee he figgered he was bein' watched and was scared to be seen round the barn."

"So he bought him a horse." Miles grinned.

V. Crumm nodded sulkily. "Said he *had* to buy him a bronc to make it sound good for why he was talkin' to me."

"I savvy," Miles nodded approvingly. "Suits me fine for Boone to be smart."

"He could just as well have bought him one of my burros, as go pick that buckskin he took off with him," she rumbled. "Would have made his story listen just as good to nosey folks as wanted to know his business with me."

Miles shook his head. "A man like Boone *had* to buy a good horse. His *friends* would have been suspicious if he'd walked out of your yard with any old bronc." He paused, grinned placatingly. "I'll settle the bill, Vee."

"Shut up!" V. Crumm pushed a hand at him. "Who's askin' you to pay for anythin'?" She suddenly chuckled. "You and that Boone Haxson! A fine horse-trader I am in my old age."

"Old my eye," grinned Miles.

"Old enough to be your ma's friend before you was born, and she'd be a long ways past fifty if she was alive to-day." She chuckled again. "I'm mighty tough, though, and believe me, boy, no damn pack of wolves is goin' to scare me away from Santa Ysabel."

"I want to know more about it," Miles said. "There's been no time to talk. I've been on the jump ever since I got off that stage yesterday."

She flapped an impatient hand at him. "Right now I'm wantin' to know what happened to you and Ellen, and how come you've got Boone Haxson swearin' he aims to ride to hell and gone with you. Just don't figger how Boone gets that way, and him runnin' with a bunch of crooks."

She listened absorbedly to his laconic account of the attempted ambush, nodded grim approval of the strategy that had turned the tables on the would-be killers.

"So that's how come you met up with Boone, huh?" She spoke in a hushed voice, and there was a curiously awed look in her eyes. "The kid you used to play with that time you visited your Uncle Jim's ranch. A bad lot, that Haxson outfit, but the kid was rememberin' you, Miles, rememberin' things he learned from you, things he didn't—couldn't learn from his no-'count dad."

"No savvy," grunted Miles, uncomfortable under her odd scrutiny.

"He learned things from you about honesty and truth and courage—the right kind of courage that stands up against wickedness."

"You're crazy," muttered Miles, embarrassed.

"Kids is queer critters," V. Crumm went on, disregarding the interruption. "Kind of copy-cats, if you savvy what I mean. Take 'em young, and it sinks in deep. Mebbe they grow up and forget, but somethin' happens and it all comes back, starts 'em thinkin' hard. That's what happened to young Boone up on the mesa last night. He was all set to ride the hoot-owl trail and runs smack into you." V. Crumm nodded her head. "Must have hit him plenty hard, Miles, got him to untyin' the crooked knots in his brain and seein' straight, like he had learned from you when you was kids together."

Miles grinned, gestured helplessly. "Have it your own way, *Violet*."

She disregarded his attempt to divert her, and continued to regard him with the same contemplative awe. "It's kind of funny about you, Miles. For all you're so quiet-spoken, and—and young and innocent-like, there's somethin' powerful strong —and—and steadyin'. There's times you get a look in your eyes that makes you feel you've run plumb into a granite wall." She nodded again. "I felt that way when you climbed down from the stage yesterday and looked over at me."

"I was wondering if you'd recognize me,"

chuckled Miles. "You didn't know me from Adam—then."

V. Crumm became suddenly brisk, as if no longer puzzled by the curious behaviour of young Boone Haxson. "Heard some talk about the killin'," she said. "A feller was in the store, told Pete that Nevada and Chino got to quarrellin' and shot it out. He said a feller with 'em come into town this mornin' with their bodies roped to their saddles." She smiled grimly: "Wasn't knowin' it was Boone fetched 'em in, nor that it was *your* hot lead the skunks run into."

Miles shrugged. "I had to do it," he said gloomily.

"Sure you had to, and good riddance to 'em." V. Crumm frowned: "That Nevada feller was on your uncle's Bar M pay-roll one time. Don't know the Chino hombre. Wasn't in town long. Reckon him and Nevada was *both* on Al Derner's pay-roll, hired killers." Her frown deepened: "Seen three more tough-lookin' fellers climb off the stage this sundown. Derner pretended not to notice 'em, but I'm bettin' he knew 'em all right."

He nodded, and after a moment's silence told her about the night at the deserted cabin, his uncle's note concealed in the knife-box.

"You got it with you?" she asked.

He found it in his pocket, handed it to her.

She read the pencil scrawl, brows puckered, lips pushing in and out. "Poor Jim," she said softly. "Died with his boots on." Her voice hardened.

169

"Bet he got some of 'em before they got him." She broke off and looked up at Miles, who was watching her intently.

"Ain't knowin' a thing about this copper ore business he writes about."

"He said you didn't," commented Miles. He waited for her to speak about the will left in her store safe.

Her mind was on another matter and she re-read the note, muttering under her breath. "I'm bettin' Al Derner thinks I know about that ore," she finally said aloud. "I savvy now about the night the store was broke into and the safe robbed." She scowled up at Miles. "Derner figgered he'd find papers, the location notice, mebbe. Reckon it explains plenty 'bout these letters I'm gettin', warnin' me to get out of town." She paused, added under her breath: "Only they won't be lettin' me get away alive, not if Derner thinks I know about that ore."

Miles said worriedly, "You mean the safe was *robbed?*"

"That's right"—her eyes took on a startled look. "Hell's bells, looks like they made off with your uncle's will makin' you his heir to the Bar M! They cleaned that safe out!" Her big body slumped limp in her chair. "My God, Miles! He'd tear the piece of paper into a million bits and burn the pieces."

Miles stood up from his chair, hitched on his

gunbelt. "It's time I had a talk with *Mister* Derner—"

She was on her feet instantly. "No! Don't act crazy! He—they'll get you."

"I'm not dodging around any more," Miles said.

"Don't be a fool." Her voice was rough, dominating again. "Talkin' with Al Derner right now won't get you nothin' but a free ride to Boothill."

"He'll take the same ride with me."

"And where does that leave me, and Ellen Frazer? The poor little lamb!" She gave him a sly look, saw that he was weakening. "No sense goin' off half-cock, Miles. You wait until you've had your talk with Boone Haxson."

Miles knew she was right, was suddenly impatient with himself. He could not afford to let anger govern him. He must keep his head.

He gave the big woman a shamefaced grin: "Was seeing red, but you're right, Vee . . ." He paused. "Must get in touch with Boone—"

"You wait until mornin'. You're dead on your feet for want of sleep, and right now you're goin' to eat." She moved to the door. "I'll fix up a big steak, with fried onions and potatoes and coffee. Come along, son, and set in the kitchen while I fix up a man-size meal." A smile touched her rugged face. "I ain't told you about the padre."

"Who's the padre?" Miles asked, following her through the door.

V. Crumm halted, looked back at him, her face oddly beatific in the soft glow of the lantern she carried.

"He's come to ring the old bell," she said solemnly. "He's goin' to ring it loud—for all Santa Ysabel to hear."

Chapter XII

Sheriff Jake Renn was in a disturbed frame of mind. He fidgeted in his chair, a small, wiry man with a drooping moustache too big for his thin face.

"Wasn't liking the way you sent Boone to get me," he grumbled. "I'm awful short-handed at the ranch. Got a bunch of three-year-olds to round up for that Kansas City buyer to look at."

"I've got work for you here," Al Derner told him coldly. "Sheriff business comes first, Jake."

The sheriff stared gloomily out of the window that overlooked the yard in the rear of the hotel. A door opened into the yard, which was walled in by a high board fence. Beyond the fence he could see the small barn where Derner stabled his buckboard team and the two saddle horses he kept for his personal use. A grey cat drowsed in the morning sunshine, apparently oblivious of the sparrow that hopped closer and closer. A peaceful enough scene, but the worried little sheriff knew it was a sham. The cat only pretended to drowse, was really watching the sparrow, claws ready for the fatal pounce.

The peace in this spacious, comfortable room in which he sat was equally false. A similar drama of life and death was in the making. Al Derner, lolling at ease in his big leather-cushioned chair, was the grey cat, and he was the sparrow—only unlike the sparrow, he was keenly aware of his danger.

He made a feeble attempt to assert himself: "That's the trouble, Al. I ain't got time for this sheriff business. I've a notion to turn in my star."

Derner shook his head, smiled thinly: "I wouldn't, Jake."

Sheriff Renn thought unhappily of his ranch. He had put his life into that ranch. Derner had him by the throat. He must do as Derner wished or face ruin, perhaps worse. The man was a devil, for all his bluff, hearty exterior.

Derner watched him intently, sardonic amusement in his eyes. He said softly: "Listen, Jake, play the game my way and you're sittin' pretty. No more trouble about that loan. I'll tear the mortgage papers up, burn 'em in front of your eyes."

"There's more to it than the damn' mortgage," Sheriff Renn muttered. "There's *murder* . . ."

The big man's face darkened. It was plain he

understood. "Jim Miles resisted arrest," he said coldly. "He was a cow-thief."

"Jim Miles was no cow-thief." The sheriff shook his head despondently. "That killing was plain murder."

"His own fault for resisting arrest," Derner again reminded him.

"It was a frame-up," muttered Sheriff Renn. His head lifted in a steady look at the other man. "You didn't want Jim Miles arrested, taken to gaol. You wanted him dead. You shot him."

Derner grinned, said nothing.

"You had me hush the thing up, spread the story that Jim had skipped the country. You didn't want his friends to know it was you who shot him." The sheriff glowered. "Folks like Luke Flagg and V. Crumm would never have believed he was a cow-thief if we'd brought his dead body back to town, told 'em Jim had been killed resisting arrest. Tellin' 'em he'd skipped the country got 'em worried, made 'em think that mebbe he *was* a cow-thief."

"You're crazy," Derner said angrily.

"I've been crazy." Renn spoke gloomily. "I ain't crazy now. Been doing some thinkin'. You wanted Jim's friends to believe he'd skipped out, so you could put over your story he was owing you a lot of money, make your fake mortgage papers look good—take over the Bar M."

Derner said viciously, "You do too much

thinking. Don't get that way, Jake. It's unhealthy." He took a bottle of whisky from his desk drawer, pushed it across the table. "You need a drink."

Sheriff Renn fastened longing eyes on the bottle. He had been keeping off liquor. It was whisky that had managed to get him into this mess, bind him hand and foot to this scheming, ruthless man. Drinking, gambling, debts—*debts*. Ready cash was always obtainable from Al Derner in exchange for pieces of paper with his name on them. And finally the blanket mortgage on all he owned: ranch, cattle, honour—*his very soul*. He was indeed in pawn to the devil. He had known well enough that Jim Miles was no cow-thief, that Derner was up to mischief when a fraudulent election had pinned a sheriff's star on his shirt. His duty as sheriff was only to do Al Derner's dirty work, and his first job had been to arrest old Jim Miles on the charge of rustling cattle. He had known the thing was absurd.

The little sheriff stared at the bottle so invitingly near his hand. He felt heartsick, mortally shamed. He knew now that Jim Miles' death had been deliberately planned by this man who was urging him to take a drink.

Sheriff Renn got out of his chair. He said, hoarsely, "I'm finished doing your dirty work, Al." He tore the star from his shirt, flung it on the floor. "This ain't worth a damn or I'd arrest you for murder."

A shape slid up behind him, and the sheriff went suddenly limp, slumped down in the chair again.

Ace Stengal looked at the knife in his hand, then coolly wiped the red stains off on the dead sheriff's shirt, and slid the knife into its sheath under his coat. He looked at Derner, smiled thinly.

"Close call, Al." He reached for the whisky bottle, took a long drink, and held the bottle out to Derner. "You need a drink."

Derner grabbed at the bottle, drank, set it back on the table, got out of his chair, his furious gaze on the dead man.

"The damn' fool! Went loco . . ."

Stengal nodded, stared thoughtfully at the lifeless sheriff. "What'll we do with him?"

Footsteps sounded from the hotel lobby. Derner looked at the door. "Dan Heeler," he said softly. He went quickly to the door, threw the bolt. "All right, Dan—come in."

The town marshal stepped inside the room, halted abruptly, startled eyes on the dead sheriff. "What the hell—"

"Jake went loco—tried to kill me—" Derner glanced at Stengal. "Ace stopped him."

Heeler grimaced, gave the slender black-haired man an oddly scared look. "I'll say he stopped him . . ." The words came awkwardly, from fright-stiffened lips, and he stood there, a dazed, stupid look on his beefy face. He repeated Stengal's question: "What'll we do with him?"

Derner returned to his chair, indicating the bottle: "You need a drink, Dan."

The town marshal wet his lips, reached for the bottle. He drank, lowered the bottle, looked briefly at the limp figure in the chair, and drank again.

The other men watched him, and something ominous in them seemed to warn him. He hastily put the bottle down, drew shirt-sleeve across wet moustache, and gave them a slow, reassuring grin. "Reckon Jake had it comin' to him. Give me a hell of a start, though, walkin' in on a dead hombre thisaways."

He hooked a chair with the toe of his boot and sat down, careful to keep his gaze away from the dead man. It was plain their continued silence was worrying him. He spoke again, his voice gruff, business-like:

"Seed Luke Flagg talkin' with V. Crumm over at the store," he said. "Luke seemed awful upset."

Al Derner broke his silence, said bleakly, "Luke Flagg can wait. I'm wanting to know about Boone Haxson."

"I reckon Boone's story is straight." The town marshal fumbled in a pocket, drew out a short remnant of dark plug-tobacco. He gnawed off a piece, pushed the plug back into his pocket, and frowned thoughtfully. "Nevada and Chino got to arguin' and Chino went for his gun and they shot it out."

"You believe this story Boone Haxson tells?"

It was Ace Stengal who broke the silence.

"Sure I believe him," asserted the town marshal. "Boone ain't got no reason to lie. He—he's too smart to try any fool play on us."

Anger stirred in him under the inscrutable eyes of the slender black-coated man. He said fretfully, "You fellers have talked to him. I ain't knowin' more'n he's told you."

Derner spoke irritably, his lowering gaze on Stengal. "Boone's all right. It was Jim Miles' outfit shot his dad. He hates the old Bar M bunch like poison. Forget him, Ace."

"I use my brains," Stengal said smoothly. His head tilted in a look at Derner, and the sunlight coming through the window put a cold glint in his eyes. "Boone's story sounds just a little too—too pat."

Derner stirred uneasily, got out of his chair, and stared out of the window into the yard. The grey cat had the sparrow between its paws, and little feathers were riffling in the wind, fluttering down on the cat's grey fur. Something else was happening in the backyard. The gate opened cautiously, showed the peering face of a man.

Derner said in a tight voice, "Looks like we've got news."

The black-coated man was instantly at his side. He moved with the swift stealth of a cat.

"Who is he?" He spoke in a low whisper, clean-cut as the flick of a whip.

"Jess Wellen," Derner said. His head turned in a grim look at the other man. "I knew we'd have trouble when Miles Clarke hit this town." He went to the door that opened on the yard, slid the bolt. "All right, Jess—come in."

Wellen climbed the steps, and for a moment had eyes only for Derner. He looked sick, like a man too weary for words. He made for a chair, saw the bottle of whisky, seized it, tipped it to his mouth.

They watched, silent, while the whisky gurgled down his throat. He gasped, choked, took another long drink, slammed the bottle on the table, his gaze still on Derner.

"Walked in from Juniper," he said in a hoarse whisper. "My God, boss—" He snatched again at the bottle, put it down, empty, reached blindly for a chair.

They gazed at him; the town marshal's eyes stupid, a growing fear on Derner's face, Stengal's black eyes narrowed, inscrutable.

"What's wrong with your hand?" It was Stengal who spoke.

Wellen looked dully at the dirty, red-stained bandage. "The feller's bullet smashed it. Hurts like hell. Reckon I'll have Doc Peters take a look at it."

Derner broke his silence. "What feller?"

"The feller that come with the girl—the Frazer girl—"

179

"Miles Clarke!" Derner's voice was savage, touched with panic.

Wellen's wandering gaze suddenly saw the limp body slumped lifeless in the chair. He jerked upright, stared with bulging eyes. "My Gawd—" his dust-grimed face went ashen.

Ace Stengal said smoothly: "The sheriff got to thinking too much. Not healthy to think too much, Mr Wellen."

Wellen lurched unsteadily to his feet, shocked eyes on Derner. "I'm needin' a drink!" he gasped.

Derner looked in a drawer, produced another bottle, and after a glance at the man's slobbering mouth, found a glass. He pushed them across the table.

Wellen filled the glass, emptied it, shuddered, put the glass down. "What's goin' on in this town?" he asked plaintively.

Derner shook his head. "You do the talking, Jess. I'm wanting to know what happened—out there." He scowled. "How come you let Clarke shoot you?"

Wellen hesitated, said sullenly, "Wasn't knowin' his name's Clarke. He rode up with the Frazer girl, wanted to know about Dunc. There was a mix-up and he shot the gun from my hand."

Derner and Stengal exchanged glances, and Stengal said in his smooth voice, "Go on talking, Mr Wellen. We want the details."

They listened without comment while Wellen

gave them the story. "Turned the broncs loose, left me afoot," he finished bitterly.

"You didn't go back to the house?" Derner asked.

Wellen shook his head. "Wasn't riskin' it. That hombre is hell on wheels. I figgered the only thing to do was get into town, tell you, and have Doc Peters fix my hand." He swore feelingly. "Sure was a hell of a walk."

"Lost your nerve," sneered Stengal. "Scared to go back."

Wellen reddened, started an angry retort. The malignant look in the man's black eyes shocked him to silence.

"So Frazer's sister suspects the truth about her brother? Is that right, Jess?" Derner's voice was worried.

"Reckon she does," mumbled Wellen. "That Clarke hombre is smart."

"Too smart for you," sneered Stengal.

Wellen refused to meet his look, made no answer.

"Any idea where Clarke and the Frazer girl went?" Derner asked.

Wellen shook his head. "Wasn't goin' back to find out."

Dan Heeler's voice broke the silence. "What'll we do with him?" He pointed at the dead sheriff. "We got to get him away from here."

Derner nodded, scowled. "How did he get into town? Ride, or in his buckboard?"

"Buckboard," answered the town marshal. "Left his rig tied outside, in front of the hotel."

"You go drive it around to my barn," Derner told him. "We'll load him into it, drive him some place up on the mesa."

"I savvy," Heeler nodded. "Make it look like he was ambushed, huh?"

"That's right," Derner grinned. "Leave him sprawled in the chaparral, gun close to his hand, one shell fired. Stampede his team into a runaway with the buckboard."

"I savvy," repeated Heeler with a callous grin. "Them horses will head back to town with pieces of buckboard danglin' at their heels."

Derner nodded, his expression bleak. "When that runaway team gets back to town you start looking for the sheriff, Dan."

"Won't be hard for *me* to find him," guffawed Heeler. He rolled amused eyes.

Derner frowned at the interruption. "After you bring the remains back to town you'll start looking for Miles Clarke, *the murderer.*" He paused, added significantly, "He won't need to live long enough to see the inside of your gaol, Dan."

The town marshal drew a long breath, reached for the whisky bottle. "I reckon that's the play." He drank, slammed the bottle back on the table, and got to his feet.

Jess Wellen came out of his stupor, rolled wicked eyes at them. "I'm settin' in on the deal—" he lifted his bandaged hand. "I'm owin' him plenty hot lead for this." He reached again for the whisky bottle.

"You go hunt up Doc Peters," Derner said. He seemed suddenly cheerful, smiled at them. "Tell Doc Peters you're looking for the sheriff, that you're swearing out a warrant for the arrest of Miles Clarke for attempted murder."

Ace Stengal shook his head: "Better still, tell Doc Peters that you already have sworn out a warrant and that the sheriff has headed up the mesa, looking for the man who shot you."

The town marshal grinned admiringly. "That'll tie up with me findin' the sheriff layin' dead in the chaparral."

"That's right," Derner's smile widened. "Smart play, Ace."

"I use my brains," the black-coated man said coldly.

"Waal"—Heeler moved to the lobby door. "I'll get things started." He halted, frowned back at them. "Will need some help with the sheriff. Reckon I'll get hold of Boone Haxson."

"Wait a minute." Ace Stengal's black eyes sneered at him. "Leave Boone Haxson out of this."

"Huh?" The town marshal's face showed bewilderment. "What's eatin' you?"

Stengal's look went to Derner. "I think," he said slowly, as if trying to make a point, "I think it is quite possible that Nevada and Chino did not quarrel and shoot it out." He paused, lip lifted in a thin smile. "In fact, it's my hunch that our young Boone Haxson has been doing some fancy lying."

They were all staring at him, did not notice the faint shadow outside the open window. The town marshal broke the silence.

"You—you mean Boone is pullin' off a double-cross?" His voice was a hoarse, shocked whisper.

Stengal shrugged, looked again at Derner: "What do *you* think, Al?" His black eyes glinted.

Derner shook his head, and his eyes had a red look in them, like an enraged bull, pawing dust, making ready to charge. He said thickly, "Dan, get this damn' corpse away from here, and then find Boone—throw him in gaol. He's going to do some talking."

"I savvy." The town marshal's beefy face was grim. "We'll sure make that hombre talk plenty." His hand went to the door-knob. "You come along with me, Jess, and have Doc Peters fix your hand. Leave a thing like that go too long and you might get blood-poisonin'."

Wellen grunted assent, followed him through the door. Derner threw the bolt, returned to his chair, and stared moodily at the dead sheriff.

"Damn the fool," he muttered. "Had it all fixed for him to arrest V. Crumm, throw her in gaol, and then he goes loco."

"It was a sure-fire scheme," Ace Stengal said,

regretfully. "A Federal job, really, but as a prominent citizen, and a victim, you would have had the right to charge her with robbing her own post office." He smirked. "I never did a better job of penmanship, Al, except on those Jim Miles mortgage papers."

"She could swear herself blue in the face the signature wasn't hers," agreed Derner, and after a moment: "V. Crumm wouldn't like a gaol cell. I'm afraid she would have committed suicide."

"Very sad end," murmured Stengal. His lip lifted in a wolfish grin.

"Nobody would ever know it wasn't suicide," smiled Derner. "Yes, a sad end for the poor woman. Imagine the headlines in Santa Fe, Silver City, Deming: 'Faced with Federal Indictment, Violet Crumm, well-known pioneer woman, hangs herself in gaol.'" Derner's head lifted in a loud laugh. He was suddenly silent, stared with startled eyes at his companion.

Ace Stengal said in a surprised voice, "Sounds like a bell!"

They sat there, listening, and an odd fear crept into Derner's eyes. He said, hoarsely, "Must be that old church bell . . . hasn't rung in fifty years."

Stengal shrugged, indicated the lifeless sheriff: "Tolling for him."

Derner made no reply. His hand went shakily to the whisky bottle.

Chapter XIII

The Mexican woman looked up from the red pepper she was slicing into a pan. She stood, rigid, listening, open-mouthed, eyes wide with astonishment. Suddenly she dropped pepper and knife and ran into the yard where two men sat on a bench under a big shading cottonwood tree.

"A bell rings!" she said, excitedly. "Listen!"

"We are not deaf," one of the men said. He looked questioningly at his companion, who got slowly to his feet, leaned on a staff of polished manzanita. He was very old.

He said in a curiously hushed voice, "The Mission bell. I have not heard it ring since the day you were born. It was the day of the massacre, when the church was destroyed."

"I am fifty years old," observed his son. "Not in those fifty years have I heard the bell."

"It calls us," his wife said. She crossed herself. "We must go." She disappeared inside the house, came out in a few moments, drawing a black *mantilla* over her head.

Her husband reached for his steeple-crown hat of plaited straw. "We go," he said briefly to his father. "The bell calls."

The gaunt old man's eyes watched them longingly. The half-century since he had last heard the bell had taken his strength. He could not make the journey to Santa Ysabel. He sat down again on the bench. It was very mysterious—*a miracle.*

He drowsed there in the noonday heat. Sunlight filtered through the spreading branches, touched his bowed grey head. It was good to hear the old bell again. Its distant clamour was music in his ears.

Presently he slept, deep-lined face peaceful, a contented smile softening his lips.

Others heard the bell, came from all directions, swarmed into the plaza, brown-faced men and women and children. Mystified, wondering, they gathered in groups, gazed solemnly at the ancient church.

The bell was silent now, but looking up at the tower, where crumbling adobe walls left large gaps, they could see a new rope, and the bell had a cleaned and oiled look:

A shape moved from the darkness beyond the massive doors, now open. A brown-robed old man appeared, stood on the top step in a halo of sunlight. A whisper, like the rustle of dry leaves in the wind, came from the awed watchers.

The Franciscan gazed down at them, a gentle smile on his thin, ascetic face, and, crucifix high in lifted hand, he began to speak:

"In nomine Patris, et Filii, et Spiriti Sancti . . ."

They were kneeling now, heads reverently bowed, women with tears in their eyes.

". . . Venite, exultemus Domino . . ."

V. Crumm looked inquiringly at Ellen, watching with her from the gate in the high wall overlooking the plaza. "What's he sayin'?"

"It's Latin," Ellen explained. "He began with the invocation, and now it's the Psalm, 'O come, let us sing unto the Lord: let us heartily rejoice in the strength of our salvation. . . .' "

V. Crumm nodded approvingly. "That's real nice," she said. "This town sure needs plenty salvation." She gazed complacently at the bell-tower. "Me and Pilar fixed up that new rope for the padre early this mornin'. Cleaned up the old bell, too." Her face clouded. "It's in my bones things is goin' to happen. I want to get you away from this town, Ellen."

"I'm not running away," Ellen said in a low voice. "Not until we find my brother's murderer . . ." She faltered. "And there's the ranch. . . . All my money is in the ranch, and—and anyway it wouldn't be fair to Duncan to run away from it."

V. Crumm did her best to scowl, smiled instead, warmly, affectionately. "I like your talk, child. Kind of that way my own self. Was never one to turn my back on trouble. Reckon it's the Irish in me."

"I'm Scottish," Ellen said with a faint smile.

"Huh?" V. Crumm grinned, made a tolerant

gesture. "I reckon it don't matter a hoot where a hombre comes from. It's guts that count—" She broke off with an angry exclamation. "There I go ag'in with my rough talk."

"I don't mind," Ellen reassured. "Courage, fortitude, ability to take punishment." She squeezed the big woman's arm. "The things that make you so—so wonderful."

"Huh?" V. Crumm gave her a pleased look. "You'd be surprised how scared I can get."

Johnny met them at the patio gate. He was excited.

"Mr Flagg's back in the store ag'in," he told V. Crumm. "He's red-eyed 'cause he ain't found the sheriff. Say's he's looked all over for him."

"Where's Miles?" she asked.

Johnny pointed in the direction of the adobe building half hidden in the cottonwoods. "Waitin' in the stable for me to find Boone Haxson. Ain't seen hide nor ha'r of Boone yet. Miles said I was to fetch him through the store and out the back way here."

"That's right," V. Crumm nodded. "I told Miles we'd smuggle Boone in through the store. You run along, Johnny, and watch out for him. Ask Pilar. It's likely Boone's hidin' out down at the barn, waitin' for Miles to show up there."

"Yes, ma'am"—Johnny's eyes were bright. "I'll scout 'round, pick up sign."

"And Johnny—tell Luke Flagg to come on

through the store. I'll be waitin' here in the patio."

"Yes, ma'am." Johnny sped away. V. Crumm's gaze followed him, her expression oddly gentle, affectionate.

"All he thinks about is scoutin' and Injuns and blazin' trails," she grinned. "Gettin' so he talks like a old mountain man, for all I make him read his grammer 'most every night."

"Johnny is fine." Ellen dimpled. "He—he has *guts*—like you."

"Done my best to have him grow up the way a man should," V. Crumm said soberly. She looked at the girl thoughtfully: "You run into the house, child. I'm takin' Luke Flagg over to the stable for a talk with Miles."

"I don't want to go into the house," demurred Ellen. "I'm mixed up in this business. I've a right to know all that goes on."

"Well—if *that's* the way you feel about it"— V. Crumm indicated the adobe building in the trees. "You run on and tell Miles I'll be right over with Luke Flagg."

Miles heard the girl's light step. He watched her, aware of a quickened pulse. She was again in her full-skirted dove-grey dress with its tight bodice. Rest and sleep had put the colour back in her cheeks. She looked wholesomely fresh; her dark hair smooth and shining, her eyes clear.

She did not see him immediately, watching her from the bushes on the slope above the little corral. She peered inside the stable. The bay horse and the chestnut mare were nosing at the hay in their mangers. The horse had a saddle on him.

Miles called softly, "Over here . . ."

Ellen turned quickly, saw him standing in the bushes. He motioned to her and she hurried up the slope.

"You shouldn't be wandering too far from the house," he said.

Her eyes widened, and then she saw that he was serious—that he was really worried. "Mrs Crumm told me I could come to the stable," she answered, defensively.

"Anything can happen, even inside these high walls," Miles said harshly. "Don't forget that we have dangerous enemies—men who think nothing of murder. They'll know we're back in town by this time. This place will be watched day and night."

"They wouldn't dare . . . look for us in here," Ellen protested feebly.

"They'll dare anything," Miles told her grimly. "Walls don't stop murderers."

"I wish you wouldn't be so—so frightening," complained the girl.

"I want to get you away from this town. Silver City, Santa Fe—anywhere but here."

"I've been over that with Mrs Crumm, and I'm telling you what I told her. *I am not running away.*"

"I'm worried about V. Crumm, too," Miles said. "I've got things to do, and don't like leaving you two alone."

Ellen looked at him curiously. He was pale, his eyes red for lack of sleep. He had a right to be worried. Two women on his hands to guard against a ruthless gang of killers, himself marked for instant death if he showed himself in the street. No wonder his anxiety, his caution in seeking the concealment of the bushes from where he could watch the approach to the stable. For her sake, for V. Crumm's sake, he could not afford a moment's let-down of vigilance. When the right time came he could be daring enough, give no heed to personal danger. He had proved his courage, his resourcefulness, when he outwitted and turned the tables on the men who had attempted to stalk them that night in the sagebrush, and he had been too smart for Jess Wellen in having guessed the ambush of the bed.

She said, remorsefully, "I'm sorry, Miles. I shouldn't make it harder for you—but I can't bear to go. I'd feel like a—a coward." She moved close to him, face lifted, lips parted in a breathless little smile. "I want to stay—with you."

Miles said something in a muffled voice, and suddenly she was in his arms.

He held her tight, said huskily, "Ellen . . ." And then he released her, stepped back, stared intently through the bushes, down the slope.

"Somebody coming," he said in a low, cautioning voice. "Boone Haxson, maybe. I've been waiting for him."

Ellen, breathless, flushed, her eyes starry, shook her head: "I think it's V. Crumm. She's bringing some man named Luke Flagg. I forgot to tell you."

Miles recalled something V. Crumm had said the evening of his arrival when she followed him to the livery barn: "Luke Flagg's another who don't believe Jim Miles is a cow-thief. Luke's been awful worried, claims there's only one answer. He thinks Jim's been murdered. Him and Jim Miles has been friends 'most all their lives."

His tired face lightened. He could use a friend right now—a lot of friends. He wished Boone Haxson would show up.

Ellen was saying something to him. She was standing very close again. The fragrance of her hair sent a tingle through him. He wanted desperately to draw her into his arms, say things that had nothing to do with Luke Flagg or anybody else. With an effort he forced his attention to the import of her words.

"Johnny said Luke Flagg is red-eyed, on the war-path. He's been looking for the sheriff and can't find him."

"V. Crumm doesn't think much of Sheriff Renn," Miles said with a bleak smile. "It's likely the sheriff doesn't mean to be found if it's an honest man who wants him."

Chapter XIV

They went down the slope, stood waiting in front of the stable door. V. Crumm and the cattleman came quickly round the bend in the path. Flagg carried a brown-paper parcel under his arm.

He gave Miles a grim smile. "Ain't seen you since you were a kid," he greeted. "Well, son, this is a hell of a mess about your uncle."

"I remember you," Miles said. "Uncle Jim used to say you were the best friend he had."

"Jim Miles and I have ridden a lot of trails together," Luke Flagg said simply. "They don't come better than Jim." He was silent for a moment, as if stirred by memories of days long gone. He was an old, gaunt man, grizzled-bearded, the eyes in his weather-beaten, lined face still sharply alert. "Yes, we've chased plenty cows together."

V. Crumm said briskly, "Luke just got in from his ranch, figgers to get the sheriff after the gang of cow-thieves that's been rustlin' his LF spread to the bone."

Miles nodded, looked inquiringly at Flagg, who was untying the brown-paper parcel.

"Got evidence good enough to send the damn'

scoundrels to the pen for life," he asserted. He shook off the brown paper, held up a piece of cowhide. "See that brand?"

They all gazed. The piece of hide was obviously fresh, the hair still glossy red. Ellen's heart turned over. The iron mark, burned in deep, was a replica of the crude sketch Duncan had sent her. "You'll like our new cattle brand . . . Jess Wellen's idea to work in my initials . . ."

She heard her own voice, startled, shaky: "It's Duncan's Box DF—"

Luke Flagg gave her a puzzled look, returned his attention to the piece of hide, reversed it to show the underside, traced a forefinger over dark lines that showed in the raw skin.

"What does *that* mark look like?" He flung a bitter, triumphant look at Miles. "You know brands, young feller."

Miles said slowly, "I'd say it's your LF Bar iron—"

"Sure it's my LF Bar iron," rasped the old cowman. "You can alter a brand on the outside, but the old iron mark always shows underneath a cow's hide. That's *one* thing a cow-thief can't change."

Miles nodded. There was a hard light in his eyes. He was beginning to understand why Duncan Frazer had been murdered.

"Been watchin' that low-down Box DF outfit," Luke Flagg was saying angrily. "A damn' cow-stealin' outfit from the start, I reckon." He reversed the hide again, traced forefinger over the freshly burned iron-marks. "Fixed their iron to set right over my LF Bar, changed it into a Box DF." He scowled. "Wasn't a hard trick: run lines up from the bar mark, put a bar on top, and turned it into a box; worked a half-circle over the L and made a D. The F was already set for 'em."

V. Crumm broke her silence. "Where did you find the cow that was wearin' this hide, Luke?"

"Come off a three-year-old steer," Luke Flagg answered. He looked at Miles. "You know that Juniper Flats country. Jim Miles' Bar M spreads over that way, down to the border, alongside my LF Bar. Never had any trouble until Al Derner got hold of the Bar M and sold off the Juniper Flats range to that rustlin' Box DF outfit. Been losin' cows ever since those low-down rustlers moved in." He glared at the tell-tale piece of hide. "One of the outfit is a hard-lookin' hombre name of Jess Wellen. The other feller wears the name of Frazer. I sure aim to send that pair of coyotes to the pen if my outfit don't catch 'em red-handed first and set 'em to dancin' on air."

Ellen wanted to scream at him, deny that Duncan was a cattle rustler. Miles' quick look held her silent.

"Of course, we lose cows to rustlers once in a while," grumbled Flagg. "Expect some losses, being so close to the border." He shook his head angrily. "Havin' a *neighbour* steal your cows is mighty different. I'm sure goin' after that outfit."

"You ain't told us where you got this hide," V. Crumm reminded.

"Found it hanging on the corral fence over at Jim's old Dry Creek camp," Luke told her. He frowned. "Used to be Jim's before Box DF moved in. I reckon they butchered the steer for beef."

"Careless of them to leave it hangin' on the fence," commented V. Crumm. "I'd figger Jess Wellen was too smart to leave evidence layin' 'round."

"It's evidence that'll send him and his pardner to the pen," Luke said grimly. He reached for the brown paper, began rolling the hide into it.

Ellen was suddenly trembling. She said fiercely, "Don't you call my brother a cow-thief!"

"Huh?" The old cattleman's hands tightened on the hide.

"Duncan Frazer is my brother." She flung the words at him. "He—he's dead." Her voice choked. *"Dead . . ."*

Luke Flagg gazed at her with shocked eyes, big hands nervously fumbling the brown paper.

V. Crumm's arm went round the girl's waist, drew her close. "That's right, Luke. Don't you go callin' Duncan Frazer a cow-thief ag'in. You're right as rain about Jess Wellen, but awful wrong about young Duncan Frazer."

"He's Jess Wellen's pardner." Flagg shook his

head, bewilderment on his weather-beaten face.

Miles pointed to the piece of hide hanging from the brown paper. "I think we have the answer that explains why you found your hide on the corral fence," he said slowly, as if reconstructing a scene. "Duncan was a tenderfoot, Luke. He didn't know Wellen's game. He must have discovered the mark of your iron and suddenly realized the truth. That's why Wellen murdered him. Young Frazer accused him of brand-blotting, told him he had learned the truth and was going to inform you—or the Law. So Wellen killed him."

"I'll be—" The LF Bar man broke off, gave Ellen a distressed look. "Mighty sorry, young lady—mighty sorry."

Ellen forced herself to speak, accept his apology: "I can hardly blame you for—for thinking the worst."

He eyed her keenly, nodded slowly, said in a gentle voice warm with admiration, "You're a brave young woman, Miss Frazer. You've got the courage to stand up against trouble. I reckon your brother had the same courage, standin' up against Jess Wellen the way Miles figgers."

He listened, sombre-faced, attentive, while Miles gave a brief account of the visit to the Box DF.

"I reckon that's proof enough," he muttered. Rage spread over his face. "We've got to hunt that wolf down pronto, Miles. String him up to a tree!"

"Won't be so easy," Miles said grimly

"Soon as I find Sheriff Renn we'll make up a posse and hit the trail," insisted the furious cattleman.

V. Crumm snorted. "Don't count on the sheriff, Luke. Al Derner owns him body and soul."

Flagg frowned, fingers pulling thoughtfully at his grizzled beard. "What you mean, Vee? What's wrong with Al Derner?"

"He's a skunk—a wolf," the big woman said fiercely.

"Some combination," chuckled Flagg. His eyes hardened. "Derner's a prominent man, has a good reputation. Not that I take to him much. Too bluff and hearty, and his eyes don't smile when he laughs."

"He's got 'most all of you fooled," V. Crumm said. "He had me fooled at first. He's a crafty, bad man, and he knows more about Jim Miles than he's tellin'."

"Huh?" Luke Flagg stiffened, flashed a startled glance at Miles Clarke.

"Use your head," snapped V. Crumm. "It was Al Derner spread the story that Jim was rustlin' cows, runnin' 'em across the border. It was him that set the sheriff on Jim, faked the evidence."

"Wasn't believing *that* story," muttered Flagg.

Anger darkened his face as he listened to Miles' laconic account of the attempted ambush in the sagebrush, the night at the cabin, the discovery of the note Jim Miles had concealed under the paper lining of the knife-box.

"You'll know his handwriting," Miles finished. He felt in a pocket for the crumpled piece of paper.

Luke Flagg took it, and gazed at it. He nodded, said sorrowfully, "That's Jim's writin'. Poor old Jim . . ."

His head lifted and he looked at Miles with grief-clouded eyes. "Proof enough, son. Proof that will hang Al Derner. Jim says in this piece of paper that the ranch was clear of debt. He wasn't owing Al Derner or anybody else a red cent, and Jim wasn't a man to lie. He hated liars same as he hated cow-thieves. Means Al Derner had him murdered so he could claim the Bar M with fake mortgage papers."

"I'm due to be murdered myself," V. Crumm told him grimly. "You remember the time the store was broke into, Luke, and the safe robbed?"

Flagg nodded. "Yes . . ."

"I didn't savvy then, but now I know it was Derner, thinkin' I knew about the copper lode and mebbe had the location papers in my safe. I wasn't knowin' a thing about the lode. Jim never told me, so all Derner got was Jim's will, leaving the ranch to Miles Clarke. Makes it awful tough for Miles losing that will. Even if Al Derner swings, his heirs can claim the ranch, unless we can prove he faked those mortgage papers."

Luke Flagg wrinkled his brows thoughtfully, shook his head, tapped the letter with a forefinger: "This is as good as a will . . . same thing as a will, written and signed by Jim." He gave Miles a brief, reassuring smile. "You won't need to worry, son."

"Right now it's Derner I'm worrying about," Miles said in a hard voice. "He's got this town sewed up, filled with his own gang, and the town marshal and the sheriff on his pay-roll."

Flagg nodded, looked curiously at V. Crumm. "What for you think you're due to be murdered?" he asked.

"Derner figgers I know about the copper lode . . . wants to shut my mouth," she told him. "He figgers if he can put me and Miles out of the way he'll be settin' pretty." V. Crumm smiled grimly. "Been gettin' mysterious notes, warnin' me to get out of Santa Ysabel, or else—" She drew a finger significantly across her throat.

"Bad as that, huh?" muttered Flagg.

"Worse than bad." V. Crumm looked at Ellen. "She's in it now. Derner won't let *her* get away. She knows too much."

Flagg growled in his throat. "I'm having a talk with Derner right now." His fingers closed on the gun in low-swung holster.

"Don't be a fool!" snorted V. Crumm. "He'd take one look at your face and go for his gun. He's got a killer ridin' herd with him, feller name of Ace Stengal."

"We must use our heads," Miles said. "No sense getting ourselves killed, Luke. Make it bad for Vee and Ellen." He paused, eyes studying the glowering old man. "If we could get your LF Bar outfit here on the jump . . ."

Flagg's face brightened. He slapped a hard thigh: "By the Lord—we'll do just that! I'll head back to the ranch and get the boys—send word to Frank Smith to fetch his Lazy S outfit along."

"Now you're talkin'!" exulted V. Crumm.

"We'll blast Derner and his gang out of Santa Ysabel," Flagg said vehemently. His eyes blazed.

"We could send Johnny with a note," suggested V. Crumm. "Save you a long ride."

The LF Bar man shook his head. Sending a boy with a note wouldn't do, he demurred. The thing was too serious, his riders would want his personal word.

"I've got to go myself . . . tell 'em what's going on. We'll swing round by the Lazy S, get Frank's outfit to throw in with us."

"Wish you'd take Ellen along with you." V. Crumm gave the girl a sideways glance. "I'm scared to death for the child. No tellin' what Derner will be up to next."

Ellen started to protest, heard Miles say quietly: "It's a good idea." He was looking at her, an odd pleading in his steady eyes. She knew what he was trying to tell her. He loved her, and because he loved her he wanted her away from this perilous place where death lurked so dangerously close.

She said in a still little voice, "If you think it is best—and if Mr Flagg is willing."

"Sure I'll take you along," agreed the cattleman heartily. "You'll be safe enough at the ranch, and Mrs Flagg will take right good care of you." He looked doubtfully at her long skirts, and V. Crumm said quickly:

"You run and get into those pants ag'in, child, while Miles throws the saddle on your mare."

Ellen nodded, sped away. Luke Flagg grinned his relief, turned to follow her. "Left my horse down in your barn, Vee—"

V. Crumm interrupted him: "You wait for her in the brush back of the big horse corral. No tellin' but what Derner's got spies watchin' out front. We'll kind of smuggle Ellen out the back gate and round by the gully to where you'll be waitin'."

Flagg nodded that he understood, took a hitch at his gun-belt, and disappeared up the path that led to the store.

V. Crumm followed Miles inside the stable, stood watching while he saddled the mare.

"Mighty queer your Boone Haxson don't show up." Her tone was worried.

"I don't like it," Miles said, and after a moment: "I'm mighty glad Ellen's getting away from this town."

She eyed him shrewdly. "You kind of like her, huh, son?" She spoke gently.

Miles drew the cinch tight, turned and looked at her. "I reckon I do, Vee. Can't bear to think of harm touching that girl." His voice was not quite steady.

V. Crumm nodded her head, said softly, "I'm prayin' that way, Miles . . . prayin' awful hard."

Chapter XV

The two riders kept their horses moving at a leisurely jog, hats pulled low against the glare of the midafternoon sun.

They topped a rise, and one of the men muttered an exclamation, halted his horse.

"Dust on the road yonder, Jess," he said.

Jess Wellen drew alongside, gazed intently, bandaged hand lifted against the sun. The wagon road from Santa Ysabel made a double loop to miss the lava beds that lay like a black tumbled sea a scant quarter of a mile away, crawled over the ridge, and disappeared in a vast stretch of tall sagebrush.

The puffs of dust below the ridge drew closer. Wellen swung his horse behind a clump of sagebrush. His companion followed, and they waited, gaze on the grey line of road where it crossed the ridge. Two riders appeared, horses taking the steep climb at a walk.

Wellen's eyes glinted. "Luke Flagg," he muttered. His lips twisted in a savage snarl. "Damned if it ain't the Frazer girl with him. I'd know her anywheres, if she *is* wearin' pants."

He glanced morosely at his bandaged hand, now resting on saddle-horn. His gun-hand, and useless for this emergency. His eyes lifted in a look at the other man. "I'm wantin' that girl, Tulsa. Won't be easy—with that old sidewinder ridin' herd on her."

Tulsa grinned, patted the gun in his holster. Grin and gesture were significant, needed no words to explain what he meant. He was a heavy-shouldered man, with small, evil eyes in a broad, swarthy face that betrayed mixed blood in him.

Wellen returned his grin. "We'll get ahead of 'em," he said. "Plenty cover for us to sneak in close to the road."

Tulsa nodded. "No call to worry. I'll 'tend to the old feller."

Wellen's scowling gaze went back to the road. The two riders were dropping down the ridge now, were suddenly lost to view in the chaparral. The man's eyes gleamed with wicked anticipation. He said curtly, "Let's go."

Ellen noticed the faint movement in the brush as the road angled sharply round a tall butte. She thought it was a coyote, was about to call Luke

Flagg's attention to it, when suddenly her ears were shocked by a gunshot. Her startled mare reared, tore into a mad run away from the road, and she had one horrified glimpse of Luke Flagg toppling from his saddle.

She heard a shout, another gunshot, and the mare gave a tremendous leap, continued the mad flight. Ellen found herself fighting desperately to keep her seat in the saddle. Brush clawed her savagely; and suddenly the mare was following a trail, running at top speed, running away, the bit in her teeth, resisting the girl's frantic attempts to stop her. Ellen guessed the second bullet must have grazed the mare. The stinging pain was driving her mad.

She managed a backward glance, saw two men swing into the trail, horses at the gallop. Horrified, she made no further attempt to halt the mare. *She must keep going . . . going . . . ride . . . ride . . .*

The sun touched the distant peaks; shadows crawled, lengthened, reached the man lying by the side of the road. His head moved, and slowly, painfully, he sat up, stared round, eyes dull, uncomprehending. A wide-brimmed Stetson lay on the ground near him. He looked at it, reached out a hand, picked it up, stared at the long gash in the dust-covered crown. He gazed at it, touched the jagged tear curiously. His fingers came away wet, sticky with dust-grimed blood. He frowned, touched the side of his head, felt the same stickiness there and on his face. More blood!

Comprehension was dawning in him, filled his eyes with horror, a growing rage. He got slowly to his feet, saw the big red-roan horse a few yards off the road, nibbling at the dry bunch grass. He started slowly towards the horse, then halted and looked at the dust cloud drifting up from beyond the bend in the road. Mechanically his hand reached for the gun in his holster, and he stood there, straddle-legged, wavering like a tree shaken in the wind.

The two men in the approaching buckboard saw him. The driver, a thin, wiry little man, let out a startled grunt, drew the fast-moving team to a quick standstill.

"My God, Fred," he exclaimed. "It's Luke!"

They hastily climbed out, ran to the old cowman. Recognition brightened his eyes. Frank Smith, owner of the Lazy S, and his foreman, Fred Hervy.

He said feebly, "Mighty glad you showed up. Don't feel so good . . ."

The Lazy S foreman got an arm round him. "He's been bleedin' some," he said to Smith. "Reckon his bronc throwed him and he hit his haid on that rock."

Luke Flagg shook his head. "Bushwhacked," he muttered. He touched the bloody smear on the side of his head.

Frank Smith bent close, studied the wound. "Bullet creased him," he told his foreman. "Knocked him from his saddle." Anger flushed his lean face. "Looks like some killin' hombre laid in the bushes for him."

"That's right, Frank," Flagg's voice came more strongly. "Must have been lying here an hour and more."

His friend was examining the wound, fingers exploring gently: "No bone broken, Luke. Awful close call. I reckon the feller that shot you figgered you were dead before you hit the ground."

Flagg looked at him, eyes bloodshot, his dusty, blood-stained face a mask of grief and despair. "The girl's gone," he groaned. "My God, Frank . . . they got the girl away from me."

"What girl?" Smith was puzzled.

"The Frazer girl. I was taking her to the ranch." Flagg's gaunt frame sagged, and, obeying Smith's quick gesture, the Lazy S foreman led him stumbling to the boulder, eased him down. Smith hurried to the buckboard, returned with a flask of whisky in his hand. He drew the cork, put the flask to Flagg's bearded lips.

The old cowman drank, pushed the flask away. "Feel queer in my head," he muttered.

"Sure you do," grunted the Lazy S man. "Just sit quiet . . . take it easy—"

"No time to lose," Luke said. "Listen, Frank . . .

hell's due to bust loose. I've found out about Jim Miles. He was murdered."

The two Lazy S men stared at him, and Frank Smith said grimly, "Sounds more reasonable than the talk that he was a cow-thief, Luke."

They listened attentively while he haltingly told them of his talk with Miles Clarke, the decision to take Ellen Frazer to LF Bar for safer keeping.

Smith rubbed a lean, pugnacious jaw reflectively: "Al Derner, huh?" He swore softly.

"We've got to work fast," Luke said. "Derner's got things tied up in Santa Ysabel, filled the town with his gunmen. Plenty more of 'em out at Bar M, I reckon." He got to his feet, his eyes clearer now. "We've got to work fast," he repeated.

Smith eyed him doubtfully, glanced at the roan horse, nibbling at the bunch grass. "You're too sick to sit a saddle, Luke. I'll take you into town in my rig, have the doc fix up your head. Fred can take your horse."

Luke started to shake his head, winced. "Don't need a doc," he said. "I've got to get back to the ranch, Frank. Want to round up the boys and head for town on the jump. Figgered your Lazy S outfit would throw in with us."

"You figgered right," grunted the boss of Lazy S.

"This damn' mess kind of changes things," Luke Flagg continued. "Ain't lettin' those killers get away with the Frazer girl." He looked at the Lazy S foreman. "Scout round, Fred, see if you can pick up sign which way they went with her."

Fred Hervy nodded, moved slowly across the road, head bent in close scrutiny. He called out excitedly, "Looks like her horse swung left, cut into the chaparral, and goin' fast."

They lost sight of him. Frank Smith said curtly, worried gaze on Luke, "I'm taking you back to the ranch in the rig. You ain't in no shape to fork a saddle."

"Took an awful fall," Luke admitted. "Ain't so young any more." He moved towards the buckboard. "All right, let's get set to go."

He climbed in stiffly between the wheels. "Feel like a freight train hit me," he grumbled.

The Lazy S man slid in by his side, gathered up the reins, and they sat there, grim, silent, waiting for Fred Hervy to rejoin them.

He was back in a few minutes. "Plenty sign," he reported. "I've a notion the girl's horse stampeded—"

"She was ridin' a mare," interrupted Luke. "I'd say that mare could run mighty fast."

"I'll say she could," Fred nodded. "Could see where she dug in her heels and sprinted like hell was on her tail." The Lazy S foreman paused. "There was two of 'em gunnin' for you, Luke. Found where they cached their broncs. Sign says they took after the girl."

"Headin' which way?" asked Luke.

"The tracks run into a trail, and I'd say that trail

heads south, towards Coyote Peak." His tone was significant.

Frank Smith broke the silence that followed his words. "Bar M is over that way," he said laconically. His head moved in a sideways glance at Luke Flagg.

The old cowman's face was haggard, his eyes bleak. He said wearily, "Let's get goin', Frank. We've got to work fast, get our boys headed on the jump for Bar M. Looks like Derner savvied the play, had us trailed from town. My own fault . . . reckon I'm gettin' too old, should have been more careful—on the watch for trouble."

"Old!" scoffed the wiry little owner of Lazy S. "I'm 'most as old, and our horns is plenty sharp yet, doggone your tough hide."

Fred Hervy had caught the roan horse. He rode up to the buckboard, looked inquiringly at the two cowmen.

Frank Smith said briskly, "You head for the ranch, Fred . . . round up the outfit and get started for the West Fork trail. Tell the boys to take rifles along."

The Lazy S foreman nodded, swung the roan. Luke Flagg's voice held him, face turned in a questioning look.

"I don't figger it that way, Frank," the old cowman said. "Somebody's got to get word to V. Crumm and young Clarke, tell them about the Frazer girl, and tell them our outfits will make straight for Bar M instead of Santa Ysabel."

"We'll lose time getting word to my boys," fretted Smith.

Luke was obdurate. "Got to warn V. Crumm," he insisted.

Smith gave in. "All right, Fred," he said. "You high-tail it for town. I'll get Luke over to his place and swing back to the ranch for the boys."

"If you say so—" Fred looked glum. "Hate to miss the fun at Bar M."

"Don't worry—" Luke Flagg gave him a wintry smile. "Like as not you'll run into hell's own fireworks when you hit Santa Ysabel."

The Lazy S foreman's face brightened. He grinned, sent the big roan into a fast lope.

Frank Smith turned the team in the opposite direction. "Goin' to jolt you some," he said, with an anxious glance at Luke. "This road has more chuck-holes than a mangy coyote has fleas."

"Damn the chuck-holes," Luke said. "Let's see how fast this team of yours can trot."

Chapter XVI

Johnny was frightened. He wanted to run, knew that if he obeyed the impulse to run he would attract attention. He must keep his head, he told himself, pretend, keep possible watchers fooled. It was no time to let panic stampede him. Got to act like old Kit Carson would when he smelled Injuns. He hugged the thought, held his feet to a careless saunter along the planked sidewalk, paused to exchange impertinent repartee with a couple of cowboys lounging at the hitch-rail in front of the Palace Bar.

"Hi, there, Slim! Why don't you git yorese'f a good bronc?"

"Ha, ha! Johnny-the-kid," gibed Slim. "How's the ol' six-gun workin', Johnny?"

Johnny faced him, legs spread, hand on the small gun in his belt. "Figger to draw on me, feller?" He glared ferociously.

The cowboy ducked behind his companion, rolled his eyes in mock dismay: "Watch out, Pete! He's on the warpath—figgers to git our skelps."

Pete rocked with laughter, flapped a derisive hand. "Ol' Dan Boone!" he chuckled. "That's right, Slim . . . he's ol' Dan Boone."

Johnny rudely thumbed his nose at them, went

leisurely up the store steps, made his nervous feet behave. He wanted to run, but he mustn't run. Pete's last words left him shivery.

Not old Dan Boone . . . Boone Haxson!

Customers were in the store, two young women looking at bolts of material Ed had spread on the long counter, an elderly rancher discussing the weather with V. Crumm while he critically examined a new plough. Two Mexicans were stacking bags of flour and sugar. Nobody watching him—only V. Crumm, whose eyes fastened on him, sharp, shrewd, questioning.

Johnny sauntered past her, whistling softly between his teeth. When he reached the back door he would run—run as fast as he could and tell Miles Clarke about Boone.

He heard V. Crumm's big voice, hearty, genial: "We got to take good seasons with the bad, Tom West. No sense yellin' our heads off when it don't rain."

"These droughts is acts of God," the old rancher said.

"Acts of God, my foot!" roared V. Crumm. "You quit blamin' God for things that don't suit you and buy this plough. You're goin' to need it when the rain comes." She flashed a look at Johnny, disappearing into the dark maw of the store-room in the rear. "Miguel," she called, "you come and 'tend to Mr West. Write him a receipt for this plough he's bought."

She grinned at the rancher, vanished swiftly into the store-room.

Johnny was already slamming through the yard gate. V. Crumm hurried down the back steps. Her powerful legs moved fast, carried her with amazing speed out of the yard and along the path that led through the cottonwoods to the little stable. Johnny's casual manner had not fooled her in the least. His eyes were like saucers, his freckles big as raisins on his scared white face. Something was wrong, and it could only be Boone Haxson.

She reached the stable in time to hear Johnny's excited voice:

"Dan Heeler had a gun on him—"

V. Crumm rushed like a tornado into the stable, grabbed the boy's arm. "You pesky young maverick—"

Miles Clarke interrupted her, said gravely, "They've got Boone Haxson in gaol."

She stared, aghast. "Knowed somethin' was wrong the minute I laid eyes on the boy."

"I acted awful careful," Johnny said indignantly. His chagrin touched her and she patted him on the shoulder. "You done fine, Johnny. You wasn't lettin' folks guess you knowed about Boone. Kind of different with me. You just can't fool me no time. I savvy you too well."

"Yes, ma'am," Johnny said meekly.

"How come you know Boone Haxson's in gaol?"

"Seen Dan Heeler grab him. Dan and another feller was settin' in Dan's buckboard outside the gaol. Boone come along on that buckskin you sold him."

V. Crumm winced. "*Sold* him!" she muttered.

"Dan called over to him," continued Johnny. "He said, 'Tie up your bronc, Boone. Want you to come along with us.' Boone looked at him kind of queer, wanted to know what for Dan wanted him."

"Did Heeler see you?" asked Miles.

Johnny shook his head. "Couldn't see me for the brush where I was hid," he assured them. "Dan sat there in the buckboard, looking hard at Boone, told him he'd found the sheriff layin' up on the mesa, dead, and that's why he wanted Boone to go along with 'em, to get the body and help pick up the killer's trail. Boone said he'd follow 'em on his bronc, and then quick as lightnin' the feller with Dan pulled his gun on Boone—"

Johnny gulped excitedly. "Looked like Boone was goin' for his own gun; . . . reckon he figgered he'd no chance, and he lifted his hands up. Dan climbed from the rig, went to him, made him get down. He had his gun on him, looked crazy mad like he wanted to kill Boone. The other feller come up tied the buckskin to the hitch-rail, and then they made Boone walk in front of them into the gaol office." Johnny drew a long breath. "That's all I seen, but Boone's in gaol all right."

V. Crumm said gloomily, "Reckon Boone slipped up some place . . . got Derner suspicious."

"I must get him out," Miles said.

"Don't be crazy," she protested. "You wait until Luke Flagg gets back with his outfit."

Miles narrowed his eyes thoughtfully. The gaol was somewhat isolated, an ancient adobe building surrounded by cottonwood trees.

"Won't need to show myself in the street," he said. "Plenty of cover in those cottonwoods. I can follow the canyon trail, leave my horse cached down on the slope, and get to the gaol easy enough."

"They'll kill you on sight," worried the big woman. "Don't be a fool, Miles."

"The gaol is the last place they'll be looking for me." He smiled grimly. "Heeler won't be expecting me to walk into his gaol office. I'll have the jump on him, if he's still there. If he's gone, I'll still have the advantage. The gaoler won't know who I am when I walk in."

"It's awful risky." V. Crumm regarded him with bright, thoughtful eyes. "Sure hate for Boone to be in that gaol," she added. "Like as not they'll kill him."

Miles saw she was won over to the plan. "I'm on my way now."

He got his horse, slid into the saddle, grinned at Johnny. "You stick close to Vee, young feller."

"I'll be worried sick, waitin' for you to get back with Boone," V. Crumm told him. "Watch your step, son."

"You watch yours." Miles looked at her soberly. "Keep away from the livery barn, Vee. We don't want them to grab *you.*"

She nodded, her own face sober. "I reckon you're talkin' good sense. Kind of feel it in my bones that things is goin' to explode in this town. Al Derner don't like havin' Jim Miles' nephew nosin' round. He's due to act quick." She paused, eyes puzzled. "Wonder what's in this talk of Heeler's about the sheriff."

Miles shrugged. "Perhaps Derner can answer that one."

V. Crumm said in a troubled voice, "They'll make out you killed him, Miles."

She watched until he was lost in the trees down by the canyon gate, her eyes clouded with gloomy forebodings. She said, worriedly, "Don't like him goin' off to that gaol. I'm scared, Johnny."

The boy's eyes gleamed hopefully. "I could kind of scout over to the gaol," he suggested. "Kind of watch what goes on."

V. Crumm hesitated. She was beset with anxious fears. If the worst came she would want to know immediately, not be forced to wait, wondering what had happened to Miles.

She said reluctantly, "All right, son. Don't let 'em see you spyin'. I shouldn't let you, but I'm all pins and needles over this business."

Johnny said, briefly, "Yes, ma'am—" He wanted to get away before she changed her mind, so he broke into a run along the path to the store.

In the street again, he held impatience in check, sauntered with the bored air of a boy who had so much time on his hands he was at a loss what to do with it. He kicked a pebble from the board-walk, stood watching it skip across the dusty street; he paused at the blacksmith shop, gazed at the leather-aproned man heating a horseshoe at the forge. Gradually he neared the big livery barn, drifted across the yard where a dusty-faced teamster was stripping harness from his mules. The high wagons made good cover, and now, head bent low, he scurried like a rabbit into the deep gully behind the barn.

Miles, crouched in a clump of buckthorn on the bluffs, saw the slight movement in the scrub. He watched, hand on gun. A bird or a rabbit, he decided, and then he caught a momentary glimpse of a face—Johnny's face.

His own face darkened with annoyance. He had told the boy to stay with V. Crumm. He could hardly believe his eyes.

Something of the truth came, drew a wry grin from him. It was V. Crumm's idea. . . . She had sent the boy to watch things from his hiding-place. V. Crumm was worried. If things went wrong and he was killed, she wanted to know the worst, not wait in an agony of uncertainty.

Miles now gave his attention to the squat adobe building half hidden in the trees. The buckboard still waited near the gaol, the buckskin horse drooped at the hitching post. The signs indicated that the town marshal was inside, probably questioning his prisoner.

He could see the narrow road twisting through the trees. All was clear there, nobody in sight. Miles drew his gun, moved swiftly, quietly, to the office door and stepped inside.

The office was empty. The town marshal and the man Johnny had said was with him were apparently in Boone's cell. The gaoler would be with them.

Sounds came to him from the corridor beyond the partly open door. Miles recognized Heeler's blustering voice.

He glanced back at the outside door, closed it, and turned the key, which he pocketed. He did not want any chance visitor to walk in on him. Somewhere beyond the other door there were three armed men.

Miles coolly considered his next move. It was too risky to show himself in the corridor. His only chance was to take them by surprise and deal with them one by one.

He stamped noisily across the floor, like a man who had no reason to conceal his presence in the office. In another moment he was behind the partly open door, tense now, gun ready.

The town marshal's voice reached him: "See who it was come in, Cisco." There was surprise in Heeler's voice, but no hint of alarm. The noisy entrance did not indicate the presence of anybody bent on mischief.

Footsteps approached along the corridor. The gaoler or the other man. Miles was not caring. He waited, gun in lifted hand.

A heavy-set man pushed into the dingy little office. The gaoler, Miles guessed, from the ring of keys he carried. He halted with a low, surprised grunt and gazed blankly about him.

"Ain't nobody here," he muttered.

Too late he heard the slight movement behind him. The steel barrel of Miles' forty-five caught him on the temple. He sagged, senseless, and Miles eased him down, dragged him behind the door, close to the wall. He prayed that the sound of the crushing impact of steel against skull had not reached the man's companions.

Apparently the slight commotion had not aroused their suspicions. Miles, crouched close to the concealing door, heard the town marshal's gruff, blustering voice:

"Al figgers you done some lyin', Boone."

No answer from Boone. An oath from the town marshal; and then another voice: "Wonder what's keepin' Cisco back in the office?"

"You go take a look," Heeler said impatiently.

The man came along the corridor quietly. Miles sensed uneasiness in him, knew that this was the critical moment. A mishap now would be fatal. This was more dangerous than the unsuspecting gaoler; he was already suspicious—wary of a trap.

The newcomer paused just inside the door. Miles grabbed his wrist, pulled him headlong into the room, and swung gun-barrel in a skull-cracking blow. The man collapsed and sprawled face down on the floor.

Miles wasted no time in a look at him. The sound of the brief scuffle would have reached the town marshal. His one chance now was to get down the corridor before Heeler had time to realize his danger.

The town marshal, tugging at the gun in his holster, rushed out of one of the cells, came to an abrupt standstill, gazed stupidly at the man running towards him, gun levelled.

Miles said softly, "Drop that gun, mister . . ."

The gun slid from Heeler's fingers, clattered on hard-packed earth. Eyes bulging, he slowly lifted his hands.

Miles backed him into the cell. Boone Haxson watched from a pile of straw where he sat. He was handcuffed, his ankles tied with a piece of rope.

He said laconically, "Was wonderin' if you'd get here."

Miles threw him a grin, said to Heeler, "Lie flat on your belly, mister. Keep your nose in the straw."

Heeler obeyed. Miles went swiftly to the corridor, snatched up the fallen gun, and put it in Boone's manacled hands. "Squeeze the trigger if he makes a motion," he said. "I've got to get the keys from the gaoler."

Boone held the gun between his hands. "I'll smash the coyote's spine if he tries anythin'," he promised gleefully.

Miles returned to the office. His first two victims were still unconscious. He snatched the ring of keys from the floor, a coil of rope from a peg on the wall, and hurried back to the cell.

"Didn't wink a eyelash," Boone said with a grin at the prone town marshal. "The doggone wolf wasn't givin' me a chance to empty this gun into him."

Miles unlocked the handcuffs. "Use your knife on the leg-ropes," he said, and turning to Heeler, pulled his arms over his back and snapped the handcuffs on the man's wrists.

Boone was already on his feet. He glanced at Heeler's legs, and proceeded to cut a suitable length of rope from the coil Miles had tossed down.

"Sure crave to slip it round his neck," he muttered. "He'd look purty doin' a fandango on air."

"We'll leave *that* job to the Law," Miles said.

"Ain't no law in the Santa Ysabel," grumbled the young cowboy.

"You're going to help us *bring* the Law." Miles gave him a grim look. "You're riding with the Law now, Boone."

"Reckon that's right." Boone rubbed his chafed wrists, an odd look of surprise on his face, as if in wonder at himself. "If you say so, boss." He grinned, bent over the town marshal and swiftly knotted the rope round his ankles. "Got him hawg-tied for sure," he chuckled.

They rolled the prisoner over on his back. Boone snatched the gaudy red bandanna from Heeler's neck, stuffed it between his lips, and securely knotted the ends.

Miles said curtly, "Now the others—" He hurried into the corridor. Boone paused to examine Heeler's gun, made certain it was fully loaded, pushed it into his empty holster, and followed Miles to the office.

His eyes widened in a curiously awed look at the pair of unconscious men. "You sure treat 'em rough." He spoke softly, admiringly.

They found handcuffs, snapped them on, tied the men's ankles with ropes, and gagged them with their own bandannas.

"What do you figger to do with 'em?" asked Boone as he straightened up.

Miles answered with a question of his own: "What do you know about the sheriff?"

"Ace Stengal killed him, over to Derner's place in the hotel," replied Boone.

"How do you know?"

"Was in the backyard watchin' through the window."

"You saw Ace Stengal kill him?"

"Yeah . . . Stabbed him in the back. Renn was gettin' tough with Derner, told him he was done with doin' his dirty work. Stengal sneaked up, stuck a knife in his back."

"Where is the sheriff now—the body?"

"Heeler has him planted up on the old road that cuts into the mesa, near where we run into you the other night."

"What do you mean, planted?" Miles asked.

"Heeler was to find him layin' there, haul the body back to town, and spread the story that you'd ambushed him." Boone's lip lifted in a mirthless grin.

"Why did Heeler jump you, throw you in gaol?" Miles frowned. "Were you seen—at the window?"

Boone shook his head. "Nothin' like that. It was the Stengal hombre . . . he wasn't believin' my story about Nevada and Chino. Told Derner I was lyin'." The cowboy scowled. "Stengal's awful smart; got Derner all worked up."

"Johnny was looking for you," Miles told him. "He said you let Heeler get the drop on you."

"Rode smack into him," admitted Boone with a shamefaced grin. "Didn't know Heeler was still here at the gaol." He jabbed a toe at the lean, hawk-faced man lying on the floor: "Was this hombre pulled his gun on me." His head lifted in a worried look at Miles. "The word is out to kill you on sight, boss." He shrugged: "I reckon the same goes for me now."

"They'll have to see us first," Miles said with a thin smile. He bent down to the heavy-set gaoler: "Give me a hand, Boone."

They carried the senseless man to the cell and dumped him on the straw. The town marshal rolled furious eyes at them.

Miles said to Boone, "Take that rope off Heeler's legs."

Boone obeyed, his expression bewildered. They dragged the town marshal to his feet. Miles prodded him with his gun.

The town marshal stumbled into the corridor. Miles shut the cell door, locked it, and put the key in his pocket.

"No savvy," muttered Boone as they moved down the corridor.

"We can't leave him here," Miles said. "Not unless we kill him."

They pushed into the office. The hawk-faced man was still unconscious. Miles went to the outer door, opened it, took a cautious look.

Boone, gun pressed against the town marshal's spine, watched, silent, puzzled.

Miles said, "Back in a moment." He went outside.

He called softly, "Johnny . . ."

Johnny stealthily emerged from the concealing brush. Miles beckoned, his gesture indicating haste.

The boy, his freckled face one big question-mark, came on the run. "Doggone—you knowed I was layin' there!" He grinned sheepishly. "How come you knowed I was there, Mr Clarke?"

"Saw you," Miles told him.

"Doggone—I ain't so good yet," mourned the boy.

"You're learning," Miles reassured. "Johnny, get my horse. He's down on the slope, cached in a clump of buckthorn near two split boulders."

Johnny nodded, excitement in his eyes now. "You got 'em, huh?"

Miles nodded. "Jump to it," he said. "We're in a rush."

He waited a moment, made sure the boy was going in the right direction, then hurried back to the office.

"All right," he said to Boone, "get Heeler into the buckboard, the front seat, on the driver's side."

The cowboy nodded, prodded the town marshal through the door. The thing was too much for him, but he had seen Miles Clarke in action before. If Miles said for him to put Heeler in the driver's seat it was all right with him, if it *was* a loco notion.

Miles saw his bewilderment, gave him an amused grin, seized Heeler's senseless companion and dragged him outside.

He waited while Boone prodded Heeler up to the buckboard seat and retied his ankles. And now, with some difficulty, they lifted the unconscious man and propped him up in the back seat, where he sat, head slumped, like a man who had fallen asleep.

Leaving Boone on guard, Miles re-entered the office, reappeared with a rifle and a shotgun and a couple of gun-filled holsters. He climbed in beside the unconscious man on the back seat, directly behind Heeler, deposited the guns on the floor of the buckboard; all but the shotgun, which he held between his knees, muzzle close to Heeler's back.

"Listen, Heeler," he said softly, "this gun is loaded with buckshot. You'll get both barrels if you try to make trouble. Understand?"

The town marshal nodded his head.

Johnny came up, riding the bay horse. He slid from the saddle, stared delightedly at the prisoners, gave Miles an awed look.

Miles said to Boone, "Put the lines in Heeler's hand. He's driving the team."

Boone was beginning to see daylight. He said softly, "Reckon I *do* savvy." He untied the lines from the whip-socket, placed them in the town marshal's manacled hands. The handcuffs gave just enough play for the fingers of each hand to grip the leathers.

Miles said, "Take the bandanna from his mouth.

Might attract attention." He eyed the man by his side, decided his gag was not noticeable under the shadowing hat pulled low over the bowed head.

"All right," he said, when Boone removed the bandanna from Heeler's mouth. "Fork your saddle, Boone."

"Want me to trail you, huh?"

Miles shook his head. "After we get out of town," he said. "Keep out of sight until we hit the old mesa road."

"I savvy." Boone swung up to his saddle, took the bay's lead-rope from Johnny. "I'll go over to Duck Creek Canyon, be waitin' for you where the road forks west for the mesa."

Miles nodded assent, looked at the office door, still open. "Johnny," he said, "lock that door and throw the key into the brush."

"Sure will," grinned the boy. He ran to the door, closed it, turned the key in the lock. "Nobody's goin' to find *this* key," he said.

"We won't even look when you throw it," chuckled Miles. He pressed the shotgun against Heeler's shoulders: "Get your team moving, mister. Not too slow and not too fast. You're the town marshal, heading out of town with a posse to look for the sheriff. You think the sheriff has had a bad accident, been murdered, perhaps, because his team has been found—a runaway team with the remains of a buckboard dangling at their

229

heels." He prodded the cringing shoulders hard. "Be very careful, Heeler, and get us out of town the back way. Savvy?"

The town marshal nodded his head, slapped the reins, swung the team into the road.

Miles nudged him again with the shotgun: "No tricks, Heeler. Head straight for the old mesa road, where you left a very dead sheriff a couple of hours ago. You see, Heeler, I know all about that murder and what you did with the body."

He slouched easily in the seat, the muzzle of the shotgun resting lightly between the unhappy town marshal's shoulder-blades, his own shoulder slyly supporting the apparently dozing man by his side.

They left the grove of cottonwood trees behind, passed V. Crumm's livery stables, circled into an alley, and finally crossed the main street into the plaza road. Nobody gave them more than a casual glance.

Al Derner caught a glimpse of them from the hotel porch, recognized the town marshal, now sending the team along at a fast trot in response to Miles' low, urging voice.

The two occupants of the back seat failed to draw Derner's attention. A couple of men Heeler was taking along to witness the finding of the murdered sheriff's body. Ace Stengal had told the town marshal it was advisable to have witnesses.

Miles drew a relieved breath. The worst was

over. He had seen Derner as they passed the hotel, was in deadly fear that the man would hail the buckboard's driver for some reason or other. He would have become suspicious if Heeler had refused to halt the team: he also would have been a dead man, a charge of buckshot in him. Miles would have killed him first and emptied the second barrel into Heeler.

They passed the old plaza church. Mexicans swarmed like bees about the ancient building. Miles realized with deep astonishment that they were hard at work repairing the walls. Men, women, and children streamed past with freshly made adobe bricks, bits of lumber, planks, beams. Through clouds of yellow dust he glimpsed a frail brown-robed man standing under the arch of the great doors. V. Crumm's Franciscan, smiling benevolently as he watched and encouraged his busy people.

Heeler swung the team into another turn and the buckboard went bouncing up a long, narrow grade. The man slumped against Miles' shoulder groaned, opened his eyes.

Miles met his dazed look, gave him a hard little smile, reached over and removed the gag. The man spat, glanced down at his manacled wrists, at his tightly-roped ankles.

"My Gawd!" he mumbled, "what the hell . . ." His head lifted in a look at the man in the driver's seat, shifted in a sideways glance at Miles.

"That's Dan Heeler, huh, settin' in front?" he asked hoarsely.

Miles nodded, pressed the muzzle of the shotgun warningly against Heeler's back.

"What did he go and tie me up for?" puzzled the ruffian.

"He didn't," Miles said laconically.

The man's gaze was on the shotgun now. He muttered a shocked oath, comprehension in his eyes, a quick, murderous fury.

"Who the hell are you?" he asked savagely.

"A prophet," Miles said with a bleak smile.

"You're loco," sneered the man.

"I prophesy the Law is going to hang you," drawled Miles.

"Ain't no law in this country."

"The Law is coming to the Santa Ysabel." Miles spoke grimly. "The hangman's noose is reaching for you and your kind."

The man gaped at him, fear in his eyes now. He said no more, sat there, frightened gaze fastened on the gun-barrel resting lightly against Dan Heeler's back.

They topped the rise and the team moved into a fast trot down the grade. Miles could see Boone Haxson, waiting at the foot of the hill, where the left fork of the road began its climb to the mesa.

Chapter XVII

The town marshal, drove carefully up the rough road that followed the twisting course of the gully. The threat of the big shotgun at his back kept him in a sweat. He winced every time the buckboard wheels dropped into a chuck-hole. A hard jolt might fatally disturb Clarke's trigger-finger, explode those twin loads of buckshot. The town marshal shuddered. His one urgent desire now was to reach the place where he had left the dead sheriff, be done with this job.

A buzzard rose heavily from a rock, flapped away. Boone Haxson, following the buckboard with Miles' bay horse on a lead-rope, swore softly. He hated buzzards. They had a way of going for a dead man's eyes.

They rounded a sharp turn, and the town marshal thankfully halted the team, gazed dully at the lifeless shape sprawled by the roadside. Boone rode up, said in a hard voice, "I reckon that's him."

Miles climbed from the back seat, bent over for a close look. After a moment he straightened, stared back at the town marshal, said in a low, furious voice: "You sent a bullet through the knife wound, Heeler. You wanted to make it look like he was shot out here, not stabbed in Derner's office."

Heeler said nothing. The bluster was gone from him. He sat there, manacled hands clutching the reins, terrified, craven.

The man in the back seat was more tough. "You ain't scarin' *me* none," he said. "Don't know a thing about this dead hombre."

"Work for Derner, don't you?" Miles asked.

"Ain't talkin'," muttered the man.

"We'll see about *you*"—Miles opened his clasp-knife and went to the buckboard. The prisoners rolled nervous eyes at him.

Boone guffawed. "Scared you're goin' to slit their throats."

Miles grinned, cut the rope from Heeler's ankles, went to the back seat and did the same for the other man. "Climb down," he told them.

The handcuffs bothered them, but they managed to swing their legs over and slide awkwardly out between the wheels. Miles got into the front seat, drove the rig close to the sheriff's dead body. He climbed out, gently lifted the body into the space between the two seats. Sheriff Renn had been a little man; in death he seemed even more scrawny, lying there, knees drawn up.

He called to Boone, "We'll need those horses."

The cowboy dropped from his saddle, helped him unhook the team and strip off the harness.

They left the bridles on and led the horses over to the prisoners.

Dan Heeler began a dismayed protest, declared he couldn't ride without a saddle.

"You'll ride, or stay here for the buzzards," Miles told him.

Sullen, worried, bothered by the handcuffs, the two men managed to climb up. Boone unbuckled a rein from each of the bridles and roped their legs to the horses.

Miles returned to the buckboard, pushed it off the road and out of sight behind a mass of boulders.

"Brush out some of those wheel-tracks," he said to Boone. "We don't want anybody reading sign on us."

Boone broke off a dry branch from a piñon-tree, dragged it over the sandy places where the wheels had sunk in.

"Cain't figger out what you aim to do with these hombres," he puzzled.

"We're taking them to an old cabin up on Sage-brush Flats"—Miles was watching him intently.

Boone shook his head: "Ain't knowin' any cabin on the flats," he said.

Miles was conscious of a vast relief. He was satisfied now that Boone Haxson could not have been at the cabin on the night of Jim Miles' murder.

"No sense takin' 'em *any* place," grumbled the

cowboy. "I'm for handin' 'em a dose of lead right here."

"Heeler is going to be useful to us," Miles explained. "We know Derner is guilty, but have no proof. We've made a beginning with these two men. Heeler's a coward. . . . He'll talk to save his own hide."

Boone nodded. "I savvy."

They adjusted the long driving reins for lead-ropes on the prisoners' horses, and got into their saddles.

Miles said, "We'll have to head back to the fork, where you met us, and go up Duck Creek Canyon."

Boone was rubbing his chin reflectively. "Seems like I remember a short-cut up the road a ways . . . old Injun trail. Save us 'most an hour, boss."

"Fine!" Miles said. "Let's go."

Shadows were crawling up the hills when they came in sight of the cabin. Miles thought of Ellen Frazer. It seemed ages since the night those log walls had sheltered them from the storm. Actually only three nights ago, he realized with some surprise. The hours had been so packed with suspense, dragging dark minutes of death in ambush. He had at last made a beginning, laid hands on something tangible that would link Al Derner to the crime of murder.

He kept a sharp watch on Dan Heeler as they approached the cabin. It was more than probable the town marshal had been there on the night of Jim Miles' murder. The memory of that cold-blooded killing was almost certain to draw some betraying sign from the man.

The town marshal was not taking notice of anything. He sagged miserably on his horse, manacled hands grasping the mane for support. He was stiff and sore, and very frightened. It was not until they came to a halt in the little clearing that his head lifted. The quick recognition in his eyes as he stared at the cabin, the sly, uneasy glance at his fellow-prisoner, told Miles what he wanted to know.

He got down from his horse, looked at the two men with implacable eyes.

"You remember this cabin, don't you," he said softly.

Heeler only gazed at him, his face ghastly. His companion said morosely, "Never seen the damn' shack before."

"What's your name?" Miles asked him.

"None of your damn' business."

Boone Haxson pushed his horse alongside, lifted his quirt threateningly: "Answer the boss, you low-down skunk!"

Miles shook his head: "Don't use your quirt on him." He looked at Heeler. "What's this man's name?"

The town marshal's dry lips formed words: "Judd Scoby," he mumbled.

"He was with you, here, the night Jim Miles was killed?"

"Wasn't sayin' I was here before," Heeler replied.

"Lying won't save your neck," warned Miles. "The truth—*might* . . ."

The town marshal's head lifted again. "All right . . . I was here, and so was Scoby—"

Scoby's furious voice interrupted him: "You crawlin' snake!"

Boone's quirt flicked him lightly across the face. "Take up that slack lip," the cowboy rasped.

"All right, Heeler," encouraged Miles. "Who else was in that party? You might as well keep on talking, or you and Scoby will be left holding the bag."

"Sheriff Renn was along with us. He swore in a bunch of us as a posse, to catch old Miles for cow-stealin'."

Scoby broke in, eager now to clear himself: "That's the shoutin' truth. Renn grabbed us for his posse, told us it was a cow-stealin' job."

Miles ignored him. "Who else was in that party?" he repeated. "Was Al Derner with you?"

Heeler's face was grey with fear. He groaned, "Sure crave to get down from this bronc. I'm settin' on blisters."

"Answer my question." Miles' voice was implacable. "I'm giving you a chance to talk, Heeler."

"Yeah—Al was along with us." Heeler glanced

238

uneasily at Scoby. "Like Scoby says, the sheriff was out to arrest Jim Miles for cow-stealin'. We was ridin' with the Law. Was Jim Miles' own fault he got killed—resistin' arrest."

"Who shot him?" asked Miles.

"There was a lot of shootin'—" Heeler was sweating visibly. "For Gawd's sake, let me down from this bronc!"

"Who shot him?" repeated Miles in the same inexorable voice. "Al Derner?"

Heeler nodded, "Yeah—I reckon it was Al who shot him."

"You saw Derner shoot him?"

Heeler nodded again. "Yeah—that's right—"

"Was Nevada there, and the man they call Chino?"

"Yeah—they was along with us."

"Why did Ace Stengal kill the sheriff?" Miles gave Boone a grim smile.

"Wasn't there when Ace knifed him," muttered the town marshal.

"We know all about the killing in Derner's office," Miles said. "Derner told you to take the body out of town, leave it in the chaparral where you'd pretend to find it when his wrecked buckboard showed up without him. Isn't that right, Heeler?"

"Yeah—that's right." Heeler's head lifted in a look of mingled fear and awe. "You're a devil, Clarke. You know everythin'."

"I know enough to put a rope over Derner's neck," Miles assured him with a grim smile. He flung an abrupt question: "Who is Ace Stengal?"

Heeler shook his head, said emphatically, "Ain't knowin' the answer to *that* one."

"*I* do." Boone Haxson met Miles' surprised look with a wry grin. "Been jumpin' round so fast I ain't had time to tell you, boss."

Miles remembered the note Boone had asked V. Crumm to give him. Boone had said he had news for him. He nodded. "Save it, Boone. Let's attend to our friends first."

They unbuckled the leather thongs from the prisoners' legs, eased them down from the horses, and prodded them into the cabin. Boone had the leather reins on his arm. He got out his knife, shortened them to a convenient length, and punched new holes for the buckles. He was enjoying the dismay of these men who had planned to kill him.

"Mighty sorry we ain't got nice easy armchairs for you," he said with affected politeness. "I reckon you'll have to set on the floor, kind of rest your backs up to the wall."

The scowling pair lowered themselves awkwardly. Heeler muttered a startled oath as his head brushed a spider web that festooned the logs.

Boone grinned: "No spider's goin' to bite you," he gibed. "Any spider that bites you fellers will sure curl up and die of quick poisonin'."

240

He buckled the straps around their ankles, stood up, brushed dust from his hands. "I reckon these coyotes won't get away from *this* gaol," he said to Miles.

"You ain't leavin' us here to starve to death?" groaned Heeler. He was breathing hard, his beefy face the colour of dirty tallow.

Miles studied him thoughtfully, his face a cold mask. He asked softly, "Where is he?"

The flicker in the man's eyes betrayed that he understood. He hesitated, glanced at Scoby, who shook his head, scowled.

Miles repeated his question, added: "Talk fast, Heeler."

Heeler licked dry lips. "In the gully back of the shed," he answered. "Was a hole there, handy. We piled in a lot of rocks."

"You helped pile the rocks, Heeler?"

The town marshal shook his head. "Judd Scoby was one of 'em—"

"You crawlin' yeller-belly!" yelled Scoby.

Miles paid him no attention, went quickly to the door, vanished into the gathering twilight.

He found the pile of rocks in the little gully, stood there for long moments, mingled grief and anger on his face. The grave of a murdered man . . . his Uncle Jim's grave.

Slowly, inexorably, the evidence was accumulating against Al Derner. It was Derner who had spread the story that Jim Miles had fled across the border. Jim Miles had not fled. His body lay under those hastily piled rocks.

Miles returned to the cabin. Boone Haxson was rummaging in a box that stood near the stove. He looked up with a contented grin.

"Found some airtights," he said, holding up a can of peaches. "Enough stuff here to feed us a couple of days, I reckon." He delved again inside the box. "Sack of beans, and coffee . . ."

Miles said, "That's fine . . ."

Something in his voice drew a quick, penetrating look from the cowboy. Miles saw the question in his eyes.

He nodded: "Yes—I found the place."

Boone's head turned in a look at Heeler and Scoby. He said nothing, just stared at them with bright, hard eyes.

Miles broke the silence. "Got to get back to town," he said. "You take care of things here, Boone."

Boone nodded, followed him outside to the horses. His face was pale.

"Listen, Miles"—he spoke huskily. "I savvy now why you gave me that queer look when I said I wasn't knowin' about this cabin up here."

"I couldn't help wondering," Miles said. "I'm mighty glad you didn't."

"I *could* have knowed," muttered the cowboy. "I could have been fooled, same as old Jake Renn."

"Renn wasn't entirely fooled," Miles pointed

242

out. "He must have guessed at least half the truth. Renn knew my uncle was no cow-thief."

"Turns me all cold when I think how close I come to bein' one of 'em," Boone groaned. "I've been a damn' worthless fool."

"Lucky break, running into each other the other night," Miles said soberly. He swung into his saddle, gave the cowboy a grim smile. "We've picked up a couple of aces, Boone. It's time to call for a showdown."

Boone suddenly slapped a lean, hard thigh. "Talkin' of aces, I picked up some news about that Ace Stengal feller. That's why I got V. Crumm to hand you the note about wantin' to see you."

"I already know he's a killer," Miles said.

"He's a low-down, crawlin' snake," declared Boone. "Listen, boss, he's thick as thieves with Al Derner in this Bar M steal. It was Ace Stengal fixed up them notes that made out Jim Miles was owin' Al Derner money."

"I already have proof those notes are forgeries," Miles told him. "How did you find out about Stengal?"

Boone grinned. "Heard him talkin' about it with Derner."

"Talked right in front of you, did they?" Miles smiled sceptically.

"Somethin' like that." Boone's grin widened. "Only I wasn't in the office where they done their talkin'."

"Listened outside the back window," guessed Miles.

"That's right." Boone grinned. "Heard enough to savvy that this Ace Stengal is smart with a pen. Derner's handin' him a big cut for fixing up the papers he's claimin' was signed by Jim Miles."

"Good work," Miles said.

"Had to do something to square the deal with you," Boone told him. "You could have killed me, that night up here on the flats."

"We're all square," Miles said. He turned his horse into the trail. "*Adiós*, Boone. If our luck holds we'll maybe pick up a couple more aces between now and next sunrise."

"Meanin' just what?" The cowboy's eyes gleamed.

"Meaning Al Derner and Ace Stengal."

"Watch your step with them hombres." Boone's eyes filled with longing. "I sure crave to set in on the deal."

Miles shook his head. "You stick on the job here," he said.

It was dark when he dropped down the slope and swung into the road. He kept the horse moving at a fast running-walk. His mind was busy with the problem he faced. At last he had evidence enough to convict Al Derner and his hired gunmen. There was no time to be lost in laying hands on the man. He doubted that Luke and his riders could make Santa Ysabel much before sunrise. For the next few hours he would have to play the hand alone, work out some plan to get at Derner.

The lights of the town broke through the darkness, a faint glimmer against the back-cloth of glittering stars.

A shape appeared in the road, vanished. Miles pulled the bay into a clump of bushes, reined to a standstill.

He listened intently for some betraying sound. The shape might have been a coyote, or a crouching man, slinking into the brush.

Minutes passed, and at last his ears picked up a stealthy rustle, the faint crack of a dry twig underfoot. Not a coyote—a man, stalking him in the chaparral.

Miles got quietly from his saddle, took a few soundless steps. He heard the faint rustle again, and now his eyes picked up the vague shape that crawled nearer. He repressed a surprised grunt, grinned, called softly: "Johnny . . ."

There was a moment's silence, then Johnny's voice, startled, chagrined: "Wasn't sure it was you, Mr Clarke."

He came forward quickly now. "You sure got cat's eyes, spottin' me in the dark."

"You did fine, Johnny. If I'd been careless, you could have got me." He smiled grimly. "We can't afford to be careless—not even for a second."

Johnny nodded gravely. "I reckon plenty fellers lost their skelps 'cause they was careless."

Miles was looking at him intently. Something in

the boy's manner sent prickles of apprehension through him.

He asked quietly, "What's wrong, Johnny?"

Johnny's voice seemed to choke in his throat. He began to tremble. "They—they got Miss Frazer—"

"Yes, Johnny . . . go on—tell me—" Miles hardly recognized that faint, hoarse whisper for his own voice.

"Couple of fellers laid for 'em, shot Luke out of his saddle—"

"Yes, Johnny—"

"Frank Smith—he owns the Lazy S—come along, headin' for town. Fred Hervy was with him, and they found old Luke layin' there. Luke wasn't dead, and they piled him into their buckboard. Frank Smith has took him to Luke's ranch. Fred caught Luke's bronc and hightailed it for town to tell V. Crumm."

"I want to know about Ellen," Miles said in a suddenly fierce voice. "Why didn't they chase after her?"

"Fred Hervy picked up sign, said it looked like the fellers that got her were headed for Bar M." Johnny gulped, added miserably: "Wish *I'd* been there. I'd have chased after 'em."

Miles hardly heard him. He was in a daze, his fine plans tumbling about his head. He could only think of the girl he loved. She was in mortal danger, was desperately needing him. He turned blindly to his horse.

Johnny grasped his arm: "Listen, Mr Clarke—I ain't finished. Fred Hervy said the Lazy S fellers and Luke's outfit would head for Bar M on the jump as quick as they could."

Miles got into his saddle, gave the boy a wild look. "They'll be too late," he groaned. "I can't wait—"

He broke off, narrowed his eyes at Johnny. "Any idea who trailed Flagg and the girl from town?"

Johnny thought it over, brows wrinkled. "Seen a couple of fellers come out of the Palace Bar and fork their saddles," he finally answered. He shook his head. "Luke and Miss Frazer hadn't left when them fellers rode away. Reckon it wasn't *them* that pulled off the ambush."

"Did you recognize them?"

Johnny shook his head again. "Wasn't close enough to get a look at their faces."

"Think hard," urged Miles. "Perhaps you noticed something—"

Johnny's face brightened. "Sure did," he exclaimed. "One of the fellers had his hand bandaged."

"Jess Wellen," muttered Miles.

"Doggone!" Johnny's tone was admiring. "It was Wellen all right . . . sets in the saddle kind of loose. . . Can see him plain as day now you made me think real hard."

Miles asked curiously, "How did you know where to look for me?"

"Seen which way you went when you drove off from the gaol. V. Crumm was awful anxious for you to know about Miss Frazer, sent me to pick up sign."

"All right, Johnny—hustle back and tell her I'm on my way to Bar M."

The bay horse shivered under the touch of spurs; and suddenly Johnny was alone in the blanketing darkness. The look on Miles Clarke's face frightened him. He shivered too, began to run. He wanted to get to his horse, feel a saddle under him, make a dust for town—and V. Crumm.

Chapter XVIII

Padre Valdez paced slowly up and down in the twilight coolness of the old mission corridor, head bowed in meditation. The day had been long, exciting, and crowded with surprising activities. He was happy, grateful, and conscious of a spiritual uplift that made him forget his bodily weariness.

Now and again he gazed about him contentedly at the miracles wrought that day by willing, eager hands. Crumbling adobe walls repaired, the accumulated litter of years removed, the ancient mission church restored to something of its former dignity. He had done well indeed to return to Santa Ysabel and plant again the Holy Cross in this long-neglected field where he had once laboured in his youth.

The padre's pleasant reflections were suddenly interrupted by approaching footsteps, and, turning, he saw that his visitors were two men. He gazed at them inquiringly, his smile benign, despite their unfriendly faces.

"The people don't want you in this town," Al Derner said bluntly.

"That is not true." The old Franciscan gestured. "The people have praised God with the work of their hands this day."

"I'm not wasting time with you," growled Derner. "You'll leave town on the next stage."

"Are you God?" asked the padre gently.

"I'm the boss of this town, and I'm telling you to get out."

"I obey only God," the Franciscan said. "I am come to do *His* will."

"You mean V. Crumm's will, don't you?" sneered the big man. He turned on his heel. "Come on, Ace. Let's get over to the gaol and see what's keepin' Heeler."

Padre Valdez watched them thoughtfully. V. Crumm was right. Wickedness had taken deep root in the town of Santa Ysabel. No wonder she had longed for the old church bell to ring, summon the faithful to arm against the devil.

The few Mexicans still lingering in the plaza looked at him solemnly as he crossed over to the gate in V. Crumm's high garden wall. They had witnessed the brief encounter and were afraid, he reflected sadly. He must strengthen them with the Living Word, make them valiant against this wicked man.

Derner was more uneasy than he cared to admit even to himself.

His carefully prepared plans seemed to be slipping since Miles Clarke's arrival in town. Too many things were happening. Nevada and Chino dead, Jess Wellen wounded, the murder of Duncan Frazer discovered, the inexplicable behaviour of Sheriff Renn, and the alarming conduct of Boone Haxson. And now this padre, his bell-ringing—the town suddenly flooded with Mexicans. V. Crumm was the answer. He had been too slow in dealing with the troublesome woman.

Two men lounged in their saddles near the gaol. One of them dropped from his horse as Derner and Stengal came up.

"Somethin' funny goin' on here," he said to Derner. "Office door is locked, and cain't get no answer from Cisco."

Derner tried the door, gave Stengal a worried look. "Cisco should be inside." He scowled. "Don't like it, Ace."

"Dan Heeler ain't showed up nuther," the rider said. "Sure is funny, him bein' gone so long."

Derner's look went to the other man, watching from his horse. "Jump over to the blacksmith and get a crowbar."

The man spurred his horse into a run. Derner pulled a handkerchief from a pocket, wiped his suddenly sweating face. "Don't like it," he repeated. "Damn it, Ace—I'm worried."

"You get scared too easy," Ace Stengal jeered. "Cisco's most likely laying inside, dead drunk."

"That don't explain what's keeping Heeler from getting back with the body," reminded Derner.

The rider returned with the crowbar, and in a few moments they had the door prised loose from the lock. Derner stepped inside, the others crowding at his heels.

Ace Stengal pointed at the piece of cord lying on the floor.

Derner nodded. "Cisco's shotgun's gone, and his rifle," he said.

One of the men sped into the corridor. They heard his startled voice. "Here's Cisco, hawg-tied in one of his own cells!"

They pushed into the corridor, stared in shocked silence at the bound and gagged gaoler.

One of the men tried to open the barred door.

"Locked," he said laconically.

"Take a look for Cisco's keys," ordered Derner. He wiped his hot face again. He was pale, a hint of alarm in his bulging eyes.

The man clattered back to the office, returned

in a few moments with the crowbar. "Cain't find no keys," he said. "Looks like we'll have to break the lock, boss."

Derner nodded assent. The man inserted the heavy steel bar and snapped the lock with a powerful heave. Derner jerked the door open and went quickly to the man lying on the straw.

He said huskily, "Cut him loose."

They cut the leg-ropes, eased the gag from the gaoler's swollen lips. He sat up, fixed frightened eyes on Derner.

"Feller come bustin' in," he said. "Laid me out cold. When I come out of it I was layin' here the way you found me." His bloodshot eyes lowered in an outraged look at his manacled hands. "Why in hell don't somebody take these damn' cuffs off?"

The man with the crowbar guffawed. "Looks like you'll be wearin' 'em for a spell, Cisco. It's my guess the hombre that put 'em on you has throwed the keys away."

The gaoler swore, lifted bound hands, and gingerly touched his sore mouth.

Derner broke his silence. "Where's Boone Haxson?"

"Don't know nothin' about nobody." The gaoler spoke fretfully. His mouth was sore and his head ached. "I'm tellin' you I was knocked cold."

"Who was here before it happened?" asked Derner.

"Dan Heeler and Judd Scoby was back in the

252

cell here, tryin' to make Boone Haxson talk." The gaoler made another effort to touch his raw lips. "Some feller come into the office and Heeler told me to go see what he wanted. Wasn't expectin' trouble; walked back to the office, and woke up layin' here in the cell. Boone and Heeler and Scoby gone—and it ain't no good askin' me where they went."

Derner nodded, said curtly, "One of you boys get a file from the blacksmith and cut off those handcuffs." He gave Stengal a look. "Let's get back to my place, Ace."

Outside, in the deepening twilight, Derner came to a standstill. "I don't like it," he said again. "Ace, it's time we head for the ranch."

Stengal nodded. "Looks like our friend Miles Clarke is pulling off some fast work."

Derner was staring at him, his expression thoughtful. "I saw Heeler drive past the hotel, and now I come to think of it, the thing didn't look right."

"How do you mean, didn't look right?"

"Heeler was holding the reins bunched in both hands, close to his chest."

Stengal narrowed his eyes. "You mean he was wearing handcuffs?"

"That's right, and one of the men in the back seat must have been Miles Clarke. I noticed the shotgun, thought the man was holding it too carelessly, close to Heeler's back."

"I think you've called the play," admitted Stengal. "Where does it leave *us?*"

The two men eyed each other worriedly; and after a moment Derner said hoarsely, "Clarke is on to something. He's found out about Jim Miles."

"How would he find out?" asked Stengal. "Nobody knew the truth about Jim Miles."

"He may have talked with Renn."

"Renn wouldn't have talked," argued Stengal. "He was in too deep."

"If you hadn't knifed him, we could have got something from Renn," grumbled Derner. "We don't know now if Clarke had a chance to get to him."

"There's a chance Clarke *did,*" admitted Stengal. "The sheriff sure got awful stubborn all of a sudden."

"Boone Haxson's another angle," continued Derner. "Nevada could have done some talking, enough to get Boone to thinking too much. Boone could have told Clarke about Jim Miles."

"How about that woman of Jess Wellen's?" suggested Stengal. "She could have told Clarke plenty."

"Hadn't thought about *her,*" muttered Derner.

Ace Stengal was watching him intently, an ugly glint in his black eyes. "I say to hell with the copper mine." His voice was thin-edged. "I'm pulling stakes, Al—only I want the split you promised."

Their eyes clashed, and Derner said gloomily, "I'm pulling out too, Ace. First thing I know Miles Clarke will have the United States Marshal on my tail. Anything can happen, and happen damn' quick."

"I'm wanting my split first," Ace Stengal said. His lip lifted in a cold smile. "You'll find me worse than Miles Clarke if you try to pull any funny business on *me.*"

"I don't keep my money in this town," Derner told him. "I keep it where I can get it in a hurry."

"At the ranch, huh?" Stengal was breathing hard. "All right, Al. . . . We'll head out that way right now. I'm taking my split, and then it's me for the border."

"Both of us," muttered Derner.

"When I head for the border I'm riding alone," Stengal said, with his thin smile.

"You don't trust me any too much." Derner attempted a reproachful look.

"I'm not turning my back on you any time," Stengal replied coldly. He saw the flicker in the other man's eyes, added menacingly: "I can take care of myself, even out at the ranch. I've been making friends with your outfit, Al. You'd be surprised."

"You make me sick," grumbled Derner. "What the hell's the matter with you?"

"You could save plenty *dinero* if I didn't live long enough to reach the border." Ace Stengal's eyes were like black agates in that growing dusk. "I'm just warning you, Al. You've got a worse wildcat than Miles Clarke to deal with if you try any low-down trick on *me*."

The gaoler came stumbling from the office, supported between the two men.

"Figger I can get these cuffs sawed off quicker if Slim rides me double over to the blacksmith shop," Cisco said.

Derner eyed him thoughtfully. Cisco was a handy man with a gun, an unscrupulous killer. If it came to a showdown with Ace Stengal he would be useful.

"All right," he assented. "Ride him over to the blacksmith's shop, Slim." He looked at the other man. "Fork your saddle and round up the rest of the bunch, have them waiting in the yard back of the hotel. We're leaving for the ranch."

"I'm leavin' with you," announced the gaoler. "Ain't cravin' to stick round this gaol no more, boss. Just as quick as I get these cuffs sawed off I'm sure headin' out to Bar M with you."

"Sure, Cisco," agreed Derner.

The gaoler limped to the horse Slim was holding ready. "Got to get me a gun," he said. "That skunk took mine."

"We'll fix you up with a gun," promised Derner. He kept his face averted from Ace Stengal. "You'll likely be needing a gun, Cisco."

Something in his voice drew a sharp look from

256

the gaoler. He grinned wolfishly: "Count on me, boss," he said.

Johnny was still a mile from town when he heard the distant drumming of hoofs. He reined into the brush, tied the paint horse, returned to the road, and flattened down behind a clump of sagebrush.

He waited, hardly daring to breathe, fiercely resolved that *this* time no sharp eyes should discover him.

The road was steep here, slowed the approaching horsemen to a walk. Johnny's eyes bulged. Even in that darkness he recognized the two riders in the lead. Al Derner and Ace Stengal. They were talking as they rode past him. Al Derner's harsh, arrogant voice was too familiar for him to be mistaken.

The riders passed, vague shapes in the darkness. Dust drifted in their wake, but Johnny managed to keep count. Fourteen men, including Derner and Stengal, the last pair talking in loud voices:

"Should make Bar M 'round midnight," one of them said.

"I reckon," answered the other rider. "Sure crave to meet up with the gent that laid his gun ag'in my haid and made off with Heeler and Scoby."

Johnny's heart swelled with pride. The gaoler's crusty voice. Cisco wasn't liking the way Miles Clarke had handled him.

Another thought came to Johnny. These men

257

were evidently on their way to the Bar M ranch, for what reason he could not guess. He only knew that Miles Clarke was headed for the same ranch. He recalled Miles Clarke's parting words: "Tell V. Crumm I'm on my way to Bar M."

Johnny forced himself to lie rigid, waiting until the hoof-beats faded into the distance. He was in an agony of impatience to carry the news of these riders to V. Crumm.

His heart thumping, Johnny ran to his horse.

The store was in darkness. He rode round to the side-gate opposite the plaza, used his key, opened the gate, and led his horse inside.

Lamplight glowed through the trees, warm, reassuring. Johnny hastily tied the winded horse and ran up the path and into the big kitchen where Ynez was drying dishes.

She gave him a startled look. He dashed past her, slammed into the hall. She dropped her towel and hurried after him.

V. Crumm was in her office, frowning over an assortment of bills spread on her desk. She heard the quick thump of Johnny's boots, and got hastily out of her chair.

One look at the boy's white face was enough. Her own face paled. She had never seen Johnny so frightened.

"Well, son." She kept her voice steady.

Johnny said breathlessly, "Al Derner is headed for Bar M with Stengal and a bunch of fellers."

"Take it easy, son—"

"Run into 'em about a mile up the road," Johnny went on. "Hid in the brush so close I heard their talk. Cisco was with 'em."

"Cisco, huh?" V. Crumm frowned. "I reckon that means Derner's found out about the gaolbreak." Worry grew in her. "Wonder why Derner is headin' for the ranch so sudden."

"Miles Clarke is goin' to run smack into 'em," Johnny said.

She grasped his arm. "What do you mean, Johnny?"

He told her of the brief meeting with Miles. She listened, grim, silent.

"Said he couldn't wait for the Lazy S fellers to get there." Johnny shook his head gloomily: "Looks like him and Ellen Frazer is done for."

V. Crumm came out of her daze, swooped at the papers on the desk, brushed them into a drawer. "We're gettin' busy right now, Johnny." She glared round the room, hands on hips, chin thrust out belligerently, fastened a look on Ynez, watching from the door: "Ynez—tell the padre I'm wantin' him in a hurry. You go get him."

"*Sí, señora.*" The Mexican woman vanished.

V. Crumm paced up and down the room. No hint of panic in her now as her capable mind attacked the problem. Johnny watched her, fascinated, drew strength, confidence from the overflow of her brimming energy. He knew

259

from the signs that she was on the warpath.

Her hard, bright eyes fastened on him: "Johnny—run over to the barn and tell Pilar to get busy hookin' up a fresh team to the stage, and then chase over to Cap Hansy's and tell Cap he's got a drivin' job to-night."

"Yes, ma'am"—Johnny leaped at the door.

"And you get right back here," she called after him. "I've got a job waitin' for you."

"Yes, ma'am."

She stood motionless, listening to the sharp rap of his boots as he sped away, and allowed herself a brief moment of sickening doubt. Johnny was right. Miles and Ellen were "done for." Nothing she did could help them now.

She was suddenly angry at herself. This was no time to let fear creep in, destroy cool thinking. And Miles Clarke was no fool. Miles Clarke was resourceful, could take on the odds and not lose his head. Miles knew that more than *his* life was at stake. He would be thinking of Ellen Frazer. For her sake he would use his wits, his splendid courage.

She puzzled briefly about Al Derner's sudden departure from town with his pack of hired gunmen. It came to her vaguely that alarm must have seized the man. He was not liking Boone Haxson's escape from the gaol, the town marshal's mysterious disappearance. Derner was a wary wolf, evidently believed that Miles Clarke had smelled him out and was making ready for the kill. It would be like him to hide at the ranch, ready for the short jump to the border.

V. Crumm shook her head impatiently. She was getting nowhere with wild surmises. Things were moving too fast. She really knew nothing, only that Miles and Ellen were in deadly peril. She had to act quickly. Perhaps she was crazy, but she could not stand idle, leaving the thing to Luke Flagg and Frank Smith. Those two fighting old-timers would do their best; only their best might be too late.

Padre Valdez smiled at her from the doorway. "You wish to see me?"

V. Crumm was all action again. "Hell's bust loose," she boomed. "We've got to work fast, throw a noose on the devil's tail."

The old Franciscan reached for a chair. He looked tired. "Tell me about this devil," he said mildly.

He listened without comment until she came to Johnny's news about Al Derner's puzzling departure from Santa Ysabel.

"Ah . . ." He spoke gravely. "This man is the devil, then?"

"Horns, hoofs, and hide," asserted V. Crumm. "We got to scotch him damn' quick—beggin' your pardon, your reverence—or God only knows what's goin' to happen to that poor lamb."

Padre Valdez shook his head sorrowfully:

261

"Alas, my daughter. You ask for a miracle."

"Sure I'm askin' for a miracle!" V. Crumm's eyes flashed. "The miracle of actin' quick, usin' the brains God give us." She paused, added softly: "The miracle of prayer, Padre—your prayers and your blessin' on us this night."

He smiled, bowed his head; and after a moment: "You have a plan?"

"I'm wantin' the old bell to ring," V. Crumm said vehemently.

"The *bell?*" The old Franciscan's eyes widened in a puzzled stare.

"That's right!" She grinned. "I'm needin' them Mexicans in a hurry. They'll come a-runnin' when they hear that bell, like they done this mornin'."

Padre Valdez looked at her respectfully. He had never known a woman like V. Crumm. Her plan was now obvious enough. Admiration for her deepened in him.

She read the swift comprehension in his eyes, smiled grimly. "I reckon you savvy, huh, Padre?"

"Yes, my daughter." He made the admission with a reluctance his kindling eyes belied.

Satisfaction glowed in her face. Her big body straightened, her fists clenched: "Start prayin', Padre, start prayin' we won't be too late."

Footsteps pounded up the hall. Johnny burst into the room, eyes snapping with excitement.

"All set," he announced. "Cap Hansy was at the barn. Him and Pilar is hookin' up the team now.

Cap says it don't make sense, but figgers you've got plenty reason for actin' crazy. Cap says your crazy streaks most always show pay-dirt."

"Doggone his impertinence!" grinned the big woman. Her face sobered: "Johnny—you crawl up to the bell-tower and get the old bell to ringin'—"

"Yes, ma'am—" Johnny was on the run. The look on her face warned him not to waste time with questions.

Padre Valdez got out of his chair: "I will be waiting at the church doors," he said.

"You're a blessed saint," V. Crumm declared fervently. "We'll smite the devil's hip and thigh, like the Good Book says." She nodded her head vigorously. "We'll stomp them crawlin' snakes into the dust."

Doubts shadowed her face as she stood there, watched the frail, brown-robed Franciscan disappear into the hall. The hours ahead were dark, every minute black with peril for Ellen—for Miles.

The bell was ringing now, a frantic, wild pealing. Alarm cried out in every deep-toned clang, an unmistakable warning of imminent danger, a desperate appeal that went throbbing into the night.

Brown-faced men began to appear in the plaza, crowded in front of the ancient mission where the padre stood in the glow of a lantern. They came from all directions, some on foot, many on horseback. It was plain they understood why the bell called. Rifles were in saddle-boots, guns in holsters, and those who owned no guns carried keen-bladed machetes, axes, clubs.

They listened, grim-eyed, silent, while the old Franciscan talked to them. The formidable look of them put an exultant gleam in V. Crumm's eyes. She turned to the waiting stage, climbed up on the driver's seat where Pilar Rojo sat beside Cap Hansy, who was holding the reins on the best six-horse hitch in her barn. She grinned at them, settled the big forty-five in the belt she had strapped on.

"Come on, *amigos*," she boomed. "Let's get goin'—"

Those without horses crowded into the big stage. Cap cracked his long whip, and they rocked away in a cloud of dust followed by half a hundred riders.

V. Crumm caught a glimpse of Johnny as he swung his paint horse into the column of horse-men. She scowled.

"The doggone little fire-eater!"

Cap Hansy, hunched forward in his seat, lines wrapped in big hands, let out an ear-splitting yell. The six horses broke into a gallop.

V. Crumm forgot about Johnny. Clinging to her seat on that wildly careening stage required all her immediate attention.

Hoofs drumming thunder, the riders followed, Johnny in the lead and yelling like a Comanche.

V. Crumm heard him, grinned fondly.

Chapter XIX

Ellen was surprised to find she had fallen asleep. She sprang from the bed, went quickly to the window, the one that overlooked the tall trees. From the moment they had locked her in the room she had had the odd feeling that it was from those close-growing trees help would come. They reached to within a hundred yards of the rambling old ranch-house, and now the shadows were deep there, the last vestige of sunlight gone. Darkness closed in, and the trees drew back into the night; not trees now, but a sinister blackness under the stars, a prison wall beyond which there seemed no escape.

Ellen tried to bolster her dwindling hopes. She must keep the bright lamp of courage burning. She was still alive, and while life was in her she must not for one moment let go of hope. She could hear V. Crumm's hearty voice: ". . . clean metal in you . . . that's what it takes in this country. . . ." Yes—she must hang on, keep the clean metal in her bright and hard against any shock the next hours might bring—*would* bring. Only three days now since she had climbed from the stage in Santa Ysabel, three days of horror that might easily have driven her to despair if it had not been for V. Crumm—*and Miles Clarke.*

Ellen was conscious of a stir in her. *Miles Clarke;* his steady eyes, his quiet, reassuring voice. While he lived she *could* dare to hope.

She had been unable to lose the two riders who had chased her into the chaparral, and finally she had glimpsed the old ranch-house.

Ellen shivered. No wonder her pursuers had been content not to overtake her, allowed her to reach the yard where she was pleading frantically with those cowboys for their protection. She would never forget that sickening moment when she recognized Jess Wellen, realized where she was, that this place where she had hoped for sanctuary was Al Derner's Bar M ranch. She was indeed trapped.

Something moved below the window, a man spoke, a low voice. Another voice answered, footsteps faded round the house. They were keeping a close watch on both windows, a man always on guard. A match flared and she glimpsed the man's face as he lit a cigarette, a lean, hard profile in that night's blackness.

Footsteps approached, coming along the hall outside the door. Not a man's heavy tread—a woman's. The door opened, lamplight flowed into the room. Ellen turned from the window, met the sly smile of Jess Wellen's wife.

The woman came in, put the lamp on a table,

moved towards the girl with the stealthy quiet-ness of a cat about to pounce. "Wasn't expectin' to see me so soon, was you, Miss Frazer?"

Ellen only looked at her. This woman knew the truth about Duncan, had witnessed his murder. She was as bad as Jess Wellen, sly, dangerous.

"Jess has sent word to the boss about you," Mrs Wellen continued. Her eyes glittered vindictively. "If it was me runnin' things I wouldn't waste no time on you, but Jess figgers it's up to the boss."

Ellen forced herself to speak: "You mean Mr Derner?"

"Sure—he's the big boss."

"I didn't know your husband worked for Mr Derner. He—he was partners with my brother—the—the Box DF—"

Mrs Wellen gave a squawky little laugh. "That was one of Al Derner's slick tricks," she said. "Al never really *sold* that Juniper Flats range to you folks. He figgered to use that fool brother of yours as a blind to cover up what was goin' on. Them cows was all rustled stock, most of 'em from old Luke Flagg's LF Bar." She laughed again. "Your brother wasn't knowin' his money was payin' for stole cows."

"He found out the truth, didn't he?" Ellen said in a stifled voice.

"Too bad for him, gettin' nosey," admitted the woman coolly. "Wasn't anythin' Jess could do but kill him like he done."

Ellen looked at her, loathing and curiosity in her eyes. "Aren't you afraid—talking about it to me?"

"What I'm tellin' you won't ever get repeated," Mrs Wellen said with another of her unpleasant laughs. "You won't have no chance to do any talkin'."

Her meaning was only too plain. Ellen's heart stood still. She was to be murdered, too.

Mrs Wellen saw the fear in her, seemed amused. "I ain't forgettin' what you done to me at the cabin," she said. "I ain't a forgettin' woman." She stood there, head on one side, eyeing the girl critically. "You're almost too purty to kill when there's places below the border that could use you. Shouldn't be s'prised none if Al Derner sends you below the border." There was wicked relish in her voice, a sadistic gloating.

Ellen saw that further talk could serve no good purpose. She groped her way to the bed, sat down, tried to fight off the fit of trembling.

Mrs Wellen watched her for a moment, picked up the lamp, and turned to the door. "I'll bring you some vittles," she said, and she went out.

Ellen heard the key turn in the lock, and after the footsteps faded down the hall, she got off the bed and felt her way through the darkness to the window.

The red spark of the cigarette told her the man was watching down there. She wondered dully what would happen if she attempted an escape through the window. There was no way of climbing down, but she could use the blankets from the bed, twist them into some kind of rope long enough to let her drop to the ground. The guard would shoot, but she would rather be killed attempting to escape than wait to be murdered in cold blood—or, worse still, sent to one of those places below the border, as Mrs Wellen had intimated.

The blankets gave her another idea. She could stand behind the door, ready for a surprise attack when Mrs Wellen returned. The woman would be carrying the lamp and the supper things. She would be unable to immediately resist when Ellen threw the blanket over her head, smothered her to unconsciousness.

Ellen reluctantly abandoned the idea, but not because she felt any compunction. She had a right to fight for her life, use any means she could devise. It was the problem of the lighted lamp the woman would have in her hand. The lamp would crash and set them both on fire. She would have no chance to put out the flames and at the same time manage to subdue Mrs Wellen.

She went back to the bed, sat down on the edge. Her head was aching. It was difficult to think things out coolly, make plans that had any sense.

She thought miserably about Luke Flagg. Of course he was dead. Jess Wellen would have made sure of it. Luke Flagg had discovered about the cow-stealing, had evidence that could have sent Wellen to prison, perhaps to the gallows. She could send Jess Wellen to the gallows herself, and Miles Clarke could send Al Derner to the gallows. Both of them thieves, murderers. Al Derner was implicated in the killing of Jim Miles, had stolen his ranch—this same house in which she was held prisoner. They would do their best to kill Miles Clarke. And that would mean the finish for her. She would be doomed. There would be no escape.

Again she fought off despair, told herself that Miles Clarke would be too smart for these men. She had seen him in action. The greater the need, the more smoothly his mind worked. She must continue to believe that Miles would meet this crisis. He would leave no stone unturned until he found her.

Ugly doubts gnawed at her. What could Miles do against all these men? She had counted them in the big yard. More than a score of them; hard faced ruffians, desperadoes, border-scum. Killing was an everyday job for their breed. What chance would Miles have? Luke Flagg had arranged to return to Santa Ysabel with his cowboys, but that fine old man was dead. Miles would wait in vain for help from Luke Flagg's LF Bar outfit.

She tried to shut out the taunting whispers, told herself fiercely that Miles would find a way. In the meantime she must play her part, refuse to let ugly fears break down her nerve.

Footsteps approached the door. Ellen listened, was suddenly thankful she had dropped the idea of a surprise attack on Mrs Wellen. The woman was not alone this time. The rap of those boot-heels came from a man. Jess Wellen, perhaps.

The thought turned her cold. Jess Wellen had decided not to wait for word from his boss. He was coming to finish it—*now.*

She sat there, stiff with fright. The key scraped in the lock, the door opened, letting in a flood of lamplight. Ellen forced herself to look. The man behind Mrs Wellen was not the woman's husband. He was small, scrawny, and he carried a tray. He was wearing a dirty apron—evidently the cook.

Mrs Wellen put the lamp on the table, waited for the cook to set the tray down.

"You don't need to wait," she said to him. "I'll set here while she eats."

The man nodded, gave the girl a leer, and went out of the room. Mrs Wellen sat down, ostentatiously placed a gun in her lap.

"Ain't settin' here long, nuther," she said to Ellen. "You come and get it now, or go hungry, for all I care."

Ellen shook her head: "I—I just can't—eat."

"Suit yourself," the woman said. "I'm givin' you ten minutes."

Ellen thought it over. V. Crumm had said, "You'll not fight trouble any easier for not eatin'. . . ." She felt that food would choke in her throat; but V. Crumm was right, food was necessary. And one never knew when chance might reach out a helping hand. She must play the game, make herself pleasant to the woman sitting there with a gun in her lap.

The gun. If she could only get her hands on that gun.

She slid from the bed. Play the game. That's what she must do; the way Miles Clarke would play it. Use her wits—be ready.

"What have you got for me?" She made herself smile, made her feet drag wearily. "I'm so tired, and stiff, I can hardly move."

"Plain beef stew, same as the boys et for supper," Mrs Wellen told her acidly. "Take it or leave it. Don't hurt me none if you starve."

Ellen reached the table, stood looking at the tin plate of greasy stew, the big tin cup of inky coffee. "The coffee smells good, and it's nice and hot—" She picked up the steaming cup and with the same motion flung its contents into the woman's face.

Mrs Wellen uttered a stifled cry of pain and rage, sprang up from the chair, spilling the gun from her lap. Ellen dived at her, arms outstretched, and her violent push sent the woman sprawling backward over the fallen chair. In an instant Ellen had the gun in her hand.

She said in a fierce whisper, "Quiet—don't move, or I'll shoot."

Mrs Wellen glared up at her with maniacal eyes,

but made no attempt to move, lay there on her back, one foot entangled in the chair. Ellen waited long enough to regain control of her breath. She hoped the brief scuffle had not been heard by the watcher outside.

She had won the first round, but what to do next puzzled her. She dare not take her gaze off the woman sprawled on the floor or relax her vigilance with the gun. Mrs Wellen would be at her like a frenzied wildcat, clawing, biting, screaming for help. Ellen guessed those thin, wiry arms would have the strength of steel.

She wondered a bit desperately if she could force herself to knock the woman senseless with a blow of the gun. It would simplify matters, give her a chance to find something with which to tie her up. She dropped the idea. She might hit too hard and kill her. She didn't want to kill anybody, although she felt she would be justified. Mrs Wellen had said *she* wouldn't waste time on *her* if she had her way. The woman was undoubtedly insane; all the more dangerous— formidable. She must take no chances with her.

She thought of the blankets. They were too clumsy to use for tying the woman, and she had no means of tearing them into strips.

A movement of Mrs Wellen's foot, entangled in the chair, drew her eyes. Those black cotton stockings were long enough to twist into cords and tie her wrists and ankles.

"All right, Mrs Wellen." Ellen spoke in a low, hard whisper. "Sit up."

As the woman obeyed, Ellen stepped behind her, pressed the muzzle of the gun against her back. "Do what I say, or I *will* shoot you. I want those stockings. Take them off—and keep very quiet." Her whisper grew razor thin. "I'm fighting for my life, Mrs Wellen—"

The woman began unfastening her shoes. She pulled them off, slid the stockings down. Ellen hardly breathed, kept the gun hard against her back, reached over and snatched the stockings as they dropped on the floor.

"Lie down flat again," she ordered. "Turn over on your face."

Mrs Wellen obeyed, lay face down on the floor. Ellen said warningly, "I've got the gun handy . . . don't stir while I tie your hands."

She had to use both hands for the tying job, and she hated to put the gun down, for fear the woman would turn on her and attempt to regain possession of the temporarily discarded gun.

It was a risk she had to take. She seized the woman's hands, drew them over her back, and swiftly twisted one of the stockings round the bony wrists. The stocking was long enough to go round several times. Ellen pulled hard, drew the knots tight. She stood up, trembling a bit, thankful the worst was over. She had the woman's hands securely tied behind her back. Mrs Wellen could not possibly make a grab for the gun now.

She picked up the other stocking and the gun, said breathlessly: "Get up, Mrs Wellen. I want you to lie down on the bed."

Mrs Wellen struggled to her feet, eyes venomous in her scalded face. Ellen shook the gun at her: "Don't talk, just get on the bed and lie face down."

She got the woman over to the bed, and tied her ankles with the other stocking. She longed for a rope so that she could tie her to the bed, but did the best she could with the two blankets, knotted together and made into a lengthy roll which she looped round the woman's waist, fastening each end to the sides of the bed. It would take Mrs Wellen quite a long time to wriggle free and roll to the floor. Even then she would be bound hand and foot, and it would be hard for her to make enough noise to attract immediate attention.

Her spirits rising, Ellen tore a strip from the woman's dress and fashioned a tight gag over her mouth. She wondered with a faint smile what Miles Clarke would think of her work, and drew the knots tight. She could feel no pity for this woman. She had stood by and watched her husband murder Duncan in cold blood—was herself a potential killer.

Ellen picked up the gun and went back to the table, looked at the stew. It was still faintly warm, and she realized with some surprise that hardly more than a few minutes had passed since she had thrown the coffee in Mrs Wellen's face. Less than ten minutes, and now the road to escape lay open. Only a very little way open, though. She had to find her way out of the house undetected, lose herself in those tall trees, be a long way from the house before Mrs Wellen could finally give the alarm. Half an hour at the most was all the time she would have.

She hated to lose a single precious minute, but she was ravenously hungry now. "You'll not fight trouble any easier for not eatin'. . . ." V. Crumm knew . . . she was so wise.

Quickly she spooned mouthfuls of the soggy mass of meat and swallowed it. It was better than nothing, and there was a lot of fighting ahead. She was a long way from being out of the woods— dark, fearsome woods where death would be lurking.

Gun again in her hand, she opened the door and peered into the hall. The darkness daunted her. She dare not trust herself without a light. Reluctantly she went back for the lamp.

She stepped into the hall, put the lamp down, turned the key Mrs Wellen had left in the lock, thrust the key in a pocket of her jeans, and picked up the lamp.

She stood for a moment, peering right and left. It was from the left they had brought her up a flight of stairs that led from a wide hall. It was possible that if she turned right she would come to a back stairs, find a door—perhaps a room where she could climb unseen through a window into the garden.

She moved slowly, cautiously, lamp in one hand, gun in the other. She was dubious about the gun. She had never shot one of the things, and this heavy, long-barrelled Colt tired her unaccustomed hand. It seemed wise, though, to take it along. There was a certain comfort in it, and it had cowed Mrs Wellen.

She found the back stairs, steep, narrow, and went quietly down to a passage. Voices came to her, and, looking along the passage, she saw a sliver of light under the door. She guessed it must be the kitchen, and now in a fever of haste, she pushed through the opposite door, closing it quietly behind her.

The place was evidently a storeroom. Ellen saw saddles, bridles, harness, leather chaps. Best of all, she saw windows. She placed the lamp on a box, turned the wick down, and blew out the light. Both the windows were closed. Ellen got one open, sliding it gently for fear of a squeak, and felt the cool night air on her face.

She waited for long moments listening, accustoming her eyes to the starlit night. The way seemed clear, and very quietly she climbed over the sill, thankful she was not wearing long skirts.

A man began to sing to the accompaniment of a guitar. She guessed the bunkhouse was near by, somewhere between the house and the corrals. Danger lay that way.

Ellen hesitated. Directly opposite was a tall hedge. She could not go that way. She must follow along the side of the house, get into the trees she had seen from the bedroom window. The thought turned her cold. It was too risky. A man was watching under those windows on the other side of the house.

Reluctantly Ellen turned the other way. Passing the bunkhouse was not as dangerous as trying to elude the vigilant eyes of the man on watch. The occupants of the bunkhouse would not be suspecting anything wrong. They were singing songs, playing cards, not thinking about her.

She moved slowly, feeling for each step, careful not to trip, and at last found herself pressing close to a tall, square building. The tankhouse, she guessed.

She edged round, saw the lighted windows of the bunkhouse. Two men were singing now, one of them in a high-pitched nasal voice, "Oh, bury me on the lone prairie . . ." Ellen felt she would never forget those long-wailed words.

The big yard lay before her. On one side was the lighted bunkhouse, the big barn beyond, and then the corrals. On the opposite side Ellen saw a dark wall of trees against the starlit sky.

It was time for boldness now. In that darkness

she would only be a vague shape, just one of the numerous outfit leisurely crossing the yard. She must be careful not to hurry, to walk slowly until she got to those trees.

Ellen drew a deep breath, moved away from the blackness of the tankhouse: It took all her resolution not to break into a run.

She became conscious of a disturbance in the night's stillness, the drumming thud of hoofs. Horsemen, a lot of them, galloping up the trail.

The bunkhouse door slammed open, framing a man against lamplight. Ellen heard his shout, started to run, heard the pound of boot-heels overtaking her. She turned on her pursuer, tried to lift the gun. He snatched it from her, held her in a remorseless grip that drew a stifled cry of pain from her.

The man muttered a startled exclamation, bent his head for a closer look into her face. "*You,* huh? How in hell did *you* bust loose."

Ellen recognized him. Tulsa, the savage-faced half-breed, the man who had ambushed old Luke Flagg and helped Jess Wellen chase her to this place of horror.

More men came streaming from the bunkhouse. One carried a lantern that made dancing shapes of them as they ran, boot-heels pounding, sending up spurts of dust.

Somebody shouted excitedly, "Here's the big boss—"

The horsemen came streaming into the yard. One of the riders reined in close to the lantern's flare. Ellen gazed at him wildly, felt her heart shrink as she met Al Derner's gloating look.

He said softly, "Well, well, if it isn't our little Miss Frazer!"

Chapter XX

They were too interested in the frightened girl to notice the faint stir in the trees beyond the fence. Appalled at the carelessness that might have drawn their attention, Miles flattened behind a clump of bunch-grass. Ellen's anguished little cry had startled him into a run that almost sent him sprawling into the gully he had failed to see in that darkness.

He watched the scene with bitter eyes, the heart in him like lead. He had arrived too late.

He could see her vaguely in the light of the lantern, see Al Derner gazing at her from his horse. His sardonic grin was almost more than Miles could bear. He found himself fighting a wild impulse to send a bullet through the man's head.

Miles scowled. It was no time to act like a madman. He was Ellen's only hope. The problem called for cool thinking if he was to get her away from Al Derner.

He heard the man's voice, arrogant, triumphant: "Take her to the office, Tulsa."

Miles did not wait to hear more, but moved swiftly through the trees. He was reasonably certain that Derner meant the old ranch office that Jim Miles had used as his private sanctum for so many years.

A woman's scream brought him to an abrupt standstill. Not Ellen's voice, a shrill, hysterical voice. He listened, heard a man's answering shout, and then Derner, loudly demanding to know what was going on.

"She got away from me!" screamed the woman. "Jess—you get lookin' for her . . . I'll scratch her eyes out—"

"She didn't git fur, Mrs Wellen," somebody shouted. "We got the little wildcat all safe."

"I'll claw her face for her," screamed the woman.

"Jess"—Derner's voice, angry, warning—"you tell your woman to keep her hands off that girl."

"Sure, boss."

Miles' face hardened. Johnny had not been wrong. Wellen was one of the men he had seen leaving town. It was Wellen who had shot old Luke Flagg and brought Ellen to the ranch. Mrs Wellen's hysterical outburst indicated that Ellen had managed an escape, only to be recaptured in

281

the yard. He understood now the scene he had just witnessed.

He slid from the blackness of the trees, reached the side of the house, quite unaware that Mrs Wellen's screams about Ellen's escape had drawn the guard away.

The first window he tried was locked. In haste now, he hurried round the corner and tried the window there. It slid up at his push, and in a moment he was inside the room, feeling his way through the darkness to the big cupboard that he knew should be somewhere opposite the door that opened from the hall.

Approaching footsteps warned him that Tulsa was coming with the girl. His hand found the knob of the cupboard door. He opened it, stepped inside, and pulled the door shut.

He was just in time, heard a man's voice as the hall door opened, saw a thin line of limelight appear under his own door.

"You sure had me plenty fooled until you started runnin'," the man said. "Figgered for a minute you was the kid Mex that helps the cook."

No answer from Ellen, only the faint push of a chair as she sat down.

"The boss said for me to wait until he gets here," drawled the man.

Another silence, broken by his guffaw. "You sure treated the Wellen woman rough," he said. "Scalded her face plenty with that coffee you throwed at her. She's wild to get her hands on you."

"She's insane," Ellen said curtly.

The man guffawed again. "She don't like the way Jess eyes you. That's the trouble with her. She don't like Jess lookin' that way at a purty gal like you, figgers mebbe Jess is fixin' to have you for his woman." His low chuckle made Miles furious.

More footsteps came quickly along the hallway. He heard Derner's voice: "So you and Jess got Luke Flagg, huh, Tulsa?"

"Sure did," answered the man.

"Good work," Derner said. "Flagg was all set to make trouble. All we've got to do now is to get hold of Miles Clarke and close his mouth for keeps."

"He ain't so easy to catch," Tulsa grumbled.

"The fool will likely show up here, looking for the girl—" Derner's tone was thoughtful.

"We'll sure grab him," chortled Tulsa.

"Don't waste time grabbing him. Empty your guns into him," Derner said savagely. "Jess is posting the boys now to keep watch for him."

"You ain't got V. Crumm fixed yet," reminded Tulsa, with another hard laugh. "She's sure a great fighter."

"We'll handle her, once we've put Clarke away." Derner spoke confidently. "We'll make a clean sweep, be sitting pretty."

"Wonder what they done with Heeler and Judd Scoby?" ruminated Tulsa.

"No need to worry about Heeler and Scoby," growled Derner. "Their own fault if they got themselves killed."

"I'd sure like to get my hands on Boone Haxson," muttered the other man. "Double-crossin' us the way he done."

"We'll get him," Derner assured him. "Boone can't do us any harm, not with Clarke and Flagg dead, and that damn' V. Crumm woman."

Miles heard Ellen's voice, low, outraged: "You dreadful monster!"

Tulsa chuckled. "She's a wildcat, huh, boss?"

"I'll cut her claws," Derner said.

"She sure is purty." Tulsa's voice was avid with longing.

"You and Jess Wellen can cut cards for her," laughed Derner.

"That's an idee, boss," guffawed the man.

"I'll think about it." Derner's voice hardened. "One more thing, Tulsa. Haven't had a chance to talk to Jess about Ace Stengal."

"Want for me to send Jess in?" asked the man.

"That's right." Derner paused, apparently considering some plan. "Ace is getting too uppity," he continued slowly, significantly. "I've no more use for him."

"Ace is some tough." Tulsa spoke doubtfully.

"He claims he's got friends in the outfit

here," sneered Derner. "You one of 'em, Tulsa?"

"Hell, no!" exploded the man.

"All right, tell Jess I'm turning Ace over to you and Cisco. Savvy?"

"I reckon I do."

"Don't let him get to me," warned Derner. "The sooner you fix the snake the better it suits me."

"I'll go talk with Cisco right now," chuckled the half-breed. "Don't you worry none about Ace, boss. We'll fix him plenty."

"Tell Jess I want to see him as quick as he gets the look-outs posted."

"I'll tell him," promised the man.

Miles heard the door close behind him. He waited a moment, gun in hand, and gently eased the cupboard door open a little and peered into the room.

Derner, his back turned to the cupboard, was talking to the girl.

"Perhaps we can make a deal," the man was saying softly. "I can do a lot for a pretty young woman like you. Seems a pity to waste you on ruffians like Tulsa and Wellen. I'm rich—and going to be a lot richer."

"I think you must be quite mad," Ellen said.

"Think it over," Derner said. "You can be the queen of the Santa Ysabel country. For your own sake you must be sensible." He smiled. "I talked to Tulsa that way just to show you what can happen if you're *not* sensible."

Miles eased the door open wide enough to show his face, caught a startled flash from Ellen's eyes. The instant recognition was too brief to draw Derner's attention, at that moment busy with the cigarette he was lighting. Miles was out of the cupboard now, moving on soundless feet.

The stony look was suddenly gone from Ellen's face. She smiled up at the man, said softly, "Do you mean you want to marry me, Mr Derner?"

Derner smiled back at her, rocked on his heels: "Well—it could come to that, eh, Miss Frazer?" His voice broke off abruptly, his big body stiffened.

Miles pressed the gun hard against the man's back. He said quietly, "Don't move, Derner . . . only your hands . . . lift 'em up—high."

Derner obeyed, his face ashen. Ellen sprang from the chair, went swiftly to the door, and turned the key in the lock.

Miles said to her, "Take his gun."

She gave Miles a starry-eyed look, lifted the gun from the man's holster, said in a matter-of-fact voice, "I knew you'd be too smart for these wretches, Miles."

He grinned, motioned at the windows: "Draw the blinds, and lock that window I left open."

She nodded, went to the windows, closed and locked the one he had left open, drew the blinds. Her coolness pleased him.

"Something to tie him with," he said when

she hurried back. His look went to a silver-mounted saddle hanging from a peg on the wall. His Uncle Jim's prized saddle. There were spurs, a bridle, a coiled lariat of braided rawhide.

Ellen saw his glance, went quickly and unfastened the lariat, brought it to him. He fished a knife from his pocket and cut off a length, gave Derner a hard smile.

He said, "Down on the floor, Derner—face down, and keep very quiet."

Derner lowered himself to the floor. Miles drew his arms behind his back, tied them, ran the lariat down to his ankles, got a noose round them, and jerked the knot tight.

Derner muttered between clenched teeth, "That hurts—"

Miles leaned over him, rapped him on the head with the barrel of the gun. "Don't talk," he warned. "Not a whisper."

He turned the man over on his back, pulled him to the wall, and propped him up, menaced him again with the gun. "When I want you to talk, I'll tell you."

Ellen's first elation was subsiding. She said, worriedly, "Jess Wellen is coming soon."

Miles nodded: "I know." He looked at the gun in her hand. "Can you use it?"

"If I must . . ." Her face paled.

"All right." Miles looked at Derner. "Listen," he said, "When Wellen comes and wants to come

287

in you call out, say 'Just a moment, Jess. . . I'll unlock the door.' Understand, Derner? If you try to warn him Miss Frazer will shoot you through the head. She'll be standing within a foot of you, the gun against your head. She won't miss."

Derner said huskily, "I understand—"

"Make sure you do," Miles told him grimly. "I'm dealing the cards for you to play right now, Derner."

Ellen sat down on a chair near the bound man. She felt trembly and wanted to conceal her nervousness from Derner. She rested the heavy Colt across a knee, muzzle close to his head. The fear in his eyes aroused no pity in her. The man was a coward. He hired killers to do his work, always kept himself in the safe background. When the killers were no longer useful he had them killed in turn by other hired gunmen. He was lower than the brutes, a ruthless, scheming, despicable scoundrel.

Miles watched her from the door, admiration for her deepening in him. He had never known a girl like her. For all her delicate beauty, there was good steel in her, a fine courage that refused to accept defeat.

The thought of what still lay ahead came close to daunting even himself. Derner had said that Jess Wellen was posting look-outs. It was going to be as hard to get away from this place as it would have been for him to get in if he had been a few minutes later in arriving. And the covering darkness would soon be gone. Another hour would bring the dawn: daylight would increase the obstacles to be overcome that *must* be overcome. He refused to accept the alternative, admit the possibility of failure. For Ellen's sake he must not fail.

He wondered grimly if Frank Smith would bring his Lazy S men with all speed, as Johnny had said he would. Luke Flagg's outfit too. They would come, once they got the word. It would take time, though, to get the outfits ready for moving, and made slim the chance that they would arrive before the dawn. It meant holding the fort until they *did* arrive. The probability of eluding the men now surrounding the ranch-house was one in a thousand. They would have to stand fast in the office, using the one ace card he now held, Al Derner.

Boot-heels clattered along the hallway, paused outside the door: "You want to see me, boss?" Jess Wellen's voice.

Miles glanced at Derner significantly, lifted his gun.

Ellen was on her feet now, gun within an inch of Derner's head. He gazed at it, slack-jawed, unable to speak.

Wellen called again, impatient, "Ain't you there, boss?" The door-knob rattled.

Derner's dry lips mumbled the words, "Just a

moment, Jess . . . I'll unlock the door—"

Miles rattled the key, turned it, and, hearing the click, Wellen pushed the door open and stepped into the room. He was wearing a broad grin that froze on his face and turned into a horrified grimace as he felt the prod of Miles' gun against his back. His eyes glazed, and slowly, mechanically, he lifted his hands above his head.

Miles kicked the door shut, reached out, turned the key, and Ellen, not waiting to be told, moved quickly and snatched the gun from Wellen's holster. Her eyes were bright as she looked at the dazed man. This was the murderer of her brother.

Obeying the prod of the gun, Wellen shambled over to the wall, eyes bulging as he now saw Derner.

"Flat on your face," Miles whispered.

Wellen got down on his knees, stretched out. Miles tapped him lightly on the head with gun-barrel: "Keep very quiet," he warned.

Ellen handed him the remaining length of the rawhide rope, and stood there, gun levelled, while he tied the man hand and foot, turned him over, and propped him against the wall.

Wellen glared at him. "You cain't get away with this," he muttered.

Miles tapped him on the head again. "When you speak—whisper," he said. "Killing *you* won't be murder, Wellen."

He said to Ellen, "Watch the door, tell me if anybody comes."

She nodded and went to the door. Miles gazed at the prisoners. "Heeler and Scoby have confessed." His eyes blasted them. "You're going to hang according to the law, Derner, for the murder of my uncle, Jim Miles."

"It's a lie," whispered Derner.

Miles shook his head. "Boone Haxson is keeping your two friends in a safe place. They'll swear they saw you shoot Jim Miles. You're going to swing, Derner." He looked at Wellen. "You too, for the murder of Duncan Frazer."

"You cain't prove it." Wellen spoke in a husky whisper.

Ellen left the door, came close to Miles, loathing in her eyes as she looked at the man. "Your wife boasted," she told him. "She said you shot my brother." She went back to the door.

"You've reached the end of your ropes and you're going to dangle from them," Miles said with a bitter smile. "I know all about your dirty game, Derner; your frauds, the forgeries of Ace Stengal, the murder of Sheriff Renn. And I know all about the copper lode; know where to look for it when I feel that way."

He looked round, saw a ball of twine on the littered desk he remembered so well. Big, jovial Uncle Jim used to sit there. He walked over to the desk, cut off two lengths of the twine, and returned to the haggard-faced prisoners.

"Won't need any more talk from *you*," he said to Wellen. He took the man's bandanna, twisted it over a piece of the twine, forced the gag between the man's lips, knotted the ends. He jerked a large silk handkerchief from Derner's pocket, went on talking quietly as he fashioned a second gag: "Won't tie *your* mouth up just yet, Derner. If anybody comes to the door I'll want you to speak up loud and gruff; say 'Go away . . . I'm busy—' " He tossed the gag on the floor, near Derner's feet, and picked up his gun. "Understand, Derner?"

The man nodded. He was sweating, his face the colour of putty.

Ellen whispered softly, "I hear somebody . . ."

Miles nodded, moved close to Derner's side, pressed the gun against his head.

A man's heavy tread came along the hallway, halted outside the door: "Hi there, boss . . ."

Miles recognized Tulsa's voice. He gave Derner a nod.

Derner called out gruffly, "I'm busy, Tulsa—"

There was a brief silence. Tulsa spoke again, his voice worried: "Cisco and me cain't find Ace Stengal no place. Looks like he's on to us."

Miles tightened the pressure of the gun, nodded again.

"I'm busy," repeated Derner. "Go away."

Tulsa went away, grumbling, obviously disturbed.

Dawn began to show through the drawn blinds, and at a sign from Miles the girl went to the lamp, turned the wick down, and blew out the light. She looked white and tired, Miles saw with concern. The strain was wearing her down.

He set his mind grimly on the probabilities. Help could come at any minute now: Luke Flagg's outfit, the Lazy S riders. He calculated the distance they would have to come, the time they would take, and decided it was honest to hope. It was hold the fort now; there was nothing else they could do.

Footsteps came along the hallway again. Two men this time. Tulsa's voice, frankly disturbed: "Let us in, boss. We found Cisco layin' dead in the yard, knifed in the back. Reckon Ace done it."

Miles prodded Derner's head, and the man said hoarsely, "Go away . . . I'm busy—"

A long silence, a low muttering, then Tulsa's voice again: "What the hell's wrong in there, boss? Sounds like you're sick."

"Go away," repeated Derner hoarsely, terrified eyes fixed on the threatening gun.

Miles waited until the footsteps faded down the hallway, beckoned to Ellen to keep her gun on Derner, and reached for the gag. No sense in leaving the man's mouth untied now. Tulsa and the others were getting too suspicious. Hearing Derner's voice was not going to fool them any more.

He forced in the gag, tied it securely, picked up his gun, and said gently to Ellen, "You might as well sit down."

She sat down, leaned back, gun in her lap, her eyes on him, puzzled but confident. "Only *you* could have done this," she said. "I never quite gave up hope, Miles." She shook her head. "I—I don't understand, though, why we are staying here."

Miles realized with a shock that she could not know about the Lazy S or Luke Flagg's riders. She was thinking that Luke Flagg was dead.

He told her briefly of Johnny's message. "We've got to wait here," he finished. "It's our only chance now they have the place surrounded."

"I see . . ." Ellen closed her eyes. "Wait—and pray," she whispered. "Wait—*and pray* . . ."

The footsteps were returning, a lot of them now.

"Boss—what's wrong in there?" Tulsa's voice was alarmed. His gun rapped hard on the door.

"Looks like the gal has knifed him," guffawed another voice.

"A couple of you fellers go take a look through the windows," Tulsa said. His gun rapped again. "What's wrong, boss? Open up or we're bustin' the door!"

Ellen was out of the chair, gun clenched in her hand. Miles, afraid she might catch a bullet from

294

the men at the windows, motioned for her to get inside the cupboard. She shook her head, moving close to his side.

"Together," she said in a whisper. "Always together, Miles . . ."

He said softly, "Yes—always," and reached for the gun she had taken from Wellen and laid on the table. They stood together, backs to the wall, opposite their prisoners, where they could watch door and windows. A gun in each hand now, he was ready to fling a bullet in either direction.

The men in the hall were not talking any more. The door began to shake under heavy kicks; and suddenly they heard the crash of window-glass, saw a hand rip the blind down. A man's face peered into the still, shadowed room.

Miles flung a quick shot. Blood spurted from the hand clutching the torn blind, and its owner yelled and dropped from sight.

A brief silence followed the crashing report of the forty-five. Smoke eddied towards the broken window. Miles waited in a half-crouch, a gun levelled in either direction. The hard mask of his face drew a shiver from the girl. She had never seen such cold fury in a man's eyes.

The poundings on the door redoubled. It was a stout door of solid timber. A man yelled, "Get an axe! No sense breakin' our toes ag'in the damn' thing."

Boot-heels clattered down the hallway, and

silence fell again, broken only by the low mutterings of the waiting men.

Daylight was coming fast. Miles glimpsed a shadow at the window. A gun roared, flared flame and smoke. Wellen groaned, a shudder ran through his long frame, and he slipped down from the wall, sprawled sideways on the floor.

Miles paid no attention to the dead renegade. He was watching the window. The man outside might find his target more surely next time. He heard Ellen's low whisper:

"Miles—that noise—horses . . ."

Other ears heard that low drumming thunder of galloping horses. A man shouted excitedly, and there was a quick rush of booted feet down the hallway.

Miles was running now. He unlocked the door, jerked it open, ran into the hall and through to the front veranda. Ellen caught up with him, stood by his side.

A strange cavalcade was moving along the trail; a six-horse stage, with old Cap Hansy in the driver's seat and screeching like a Comanche. Horsemen followed the careening stage, half a hundred of them, dark-faced riders with guns in their hands.

Ellen clutched Miles' arm. "V. Crumm!" she exclaimed. "It's V. Crumm!"

V. Crumm was yelling, too, and brandishing a gun. She saw them, spoke to Cap Hansy. He slowed the running team, swung the stage round to the veranda steps, and slammed on his brake. The riders followed; dust drifted past.

V. Crumm was suddenly limp in her high seat. She made fanning motions with the gun. Cap Hansy said testily, "Easy with that gun, Vee, or you'll blow a hole in me."

The dark-faced riders grouped their horses round them, eyes grim, watchful. Johnny's dusty face wore a triumphant grin.

Miles came out of his daze. He said simply, "Thanks, V. Crumm. We were needing you a lot."

"Figgered you would," V. Crumm said. Her hand lifted: "Listen—I reckon that's Luke's outfit comin', and the Lazy S fellers." She let out a delighted whoop, started climbing down from the stage.

Dust was lifting on the trail. The cowboys tore past the house to the yard where the frightened renegades were hurriedly throwing saddles on their horses. Ellen heard the crackle of six-guns, shouts, yells of pain, and then suddenly it was over.

Luke Flagg and Frank Smith rode up. Luke was wearing a bandage under his hat, also a satisfied grin.

"One big round-up," he exulted. "Wasn't more'n a couple of 'em got away."

"Two or three layin out in the corral, dead," Frank Smith said. "Mighty glad we got here in time." He stared curiously at the big stage, at the silent, brown-faced riders, and gave V. Crumm an admiring grin. "Looks like you beat us to it, Vee."

"I ain't one to set and fiddle my thumbs when old man trouble's on the prod," she said complacently. She gave Miles a keen look. "Heard some shootin' when we come along the trail. Sure got me worried."

"Derner's inside, tied up," Miles told them. "Jess Wellen's inside, too—dead."

The Lazy S foreman came clattering from the hall. "Found another of 'em," he said to his boss. "That Ace Stengal feller—hidin' in the tank-house."

"The little snake," grunted V. Crumm. "He's the feller that stabbed poor old Jake Renn in the back. We're sure goin' to pack the Santa Ysabel gaol full to-night." She was watching Miles again, concern in her eyes. "You look awful done up, Miles. You and Ellen run along and leave things to us. You done plenty."

She was right, Miles realized. He had never felt so tired. "I'll get my horse," he said. "Left him cached in the brush."

He found Ellen walking by his side, stopped, and looked at her. "I'm going with you," she said. Her colour was high, her eyes shining—and very tender. "You haven't asked me, but I'm never leaving you again."

Miles was suddenly not tired any more. "Hasn't been much time for—for asking," he said, and drew her into his arms.

The sun lifted above the mountains, bright, warming. It seemed to them that no day had ever been so fair, so radiant with rich promise.

About the Author

Arthur Henry Gooden recalled that "I was still a babe in arms when my parents took me from Manchester, England, to South Africa for a four-year stay in Port Elizabeth, then back to England for a brief time, and finally the journey that made me a Californian. Reaching the San Joaquin Valley in those days meant work from sunup to sundown. Always plenty for a boy to do. But there were compensations—my rifle, my shotgun, my horse. By the time I was ten I was master of all three and the hunting was good." Gooden began his career as a Western writer working in Hollywood beginning in 1919. *The Fox* (Universal, 1921) was the first feature film based on one of his screenplays and starred Harry Carey. For what remained of the decade, Gooden worked in the writing department at Universal, turning out scenarios for two-reelers and feature films as well as serials like *The Lawless Men* (Universal, 1927) based on Frank Spearman's popular character, railroad detective Whispering Smith. In the early 1930s Gooden left Hollywood to live in a stone cabin in the foothills of the San Jacinto, overlooking the sand dunes of the

Colorado Desert. The life he led there was primitive: no electricity, no gasoline, no telephones, but he had his typewriter and began writing Western novels, beginning with *Cross Knife Ranch*, first published by Harrap in London in 1933. In fact, although he would eventually have various American publishers, the British editions of his novels continued to be published by Harrap until 1951. *Smoke Tree Range* (Kinsey, 1936), one of his finest stories, was brought to the screen by cowboy star Buck Jones in 1937, Gooden's only screen credit during that decade. Gooden had a distinguished prose style and was always able to evoke the Western terrain and animal life vividly as well as authentically address the psychology of many of his complex characters with the sophistication of a master storyteller.

Center Point Large Print
600 Brooks Road / PO Box 1
Thorndike ME 04986-0001 USA

(207) 568-3717

US & Canada:
1 800 929-9108
www.centerpointlargeprint.com